BLIND SPOT

Laura Ellen

Houghton Mifflin Harcourt
Boston   New York

www.hmhco.com

Text set in Minion

The Library of Congress has cataloged the hardcover edition as follows:
Ellen, Laura.
Blind spot / Laura Ellen.
p. cm.
Summary: "Tricia Farni was last seen alive the night she fought with Roswell Hart—
a night Roz can't remember. Can Roz piece together the events of that night, despite the
eye disease that robs her of most of her vision, in order to clear her name
and find a murderer?" —Provided by publisher.
[1. Mystery and detective stories. 2. High schools—Fiction. 3. Schools—Fiction. 4. Blind—
Fiction. 5. People with disabilities—Fiction.] I. Title.
PZ7.E42838Bl 2012
[Fic]—dc23
2012028976

ISBN: 978-0-547-76344-6 hardcover
ISBN: 978-0-544-23284-6 paperback

Manufactured in the United States of America
DOC 10 9 8 7 6 5 4 3 2 1
4500468031

For Breanna, James, and Megan,
may they always follow their dreams,
and for Jeff, who helped clear the
path so that I could follow mine.

Revelation

Winter stopped hiding Tricia Farni on Good Friday.

A truck driver, anxious to shave forty minutes off his commute, ventured across the shallow section of the Birch River used as an ice bridge all winter. His truck plunged into the frigid water, and as rescuers worked to save him and his semi, Tricia's body floated to the surface.

She'd been missing since the incident in the loft six months ago. But honestly, she didn't come to mind when I heard that a girl's body had been found. I was that sure she was alive somewhere, making someone else's life miserable. Maybe she was shacking up with some drug dealer, or hooking her way across the state, or whatever. But she was definitely alive.

On Easter morning, that changed.

The body of seventeen-year-old Tricia Farni was pulled from the Birch River Friday night. A junior at Chance High School, Tricia disappeared October 6 after leaving a homecoming party at Birch Hill. Police believe her body has been in the water since the night she disappeared.

I couldn't wrap my brain around it. Tricia was a lot of things, a drug addict, a bitch, a freak. But dead? No. She was a survivor. Something — the only thing — I admired about her. I stared at my clock radio, disbelieving the news reporter. Ninety percent talk, AM 760 was supposed to provide refuge from my own wrecked life that weekend. I thought all those old songs with their *sha-la-la-las* and *da-doo-run-runs* couldn't possibly trigger any painful memories. I guess when a dead girl is found in Birch, Alaska, and you were the last one to see her alive, even AM 760 can't save you from bad memories.

While the rest of Chance High spent Easter Sunday shopping for bargains on prom dresses and making meals of pink marsh-mallow chicks, I lay on my bed, images of Tricia flooding my brain. I tried to cling to the macabre ones — the way I imagined her when she was found: her body stiff and lifeless, her brown cloak spread like wings, her black, kohl-rimmed eyes staring up through the cracks in the ice that had been her coffin all winter. These images made me feel sad and sympathetic, how one should feel about a dead girl.

Another image kept shoving its way in, though. It was the last time I'd seen Tricia. The last thing I remembered clearly from that night, minutes before she disappeared. She and Jonathan in the loft. It made me despise her all over again. And I didn't want to despise her anymore. She was dead.

What happened to her that night? And why couldn't I remember anything after the loft, not even going home? All I had were quick snapshots, like traces of a dream: Jonathan's body against mine; arms, way too many arms; and Mr. Dellian's face. Puzzle pieces that wouldn't fit together.

I'm used to piecing things together. My central vision is blocked by dots that hide things from me, leaving my brain to fill in the blanks. My brain doesn't always get it right. I misinterpret, make mistakes. But my memory? It's always been the one thing I could count on, saving me time after time from major humiliation. I can see something once and remember it exactly — the layout of a room, the contents of a page, anything. My visual memory makes it less necessary to see, and I rely on it to pick up where my vision fails.

How could my memory be failing me now?

I went over that night again, much as I would with my vision, putting the pieces together to make something sensible and concrete. But the more I focused on those tiny snippets, the farther they slipped from my grasp.

Then "Copacabana" started playing on the radio.

I slammed my fingers down on the power button to stop the lyrics, but my mind went there anyway. A replay of the day Tricia did a striptease during lunch. The day I helped her buy drugs . . .

There's none so blind as they that won't see.
—Jonathan Swift

Pieces

Forty days before

It should've been a breeze, a no-brainer. I was returning to the same halls I'd occupied last year. A seasoned vet, not some scared, insecure freshman. But still. I passed through the black doors of Chance High that first day of sophomore year and found myself in Hell.

Okay, I exaggerate. Hell didn't reveal itself until minutes later, when I met Tricia and realized I'd been placed in a special ed class. But the sensory overload that hit me when I first entered the building certainly began my journey. Nauseating combinations of musk, coconut, cherry blossom, and industrial cleaner assaulted me. Out-of-focus faces in globs of color swirled around me like the psychedelic covers on my dad's old acid rock albums. A cacophony of squeals stabbed at my ears. I went from zero to panic in less than sixty seconds, and the fact that I had to get through it on my own only made it worse.

Before, Missy Cervano had been my compass, my shelter, my shield. Last year we'd attacked the first day of school together, scurrying down the halls, mice in a maze, trying to find our lockers, ducking into corners, and flattening ourselves against walls to avoid the intimidating seniors. We'd survived because we had the perfect social weapons: each other. Best Friends Forever. Forever ended a few months ago when she suddenly stopped talking to me. Music was my only safe haven now. Lyrics never change like people do.

I took a steadying breath and popped in my ear buds. My *F.U. World* playlist cut through the chaos surrounding me and urged me forward. Clutching my class schedule, I skirted the boundaries of clique after clique arranged like planets along the hallways. Posers and wannabes orbiting around them, like satellites waiting to crash through the atmosphere. At least they could pretend to belong. Without Missy, I couldn't even do that anymore.

I passed the office and the cafeteria and turned left down a nearly empty hallway in a section of the school where I'd never been. The lack of people allowed me to move closer to the wall, and I squinted at the room numbers. I was looking for room 22, Life Skills.

Life Skills wasn't on my original schedule. Auto Maintenance was. A total waste for someone who'd never drive, I know. And in my defense, I'd totally planned on signing up for Art. Except Missy gave me that "oops, my bad" look when we were coordinating our schedules last spring. Then she started babbling about how she'd understand if I didn't want to take Auto, and how Rona would be in there to keep her company if I didn't, and how maybe they'd take driver's ed together too . . . Whatever, it didn't matter now anyway. I'd been switched to Life Skills, which according to Mom was some new school policy. A required class.

The farther I walked, the more deserted the hallway became,

and a nagging suspicion about Life Skills began to take over, twisting my stomach, disrupting the leftover shrimp lo mein I'd had for breakfast. For a new, required class, shouldn't there be more people on this route?

I consulted my map. My fingers followed the thick black lines that I'd drawn the night before. This was the way. A right at the next hallway and I'd be there.

At that last turn, I stopped. Someone in a brown, hooded cloak twirled, twirled, twirled in the middle of the hallway, like a little girl in a frilly Easter dress. A garment like that meant immediate social suicide, but in a deserted hallway, I knew it meant something else too.

Special Ed.

I maneuvered around the twirling girl and approached the classroom. As I brought my eyes up from the floor to look inside, I spotted the spokes of a wheelchair.

No, I thought, my stomach tightening. I slid the dots blocking my central vision to the side so I could see the chair's occupant. He was talking to someone out of sight range, but I could hear his voice; he sounded normal. Simply a guy in a wheelchair.

I relaxed, took a few steps closer — and noticed the slumped body to the left. He was humming and rocking, hands twitching uncontrollably. My eyes flitted to the girl facing me. Short and plump, a permanent smile plastered on her face — the perfect model for a Special Olympics poster.

There had to have been a mistake. This was not my room. I hurried past, hoping the next room was mine. But there wasn't one. Only a pair of bathrooms with blue HANDICAPPED signs.

Welcome to Hell.

I turned around. The girl in the cloak stopped spinning and stared at me. The thick layer of eyeliner against her white-blond hair and ghostly pale skin made her eyes hang in midair, faceless. I moved past her, rounded the corner, and once the hall was clear, yanked my magnifying glass from the side pocket of my backpack. The enlarged numbers on my schedule told me what I already knew. That was my classroom.

Why? I didn't belong in there. I wasn't a freak.

"There's been a mistake," I said, handing my schedule to the counselor. "I don't belong in Life Skills."

She typed something into the computer and then peered over the top of her wire-framed glasses. "You *are* Roswell Hart, aren't you?"

"Roz." I tried to make eye contact with her by directing my blind spot to her ear and using my peripheral vision to see her face. But she thought I was looking behind her. She looked over her shoulder and then turned back to me, a puzzled frown on her face.

I hate it when that happens. I tried to save face by pretending I *was* looking behind her, and at the ceiling, and down at the ground. "Eyelash on my contact," I muttered, pulling at my eyelid. "Yes, I'm Roswell Hart."

"There's no mistake, sweetie." She handed the schedule back to me. "Life Skills is in your IEP."

"What? No. It isn't." My Individualized Education Program — a list of adaptations some school officials came up with to help me "succeed" in the classroom: extra time for tests, oral instead of written tests, prewritten class notes, class materials in large print, books on tape, and so on.

I didn't need any of it. As long as I sit in the front, I get along just fine. Yes, it takes a while for me to read the board—I have to move my dots from spot to spot until I have pieced together a sentence—but it's better than being singled out for "special" treatment. I had told this to Mr. Villanari, my IEP advisor, when we discussed my IEP last spring. He told me if I didn't think I needed any special help, I didn't have to use it. That's how I knew. "There's no Life Skills in my IEP—ask Mr. Villanari."

"Oh, Mr. Villanari is no longer your IEP advisor. Mr. Dellian is." She gave me a sappy sympathetic look. "And he's decided that after that unfortunate event last year, everyone with a disability must take Life Skills. It's for your own good, sweetie."

"Disability." How I loved to hate that word. I used to think I had "ability," that I was normal. That's because I thought everyone saw like me—disjointed and fragmented, every object in visual range like pieces of a puzzle in need of constant reconstruction. When it's the only way you know, your way is normal. Until told otherwise. For me that happened in fifth grade, when Ms. Freemont thought I was dyslexic because I'd read words wrong out loud.

After my optometrist rechecked my glasses' prescription and found nothing wrong, everyone figured it must be some mental problem, a learning disability, whatever. They ran me through tons of tests, finding nothing. Then in the middle of eighth grade, Mom suddenly thought to mention that my dad can't drive because of some eye disease. Something *I* didn't even know. I saw an ophthalmologist and voilà! They got their diagnosis: macular degeneration. And I got my label: disabled.

Don't get me wrong. With Mom dating anyone who checked out her ass and Dad chasing UFOs across the country instead of hanging out with me, I'd had my share of labels before that. But "Broken Family," "Single Mom," "Absent Dad," no matter what the teachers tagged me with, it didn't matter; half the class had them too. Disabled, however, opened a whole can of labels that stripped me of my identity. I went from Roswell Hart with straight As and a permanent spot on the honor roll to Legally Blind, Visually Impaired Roswell Hart, a Disabled student with an IEP.

"Look," I said, fighting the urge to "sweetie" her back, "I have bad vision, but my life skills are just fine."

"Your parents can speak with us about it. But until then, the only change I can make is to place you in another Life Skills class." She looked behind me. "Next!"

The first bell rang. There was an instant swarm as I entered the hallway, and then I was left alone with only a few stragglers. A frustrated scream thrashed around inside me, clawing at my ribs. I didn't want to go to that class, that black hole the school was shoving me toward. But what could I do? The school had made that decision for me. The class was on my schedule, a requirement now for losers with labels.

My legs carried me back toward the Special Education hallway, but my body was rejecting the situation. Bile crawled up the sides of my stomach, and I struggled to keep my breakfast down. When

I reached the hallway outside Life Skills, I flung open the bathroom door and barely made it into a stall before the vomit broke free. Chunks hit the gray linoleum with a splattering slap.

"Classy." Cape-girl hung over the stall wall above me. "Is this a first-day thing, or are you bulimic or something?"

"Huh?"

"The puke. You do it to stay skinny?"

Before I could answer, she'd disappeared. Her high heels click-clacked on the tile outside, and then she shoved my door open, a handful of paper towels in her hand. "God, that is rancid! What did you eat for breakfast?" She covered her nose and tossed the brown paper on top of the half-digested shrimp swimming in a salmon-colored sea. Clutching her cloak with one hand, she pushed the towels around with the toe of her thigh-high black leather boot. "I puked at school once," she said, still holding her hand over her nose. "Jimmy Benson shared his fifth of vodka with me during gym." She turned smoothly on her toes and went back to the stall next door. "You coming? Or you gonna stay in here with your puke?"

I should've washed my face, recentered myself, and moseyed into that hellhole of a class. But something about her fascinated me. I couldn't tear my eyes away. The cloak suggested some out-of-touch lost soul, but she sure didn't talk that way. Like an alien abductee caught in a tractor beam, I followed her.

"I'm Tricia," she said. Her butt rested on the railing, feet balanced on the toilet lid, hiked-up cloak revealing a red vinyl miniskirt. She slipped a thin, home-rolled cigarette from her cloak pocket and flicked her lighter until an orange flame lapped at the paper. She sucked in as she lit it, holding the smoke in her lungs before exhaling. "Want some?"

"Is that weed?" I waved the smoke away and glanced up at the ceiling, expecting a sprinkler or smoke alarm to go off at any moment.

Tricia smiled. "Don't worry. No one except Rodney will come looking in here, and he and I are like this." She crossed her fingers.

"Rodney?" *Could I get high sitting here?* I tried not to breathe.

"Mr. Dellian. Mr. D. The SPED teacher? He's also the hockey coach. Makes for some hot teacher aides." Tricia took another long drag. "It's all legal anyway," she said, holding in her breath. "I use it for medicinal purposes." She grinned and let her breath out again. "I have a prescription and everything."

"You have a prescription for pot?" I breathed into my sweatshirt collar. "Why?"

Tricia's dark, outlined eyes bore into me as she took another drag. The end of the joint flared a bright orange. Its thin paper crackled in the silence.

I no longer wanted an answer, just out. I reached for the stall door.

"They stuck you in Life Skills too, huh?" Her voice startled my hand from the door. "So, what's your poison?"

I turned, frowning. "My what?"

"Poison, you know, learning disabled, physically challenged, or, my personal favorite" — she gave an evil grin — "severely emotionally disturbed."

"I don't —" Okay, so I did. But she didn't need to know it. "It's a mistake."

"Sure it is." She blew smoke in my face and jumped off the railing. "If you plan on hiding out in here, don't. Since Renny's suicide, Rodney's been pretty hot and heavy about this Life Skills class."

"Renny?"

She glared at me. "The Down syndrome kid?" She jammed the lit end of the joint against her palm, barely flinching as the butt burned her flesh. "We're late. Tell him you got lost. He'll let it slide."

When we reached the door, Tricia yelled, "Found her!" and yanked me into the classroom. "She was ditching in the bathroom."

"No, I wasn't!" Her betrayal didn't shock me; after all, she was a pot-smoking SPED student in a cloak. How smoothly she pivoted from ally to prosecutor, however, did. "I . . . got lost."

"Sure," Tricia said. "That's why you were outside before the bell rang." She flopped down in Mr. Dellian's chair and put her feet up on his desk, not bothering to cross them. "You should give her detention."

"Thank you, Tricia. I can handle this myself." He turned to me. "Life Skills is not a blow-off class. I won't tolerate tardiness and unexcused absences. Understood?"

So much for peace, love, and understanding. It probably wasn't the best time to tell him I didn't belong in there. But like an idiot, I gave it a try. "Yeah, but I'm not even supposed to be in here." I darted my eyes up to his face briefly and then looked at the ground. "I told Mr. Villanari last year. I don't need any help."

"Mr. Villanari is no longer in charge of your IEP. I am. And I think you need this class."

The tone in his voice told me I'd struck a nerve, but I couldn't let it go. I had to make him see that I wasn't like Tricia and the others. "Mr. Dellian, I get your reason for this class and all, but I don't belong in here. I'm not like" — I gestured at the class — "*them*." I focused on Dellian's shoulder. "I'm totally normal, and I swear, I'm not suicidal."

The muscles in Dellian's arm flexed. "Normal? You think these kids aren't normal?"

"No! I —" I stopped. The class was dead silent. I didn't need Tricia to tell me I'd said too much.

She did anyway.

"Smooth. Even Asperger's over there has better social etiquette. Think I know your poison now. Mental retardation?"

"Enough!" Mr. Dellian growled at Tricia, and then looked at me. "You're in here because I say you're in here. Now sit!" He glanced back at Tricia. "Both of you."

I had no desire to be near the now pissed-off Mr. Dellian, nor by the freak-show named Tricia. Besides, what could I possibly need to see on the board? So I headed to the back of the room.

The short girl held out a plastic container as I went by. "Cookie?"

"Don't give her one, Ruth," Tricia said. "She's a puker."

"Tricia," Mr. Dellian said with a sigh. "Please, find a seat."

"No, no. Stay there. I like that view!" A guy in jeans and a hockey jersey walked into the classroom. "Thong or bikini?"

Tricia's voice took on a seductive tone. "Maybe neither."

The newcomer handed Mr. Dellian a stack of papers. "There was a traffic jam at the copier." He took a cookie from Ruth. "Mmmm, chocolate," he said, then nodded his head toward me and grinned.

My heart stopped. Jonathan Webb. A senior and a huge hockey star; everyone called him Zeus, the lightning-fast god of the ice.

"Class," Dellian said as he set the papers on his desk, "Jonathan will be my aide this semester."

I almost laughed out loud. Missy would die to be in a class with Jonathan — well maybe not this particular class, but still. She'd been crushing on him since the summer before freshman year. He lived a few blocks away from me, though I'm sure he didn't know that. Missy and I used to ride our bikes by his house, hoping to see him. Sometimes he'd be outside washing his cherry-red Corvette. We spent hours planning ways to cross his path — a flat bike tire, a lost dog, a twisted knee — each time victims in need of saving. We always chickened out, though. Neither of us had ever spoken to him.

"While we're making introductions" — Mr. Dellian walked to the slumped-over guy who'd been humming and rocking earlier — "most of you know Bart, and over there —" He pointed at the girl with the cookies. She grinned at me. "I'm Ruth."

"JJ," the guy in the wheelchair said.

"Roz," I said.

"No!" The dude wearing an oversize cowboy hat at the front of my row whipped around and glared at me. "It's *my* turn." He faced forward again. "I'm Jeffrey."

"She probably couldn't see over that hat," Tricia said.

"I could too!" I snapped, realizing, as I did, that she was teasing him, not me.

"It's my Indiana Jones hat." He turned back around. "Do you like Harrison Ford? I have all his movies. You could come see my collection."

"Aah, retards in love," Tricia said. "When's the wedding?"

"T." Mr. Dellian lowered his voice and moved in front of Tricia. "Take a seat."

Tricia let her legs fall, one by one, to the floor. She strolled to the back of the room, lingering too long as she passed Jonathan, and then dragged a desk across the floor and pushed it against mine. "This better?"

I scooted away, but she followed with a sadistic smile. I surrendered and slid my butt to the edge of my seat instead.

"There seems to be some misconception about this class. So let me explain." Even as I stared at my desktop, I knew Mr. Dellian was looking at me. "Sometimes academic classes alone cannot prepare you for the world outside, especially if you have a physical, emotional, or intellectual disability hindering your success."

My ears began to burn. It was bad enough sitting there in that class. But in front of Jonathan? How humiliating.

"Except for Bart, all of you take classes with the rest of the school, and this can be tough sometimes. If you're not prepared to interact with others who don't understand your unique needs, the stress can be overwhelming, as it was for Renny. Renny was having trouble, and no one knew it because he was refusing help. It's hard to admit to yourself sometimes that you are overwhelmed and need help. That's what I hope to teach you in this class: How to recognize that you need help and how to —" Dellian sighed as the bell cut him off.

I couldn't escape fast enough. I leaped forward, reaching the door at the same time as Jonathan. He smiled and gestured for me to go in front of him. "After you."

Funny. I never liked Jonathan. Not like Missy. But that simple interaction sent my mind reeling. *Do I laugh? Smile? Say something clever? But that would all mean making eye contact. What if he thinks I'm looking behind him? Not interested? Blowing him off?* I'd almost decided to smile and just look at the ground, act shy, when Mr. Dellian zapped me back to earth.

"Miss Hart, you should be sitting up front."

I stole a glance at Jonathan from the corner of my eye. He'd paused, as if waiting for me. "I'm fine back there."

"Are you?" Dellian stepped backwards to let JJ wheel by. "I distinctly remember Mr. Villanari telling me the only accommodation you admit needing is a seat up front."

I wanted to disappear, meld into the cement wall and fail to exist. It was as if Dellian was suddenly bent on proving I was a freak. "Whatever," I muttered and sped out without looking back.

The rest of the day sucked like that too. Missy was in most of my classes, just as we'd planned last spring. She made it obvious I was invisible. Whatever. I listened to music until each class started. Earphones make it easy to pretend you don't care.

Sixth hour, AP History, was supposed to be my highlight,

though. It wasn't the subject. I'd rather read about Sasquatch or the search for alien life forms than about dead presidents. It was what it represented. A junior course; only a handful of sophomores were allowed to test in. Missy squeaked by with the minimum score. But I smoked that test, not a single point missed, and I even refused the extra time they offered so I wouldn't be accused of "special" treatment. Missy had always been the perfect one, the popular one, the pretty one. Acing the test meant I was the smart one.

Now, however, AP History meant more than a simple victory in a jealous rivalry; it was the sole representation of the real me. Being in that AP class validated me. It justified my belief that I did not belong in a special education class. I was AP History material, and I'd clung all day to the idea that AP History was my salvation. It would deliver me from evil.

Unfortunately, it wasn't deliverance. It was the doorway to another level of Hell.

Sixth hour started with my usual level of frustration. I'd misplaced my map and spilled water on my schedule. To make a long story short, I was still trying to decipher the room number well after the bell had rung. It was 200, 203, or 208. Through a process of elimination, I finally found it — but class had been in session for at least fifteen minutes already. I opened the door, heard the teacher's voice, and froze.

"Well, Miss Hart? Are you joining us?"

"I'm looking for AP History?"

"And you found it."

"But . . ." I frowned. "Why are you here?"

"I could ask you the same question," Mr. Dellian said. "Once again, you're wasting my class time. If you are staying, take a seat."

I'm sure my mouth dropped open; I was so shocked and infuriated, I think I even forgot to breathe. I know I forgot to sit. I just stood there and stared at him. Dellian was my AP teacher? How had I missed that? This was supposed to be my salvation! My chance to prove I didn't belong in Special Ed. I wanted an AP teacher, not the SPED teacher, *my* SPED teacher.

"Miss Hart," Mr. Dellian said in a tone that was half exasperation and half boredom, "we sit in this class."

I smelled Missy's signature scent, lavender and vanilla, and, repulsed, moved toward the center aisle. I suppose most people can see the empty seats in a classroom right away. I can't. Not until I'm a few feet away. And being pissed doesn't help me focus. I realized halfway up the center that all seats were taken. I backtracked and moved up the next aisle, only to discover it too was full.

"Today, please," Mr. Dellian said, fueling giggles from the rest of the class.

"Over here," a voice called.

I focused on the waving arm. It was pointing at a desk up front. On my way, I passed an empty seat in the back of the same row and, desperate to sit, took it instead.

Dellian droned on and on about class expectations and assignments. I only half listened, still annoyed. "Be sure to consult your syllabus for tomorrow's assignment," he said as class ended. "No assignment means an F in my classroom."

This caught my attention. "Wait, syllabus?"

"Syllabus." Mr. Dellian repeated. "And Miss Hart? You have

detention. You're not new; you're not a freshman. There's no excuse for being over fifteen minutes late to my class." He shoved a pink paper across his desk at me.

"But—" I snatched the paper from his desk. "Whatever." I rushed out of the room and slammed full force into someone blocking the doorway.

"Sorry," I said to the blue button-up, collared dress shirt. Its owner smelled of watermelon bubblegum. My eyes fell to the sleeve. It was the one that had waved me to a seat.

"That was my fault. Did you get a syllabus?"

"No, just detention." I darted a quick glance up at him. He was tall, too tall, with a crazy, out-of-control mop of brown curls. That was the puzzle piece I needed. I knew him. Greg Martin. Missy's neighbor. A junior. I'd had a crush on him until fifth grade, when he started following Missy around like a sick puppy dog. "Thought you went to that private school?"

"Trinity. I transferred. So, you remember me?"

"Hard to forget Missy's number-one fan." I focused on his ear. A dark blue smudge stood out on his cheek. "You've got something on your face."

He rubbed at it. "Erasable ink. I get it on my hand too." He showed me a smeared blue hand. "I hate making mistakes, and a pencil is so . . . rudimentary. What do you mean Missy's number-one fan?"

I shrugged, perplexed at how inked-up skin could rank higher in sophistication than writing in pencil. I began walking toward the sophomore hallway.

"I haven't seen you around Missy's house much," Greg said.

"We're doing our own thing right now." I turned toward the dead-end hallway that housed my locker. "See ya later," I said with a wave.

But Greg hurried after me. "I can make a copy of the syllabus for you."

"Beats asking Dellian, I guess. Thanks." I shook my head. "I can't believe he's teaching that class." I pulled up on my locker handle. Locked. I'd forgotten to leave the dial on the last number. The numbers were too small; I'd spent lunch with my face pressed up against the metal trying to get it open. I couldn't do that blind girl thing in front of him, though. I began haphazardly guessing at the numbers.

"Is he even qualified?" Greg asked. "He's used to mental cases and boneheads."

"Not everyone in Special Ed is a mental case or a bonehead." I spun the lock in frustration while I waited for him to stop talking and go.

"I meant the hockey team," he said. "He teaches Special Ed? That's even worse! A remedial teacher instructing an advanced placement course — that's just wrong." He set his books down on the floor. "Here, what's your combo?"

It was like listening to someone insult my mom — okay for me to do, not okay for someone else. I took his comment as a direct assault and glared at him.

His face scrunched up. "What?"

But "what" would've required a discussion about Life Skills, Special Ed, and me. Besides, I hated confrontation. "I don't have time for this." I stopped spinning the dial. "I've got detention."

"I'll get you that syllabus!" he yelled as I hurried away.

"Don't bother," I muttered out of earshot. "I'll get my own."

By the time I got home from detention, I just wanted to lose myself in music. One time in sixth-grade health class we watched a movie about this girl who would cut herself. She had scabs up and down her arm. She said feeling the razor slice her skin, the sting, the rush of pain, released all the anger and pain inside her. I remember thinking, *Why doesn't she just listen to some music?* because that's what music was for me. My razor. The angry lyrics, thrashing chords, banging drums — they open me up and bleed for me.

I flopped onto my bed, cranked *Saliva,* and glared up at the UFO photos that line the ceiling. I can't actually see the alleged alien aircrafts in the array of amateur shots, not unless I stand on tippy toes, face pressed against them. But I like the way my less-than-stellar vision blurs the backgrounds together into a gray-black sky. It's like staring into my own world. One where anything is possible.

Soon I'd mellowed enough to think. The counselor said my parents could get me out of Life Skills, and since appealing to Dellian's nonexistent soft side was out, and my dad was somewhere in New Mexico tracking UFOs, Mom was my only option. Convincing her wouldn't be easy, especially if she had to make dinner.

I ran upstairs and tossed frozen lasagna into the oven. While it baked, I went back down to my room to work on my History assignment — made possible thanks to Greg, who had slipped a neatly folded syllabus into my locker while I was in detention.

I was just finishing when Mom opened my door. "Do you have to play that garbage so loud?"

Garbage? Please. Mom's musical tastes are dictated by whatever loser she's dating—her last was a country fan. She even started wearing a cowboy hat and matching boots. Thank God they didn't date long. Then there was that new wave punk throwback she dated. He was actually pretty cool, and I liked his music, but Mom dressed like Adam Ant the whole time. And that wasn't cool or pretty.

"There's lasagna baking, if you're hungry." I reached over to turn down the music and noticed a to-go container in her hand. "Or not."

"Sorry, baby. I met someone at the club. Tony. He's real nice, took me out to eat." She checked herself out in my mirror. "So, how was school?"

I flipped my feet down onto the carpet. "They screwed up my schedule."

"Get it straightened out?"

"You have to. You said Life Skills is a new requirement for everyone. It's not. It's a special education class."

Mom leaned against the wall. "I know."

I stared at the door frame above her head. "You let them put me in there? Why?"

"Because you never listen to anyone, always insisting on doing everything yourself, your way. That kid who killed himself? He was like that. You don't know how to be disabled, Rozzy. They'll teach you."

"Teach me to be disabled? As if it's a job? That's ludicrous!

Daddy's lived his whole life with this eye disease. No one taught him to be disabled!"

"Maybe if they had, he wouldn't be chasing flying saucers in an RV driven by his twenty-year-old girlfriend."

Critical mistake, bringing Dad into it. I backpedaled. "Mom, I'm not suicidal. And I'm only bent on doing things myself because I *can*. I've been fending for myself long before anyone ever called me disabled." I softened my voice. "Please, Mom? I don't need this class."

She gave a long, exaggerated sigh. "I'll call tomorrow." I shot off the bed and hugged her. "But if they say you need it, you need it. Okay?"

Thirty-nine days before

I'd found a way out of Hell. Unfortunately, with Mom never up before noon, I knew I'd have to endure one more day of Life Skills. I circumvented the spinning Tricia without looking at her and headed to the back of the room. Within seconds, Tricia's desk was next to mine. She plopped down, pulled a canister of Insta-Whip from her cloak, and began squirting whipped cream into her mouth. It sounded like a dentist sucking spit from someone's mouth.

She caught me staring at her and held out the can. "Want some?"

"No. I'm good." I tuned in to the "academic" conversation Dellian and Jeffrey were having.

"But who would win a fight between Han Solo and Indiana Jones?" Jeffrey asked.

Mr. Dellian glanced at his watch. "Indiana Jones, I suppose, unless Han Solo used the Force."

"No! Han Solo isn't a Jedi," Jeffrey said. "He can't use the Force."

JJ, the guy in the wheelchair, snorted at this. I couldn't help smirking too. Even in a SPED class, Dellian was out of his league.

Dellian shrugged. "Perhaps Luke Skywalker taught it to him."

"You can't teach the Force!"

Jeffrey's loud outburst startled everyone, including Dellian. We all snapped our heads up to look at him as Mr. Dellian reprimanded. "Jeffrey, enough."

But Jeffrey wouldn't let it go. "No! You haven't answered me yet. Who would win, Han Solo or Indiana Jones?"

"Indiana Jones. Now, it's time for class, Jeffrey." Dellian turned to the rest of us. "As I was saying yesterday, this course will teach you to be self-sufficient. *Self-sufficient*, however, does not mean doing everything by yourself. To succeed, you must stand up for yourself, and that includes asking for help when you need it." He looked at me as he said this. He probably figured since I didn't ask him for the History syllabus, I wouldn't have the assignment. Bet he was dying to give me an F. I couldn't wait to see his reaction when I turned it in that afternoon.

"You'll be assigned a partner. If your partner is having a bad day, *you're* having a bad day. Understood?" He picked up a clipboard. The names of six students were apparently too much for him to memorize. "Because Bart has autism —"

"So do I!" Jeffrey interrupted.

"It's not a competition, Jeffrey. Please let me finish." I watched Bart as Mr. Dellian said this. He seemed unaware that he was being talked about. He just ate a chicken nugget, flapped his arms, ate another nugget, flapped again . . .

"Since Bart needs extra assistance," Mr. Dellian continued, "I'll be his partner. JJ and Jeffrey; Roz and Tricia; and our aide, Jonathan, will be your partner, Ruth."

"Maybe you should put Ruth with Tricia?" I said. "I'm switching out of here."

"Oh?" Dellian tilted his head. "How's that?"

"My mom's calling today. To say I don't need it."

"Well, I look forward to that conversation." His tone made me wish I'd kept quiet. "You're with Tricia." He started on a new topic — a job program for the juniors and seniors.

"Guess you're stuck with me." Tricia squirted a massive blob into her mouth. "Careful," she said through the whipped cream, "I bite when I've got the munchies."

The rest of the day dragged on like yesterday, second verse same as the first. As I took my lunch from my locker, I smelled watermelon bubblegum and glimpsed a tall figure coming my way. So much for lunch at my locker. I slammed it shut and pretended not to notice him as I headed toward the lunchroom.

The scent stayed with me. In my peripheral vision, I saw him to my left. He said nothing while we walked down the hallway. We reached the stairs together, feet falling in perfect unison, but still, we both pretended not to notice each other.

I stifled a manic giggle. If I ducked into the bathroom, would he follow me? When we neared the cafeteria, side by side, it became too awkward. I stopped. "Hi, Greg."

He stopped too. "Oh, hi!" he said. I tried to walk away then, but again he followed me, again saying nothing.

"Uh, thanks for the syllabus?" I tried.

That worked. Too well. "So you got it, then? Good, I worried I had the wrong locker." He bobbed his head, his mop more unruly than yesterday. "I was fairly confident it was the correct locker."

The area outside the cafeteria smelled like a perfume counter. And it was loud. Chatter echoed off the walls. Groups clogged the pathway. I hesitated a few yards from the entrance. Missy had to be at the center of one of those clusters. I should've grabbed my ear buds so I could look unbothered by her popularity. Of course, I hadn't planned on coming down here in the first place.

Greg slowed his pace too, still rambling. "I remembered there were three twos in the number, and it was in the right vicinity —"

Strong hands squeezed my shoulders from behind. "Hey, Beautiful!" Jonathan Webb draped his arm across my back.

I gave him an overly toothy grin. I couldn't help it. He made me lose all muscle control.

"Your mom get first hour straightened out?" He smiled at some girls to the right of us and then turned his full attention back on me.

"Working on it." I tried not to blush, but I could feel the blood in my cheeks.

"It'll be a drag without you." He gave my shoulders another squeeze before letting go. "See ya 'round, Rose." As he joined the group of girls, I glanced around to see if anyone had heard his mistake.

Greg had.

Why was he here anyway? I left him standing there and pushed through the crowd into the cafeteria. I threw myself down at a nearly empty table in the back, grabbed my apple out of my bag, and ripped a bite from it.

"Hey, Fritz. Ricky," a girl said to the guys at the end of my table. Fritz and Ricky. Two skateboarders who always wore shorts, even when it was forty-below outside. I heard the hand slaps of two high-fives, and then the girl slid in across from me. "Saw you talking to Zeus! Yummy!"

I looked up from my apple. Bright fuchsia sweater. Long raven-blue hair. Chin-length gold hoop earrings. Heather Torres. She hung on the fringe mostly, not popular, not a loser — although there was some controversy with her in fifth grade, I think. A fashionista, her every outfit was loud and dramatic, over-the-top, and truly out of place in Birch, Alaska, where fashion trends are a full year behind the rest of the world. I'd always admired that about her. She stood out and didn't care. "Yeah, yum." I rolled my eyes. "He can't even get my name right."

"No?" She stuck her lip out in a sympathetic pout. "Well, he did have his arm around you, so there's that. And Missy. Was. So. Green." She gave me a smile that said she knew the score between me and my ex-BFF. "Rona was all 'Helen Keller and Zeus? Not gonna happen, Missy. Not gonna happen.' But Missy thought it was happening." She stuck her hand out for a high-five. "Totally worth it?"

Helen Keller? Nice. It meant that not only had Missy told Rona about my eyes, but they'd laughed about it enough to give me a nickname. Who else had Missy told? Did the whole school know now? I cringed, but obliged Heather with a "Totally" and a high-five. I took another big bite of apple and prayed she wouldn't ask.

She didn't. Not right away. First she took a bite of her burger and shoved a bunch of fries into a vat of ketchup. "So, why 'Helen Keller'?"

I shrugged. "I can't see that well."

"You need glasses?"

Everyone always says that. Like a conditioned response. I studied the core of my apple. "I have contacts but . . ." I hated this part. It wasn't the questions people inevitably asked; it was their reactions. They fell into one of two categories: pity or discomfort. And I still didn't know how to handle either. "Legally I'm considered blind."

"Like cane-and-seeing-eye-dog blind? You don't look blind."

"I'm not. My vision isn't good enough to drive, though, so I'm 'legally' blind."

"Is that why you never look at people? I always thought you were just a bitch. No offense." She shoved the ketchup-soaked fries into her mouth.

Bitch. I'd heard that one before. Missy used to call me that and accuse me of ignoring people. From a distance, say when I'm walking down the hall, I can't see people's eyes, so I may hear them talk or may see them wave, but I don't know if they are looking at me or someone else. It's humiliating when you think someone's talking to you and they aren't. Just as humiliating when the guy you're crushing on thinks you just blew him off because he waved and you didn't wave back. That's why I stare at the ground or fiddle with my shirt or pretend to be reading when I'm in a crowd. Anything to avoid humiliation. "I can't really see faces, so . . ." I shrugged.

"But you can hear?"

"Uh, yeah?"

She smirked. "Well, Helen Keller couldn't! She was blind and deaf; mute, I think, too. Leave it to Rona to get it wrong. So can you see—" She looked across the cafeteria to search out a test object, then stopped and smiled at someone behind me.

I turned. Greg's finger went into my eye.

"Roz, I am *so* sorry!" He crouched to peer in my eye. "Are you okay?"

My eye stung. I blinked rapidly to make it tear up. "Is there salt on your finger?"

"Ink. Sorry."

I dabbed my watering eye with a napkin. "'S okay."

"So that was 'Zeus'?" Greg said, making punctuation marks with his hands. "The guy Missy likes?"

I blinked again to clear my eye. "Yep."

"I need more ketchup," Heather said.

Greg watched her leave. "Why aren't you eating with Missy?"

"Are you conducting a social survey or something?" I asked.

"No, I was just wondering." He sat down. "Is Zeus the reason you and Missy aren't talking?"

Greg's crush on Missy. Of course. He was hoping I'd taken Jonathan out of the picture so Missy could focus on someone else, like Greg. "No, he's not. We just met." I felt suddenly sorry for Greg with his knit sweater, Oxford collar, and ink-smudged chin. Missy'd never flit from Jonathan to Greg. He was wasting his time on her. "We've all changed, Greg. Me, you, Missy—we're not kids anymore. You know what I mean?"

"Yeah." He gave a nervous cough and I knew I'd embarrassed

him. Which embarrassed me. I looked into my bag and pulled my sandwich out.

"If I offended you yesterday somehow, I'm sorry. Okay?" He stood up.

"Okay." I slowly chewed my sandwich and willed him away.

Heather bounced up. "Too soon? I can go —"

"No! I mean —" I glanced up at Greg. "You can eat with us —"

He was backing up, though, flustered, no doubt, by my awesome hospitality. "I see . . . friends."

"Awk-ward," I said when he'd moved away.

"Oh, come on, he's cute," Heather whispered. "Not Zeus cute. Shy cute. Way too Ivy League–ish for me, though. What's his story?"

"Missy's next-door neighbor, just transferred from Trinity."

"He ask you out?" she said, her voice still low.

"Hardly." I laughed. "He's hot for Missy. Keeps lurking around me for info, practically stalking me." Heather made a face and mouthed something at me that I couldn't make out. "What?"

She pointed to the end of the table with her french fry. Oops. Greg was eating with Fritz and Ricky, and by the way he sat motionless, staring at the lunch bag in front of him, I was pretty sure he'd heard me.

I took a front-row seat in AP, and as I pulled out my assignment the smell of watermelon bubblegum caught my attention. *He must shop wholesale for that gum,* I thought and looked up.

"I'm not *hot* for Missy," Greg muttered, darting a glance in her direction, "and I'm not stalking you either. That's my assigned seat."

"I'm sorry I said that." I paused. "Assigned seat? We have assigned seats?"

"Please put your assignments in this basket," Mr. Dellian said.

Greg walked his over. I followed, giving Dellian my best I-don't-need-Life-Skills-see?-I-got-the-syllabus-all-on-my-own smile.

Dellian looked unimpressed. "Miss Hart, if you don't want to be marked absent, I suggest you take your assigned seat."

I rolled my eyes at Greg's smug expression and slid my books off his desk. "I wasn't given an assigned seat."

"You were sitting at a desk yesterday, correct? That's your assigned seat."

"Oh." I couldn't see the board back there, though. Perfect opportunity to demonstrate my life skills. I turned back around. "Could I move?"

He hesitated a moment, as if my asking to move was a really difficult question. "No, you're *fine* back there, aren't you?" — a smug smirk in his tone. "Take your assigned seat, Miss Hart."

Even though the rest of the class didn't know those were my words from Life Skills yesterday that he was repeating, I knew. My cheeks flushed, anger rising. I went to his desk, all too aware that everyone was now listening. "You want me to admit it? Fine," I whispered. "You're right. I can't see from back there, okay? Now can I move?"

"You can't see?" he said too loud to be accidental. "Perhaps you should invest in a pair of glasses, Miss Hart." The class laughed.

As if I hadn't heard that before. I folded my arms and said nothing.

He postured against his desk. "You had bad eyesight yesterday, didn't you?"

"Yeah, it's kind of an ongoing thing."

"Yet you chose to sit in the back. Bad choice, wouldn't you agree?"

"Okay, I get it! I should've sat in the front, but I was late. God! Why are you being such a —" I stopped myself too late.

"I won't tolerate disrespect in my classroom," Mr. Dellian said in a voice as thick as ice. "I can and *will* kick you out of here."

"I'm sorry —"

He didn't let me finish. "In my classroom, students are assigned the seat they take on the first day. I don't change my seating chart once it's complete. Now —"

I expected him to say "I'll let it slide" or "Don't let it happen again," not "Take your seat in the back, Miss Hart."

"What?" I stared in disbelief. "You have to let me switch! It's —"

"It's what?" he asked.

I heard the challenge in his voice. What an ass. He wanted me to say "It's in my IEP." To admit out loud that I had a disability, that I needed special help — *his* special help. Well, I wasn't going to play his stupid game anymore. I wasn't going to beg him for a seat up front. I didn't need it that badly. I focused my blind spot on his face and glared at him.

"I'll switch with her," Greg offered.

"How gallant of you" — Dellian consulted his seating chart — "Mr. Martin. But then I'd have to mark you both absent."

Greg shrugged at me apologetically.

"Are we finished? I'd like to start class." Mr. Dellian's bored tone made me want to scream.

"Yes." I marched back to my assigned seat and silently screamed a thousand obscenities while he shuffled through the assignments, all smug and arrogant.

"Oh, and Miss Hart?" Mr. Dellian said without looking up. "I had a lovely discussion with your mother earlier. We decided to keep you in your Special Education class. We both feel you need it."

My body exploded. Hellfire. Brimstone. Lava dripped from my pores. I wanted to fly across the room. Tear the flesh from his limbs. I glared at the back of his head. Burned holes in his skull while he rifled through the pages as if he'd merely commented on the weather.

Everyone else knew the weight of his comment, though. The tension that settled over the room told me they were watching, waiting to see what I would do. If only I had telekinetic powers. I'd burst him into flames, his desk combusting with a boom. The best I could do was focus my central vision on him, making the reddish-orange dots that block my vision engulf him, make him disappear.

Slowly my laser gaze slipped from Dellian to the empty desk next to Greg. I don't remember making a conscious decision. But I guess I did.

I thought, *Screw you, Dellian!*

And then I stood, walked back up to that front-row seat, and made it mine.

"Rozzy, why do you do this?" Mom said when I told her Dellian was now marking me absent for sitting in the front. "He's trying to help you!"

This was *my* fault? "He tells me to stand up for myself in Life Skills and then when I do, he punishes me? How is that helping? It makes no sense!"

"With that attitude of yours, I'd mark you absent too."

"Whatever, Mom," I muttered. "Can you at least admit he's being stupid?"

She sighed as if I were exhausting her. "Trying to keep you from self-destructing so you don't end up like that poor kid is not stupid, Rozzy. You have to start accepting the fact that there are things you can't do. Maybe that AP class isn't such a good idea."

"What? No!"

"You have a disability, Rozzy. No one expects you to become a brain surgeon."

"So what? I should take Underwater Basket Weaving instead of AP History? Why even bother with school? I'll just quit and find men to live off of like you do."

Too far. "You can take the bus to school," Mom said, heading back to bed. It didn't matter anyway. It was obvious I was on my own on this one. Dellian had her snowed.

"'Half of the harm that is done in this world is due to people who want to feel important,'" Greg said as we left AP. "T. S. Eliot. Have you told your parents about Dellian's power trip?"

I snorted. "Tried. Mom thinks he walks on water, though."

"Mine too. Hockey coach, yearbook advisor, Special Education teacher — Principal Ratner is so impressed with Dellian's multiple talents that he didn't even think twice when Ms. Ludlow moved out of state at the last minute. He handed AP over like an offering to the gods." Greg shook his head in disgust. "Anyway, when Mom talked with Mr. Dellian, he said we're just using your impairment as an excuse to sit together."

I stared, horrified. His mom? Talked to Dellian? My "impairment"?

"Oh, I'm sorry." He frowned. "Is *impairment* not the right word?"

"It's . . . fine," I said. There was so much wrong with what he'd said, I didn't know where to start. "You know about my . . . ? You told your mom?"

"Missy told me about your impairment, and Mom's the school nurse. I thought she could help you with Mr. Dellian."

"Oh." Heat rushed to my face as I imagined all the things Missy probably told him. I tried to steer the conversation away from my eyes. "That's kind of stupid, isn't it? I mean, why would it matter if we sat together? Your mom bought that?"

"I know. Stupid." Greg gave a little laugh and pushed his hand through his curls. "So stupid. No idea why she'd believe him. As you said, I guess she thinks he walks on water too." He shrugged as we reached my locker. "Maybe you should sit where he says. If you're worried about not seeing the board, I'll take notes for you."

God, now he feels sorry *for me.* "I don't need your notes," I said. "I'm not giving in. He's wrong, not me."

"He *is* wrong. He's also in control. If you sit in the back and get notes from me, you take back control."

"Control? I'll be sitting where he wants me to sit instead of where I need to sit; getting notes from you instead of taking them myself. That's not being *in* control; that's *being* controlled." I pulled up on the locker handle. Ugh, why couldn't I remember to keep it unlocked? I turned back to end the conversation so he'd leave. "It doesn't matter. I'm going to tell the principal."

"You want to go now? I can vouch for everything."

"I have to catch my bus. I'll try tomorrow."

"Let me know when you do," he said, turning to go. "I'll back you up."

As I walked to my bus, I wondered how Dellian could have everyone so snowed. The adults, anyway. Tricia, on the other hand, seemed to have Dellian snowed. She had him walking on eggshells around her — I actually kind of admired that aspect of her.

Yes, she was a freak. Twirling in the hall, wearing a cloak no hard-core *Star Wars* fan would even wear in public, ignoring all the snide comments people made. And she'd turn on you quickly, morphing into a witch without warning, claws out, ready to take down anyone. Brutally mean one minute, sincerely sweet the next;

it was obvious Tricia was psycho. But was she truly psychotic, or was it an act to keep Dellian off her back?

Was "psychotic psycho" the way to handle him? Would he leave me alone if I were erratic and unpredictable like Tricia? Tempting, I thought, as I boarded my unusually crowded bus. But I wasn't capable of psychotic behavior, not in front of Jonathan, or anyone really.

The bus pulled through the school parking lot and into the left-turn lane, bringing me out of my thoughts. We were headed out of town. *Crap,* I thought, standing up. "Driver? I'm sorry. I got on the wrong bus." I couldn't see the bus numbers on the side, but my bus was always parked in the second slot. I'd just assumed it was mine, without checking with the driver.

We lurched to a stop and I hurried past the other students, ignoring their dirty looks and "What are you, in kindergarten?" comments. My bus was long gone by now; I trudged toward the city bus stop — embarrassed and humiliated. The familiar burning at my ears brought me right back to Dellian.

What did he want anyway? All his talk about the Americans with Disabilities Act in Life Skills — he had to be doing this to make a point. The whole premise was ridiculous. What teacher marks a student absent for sitting in the front? Especially one with an IEP that says she must sit there? It was a game. He wasn't for real. Whatever his point, whatever his game — I thought as I climbed aboard the *correct* city bus — I was going to prove to him once and for all that I *have* life skills.

Twenty-nine days before

One Friday, Tricia wasn't spinning in the hall. Nor was she shooting whipped cream at her desk. It didn't faze me much; even freaks get sick. I was munching on one of the brownies Ruth had brought when Mr. Dellian stormed in.

"Miss Hart! Where's your partner?"

"I . . . don't know."

"Find her! When she's not here, you get her here, understood?"

Jonathan shook his head in sympathy as I walked by.

The hall was deserted. With no idea of where she'd be, I decided to just pretend I'd scoured the school looking for her. I ducked into the girls' handicapped bathroom and was attempting to prop my butt up on the rail Tricia-style when I heard a sniffle next door.

"Tricia?" I pushed on the other stall door. It was locked. "Come on. Mr. Dellian wants you in class."

"Go to Hell."

"I'm already *in* Hell. Come on, open up! I've got better things to do than babysit you."

A leg plopped down on the ground and the lock turned.

I shoved the door open. Tricia was hunched against the wall, staring hard at the toilet paper roll. "What're you doing?" I asked.

She lifted her right hand, revealing a syringe clenched in her fist. "I'm out of pot."

The sight of the needle made me shiver. I'd never seen a drug needle before, except in movies. "And that's your alternative? Ever try a plain old cigarette?"

"I don't want to use it." Tricia turned her hollow eyes toward me. "Pot keeps the edge off. I've been clean for three months."

"Well, you have a prescription for it, right? Can't you go get more?"

"I don't have a frigging prescription!" Her voice turned to a little-girl whine. "Rodney took my stash. He says I have to do this on my own, but I can't. I can't." She brought her hands up to her face. I winced at how close the needle came to her eye. "Go get me some, okay?"

"Get you some *weed*? Are you insane?" I stared at the needle. This was way over my head. "I'll go get Dellian —"

"No! He'll send me back to rehab." She started to cry. "I'll kill myself before I go back there."

She wasn't my friend, or even someone I wanted for a friend; she was just a messed-up freak in the bathroom in need of serious help. The intelligent part of me knew I should get Dellian, or the nurse, or the principal, someone in authority who could help her. But the pleading whine in her voice and her crumbled state struck a chord with me. The whipped-cream-squirting, cloak-twirling, I-don't-give-a-shit routine was all an act. Underneath she was a defeated, deflated shell of a girl struggling to reright herself. Fighting for control. Broken.

Like me.

SPED wasn't where I belonged, despite what the "authorities" said; maybe rehab wasn't where she belonged either. As messed up as it sounded, maybe smoking pot to stay clean was the right way for her. And Dellian had taken that away.

"The pot, it really keeps you from" — I gestured at the needle — "that?"

Tricia slapped at a tear dripping down her chin and nodded.

It's just pot, I told myself. *Doctors write prescriptions for it all the time, right? It's gotta be safer than whatever is in that needle.* "Okay. Where do I get it? The vending machines are fresh out."

Tricia smiled slightly. "Go ask Jonathan."

"Jonathan? Webb? How would he know?"

She leaned her head against the stall. "Just go ask him."

I hesitated outside of class. I needed a lie. I couldn't waltz in and announce, "I need Jonathan in the girls' bathroom and, oh by the way, a bag of pot too."

"I found Tricia," I said, opening the door. "But she's . . . sick. I need someone to help me bring her back in here." I didn't wait for Mr. Dellian to respond. "Jonathan?"

Jonathan followed me out the door. "She's not puking everywhere, is she?"

"No." Clear of the classroom, I pulled him to the wall. "She's in some sort of drug withdrawal." I scanned the empty hall. "She needs some pot."

Jonathan frowned. "She's addicted to pot? Is that possible? I'd always heard —"

"I don't know what she's addicted to!" I hated how out of

control my voice sounded. I lowered it, hoping a whisper would disguise the panic. "Something in a needle. Pot keeps her from shooting up. Can you help me find some?" My voice wavered as I gave in to the panic. "Or should we just get Dellian?"

"No, no teachers. She'll get in more trouble." Jonathan put his arm around my shoulder. "Relax. We'll help her."

I took a much-needed breath and nodded.

"My friend Ethan can find some." He looked at his watch, his arm still around me. I liked how it felt. Warm. Safe. "She have money?"

"I don't know. I have" — I pulled some cash from my pocket — "fourteen?"

He took the bills from me. "I don't think that'll cover it." He opened his wallet. It looked empty. "I only have a twenty, and I gotta buy gas today."

"I have my ATM card." As if I had money. Social Security deposits a check every month to my savings account. Mom's compensation for "being saddled with a disabled kid." It's our grocery money.

"Cool." He looked at his watch again. "There's one about a block from here. We can be back before class ends. Where is she?"

We entered the bathroom. Jonathan knelt down next to Tricia, carefully releasing the needle from her grasp. "We're gonna help you," he said. "Can you hold it together a while longer?"

Tricia nodded. "I can't pay."

"It's already covered." He smiled up at me. A brilliant, awesome smile.

I couldn't help grinning.

Tricia's eyes slid to me, a dead expression on her face.

My grin slithered away. "We'll be back." I hurried out.

"I'm really sticking my neck out for you two," Jonathan told me. We were sneaking out the back entrance, by Auto Shop. "I could get kicked off the team for this."

"I know," I said. "This isn't my usual thing either."

We ran around the side of the school to the seniors' parking lot. Jonathan jumped into the driver's side of his Corvette and leaned across to unlock the door for me.

"What *is* your usual thing?" Jonathan asked.

Not sure what he was asking, I shrugged. "I don't know."

He started the engine. Some techno-bass dance music boomed through his stereo speakers. He turned it down. "You don't know what you like to do for fun?"

I took in the interior smell — leather, musky cologne, baby powder air freshener — and scrambled for something to say. Listen to any kind of music *except* techno-bass dance hits? Collect UFO photos? Watch *Ghost Team* episodes? I doubted any of that would scream *fun* to him. *Nerd,* maybe. *Run for the hills,* maybe. But definitely not *fun.* It didn't matter anyway. He'd already moved on to the next question.

The one I was dreading.

"How come you're still in that class? Thought they made a mistake?"

I stared at the black-and-white bunny air freshener hanging from the mirror. What would happen if I told him it wasn't a mistake, not as far as the school was concerned? Would he still talk to me? It's not that I was super into him, not like Missy, anyway.

But he *was* Jonathan Webb. Everyone wanted to be with him. Me included.

And I was. Sitting in his car. With him. Talking. Granted, we were on our way to get money for a drug deal, but still. Being there with him made me feel normal. I didn't want it to end with him learning I was a freak.

In my peripheral vision, I saw him watching me, waiting for an answer. I could lie. He was Dellian's aide, though. He'd eventually figure it out, and then I'd look even stupider for lying. "Long story," I said with a shrug.

"Someone as beautiful as you?" He smiled that brilliant smile again. "It's obvious you don't belong in there."

Beautiful? No one had ever called me beautiful. Not even my parents. And I didn't believe I was or could be. Beautiful was a category reserved for runway models and actresses and Missy Cervanos. Not girls with vision-robbing eye diseases.

Yet Jonathan had called me beautiful. Twice. Something in the way he said it made it seem a basic truth, like rain is wet and sun is warm. He said it as if he believed it, and I wanted to believe it too. Desperately.

I think I blushed, gave an embarrassed laugh, and said something like "thanks."

He grinned. "I'll be bummed, but I hope you get it straightened out."

"I don't think I will. Dellian won't let me switch. He thinks I need the class because I don't see that well."

"So get glasses." He pulled in to the bank's parking lot.

Funny how everyone always thinks that's the solution. "I have contacts, but they only help some because . . ." My heart started racing. I hesitated, afraid to continue. Would I still be beautiful if I explained it to him? Which category would he be in, discomfort or pity?

He gave me a funny look. "Did you want me to go up to the ATM with you?"

"Oh." No questions? There were always questions. Unless he was too freaked already to ask. "No." I opened the passenger door. "Be right back."

"Take out eighty."

"Eighty?" My mouth fell open. "That much?" My account was for groceries only. A twenty I could explain, but eighty?

"Maybe more. Not really sure." He tilted his head. "Don't have the funds?" When I shook my head, he motioned. "Come here."

I brought my legs back inside and shut the door.

He leaned over. His fingers gently pulled at my hair. He isolated a strand. Twirled it around his finger. His musky scent floated in the small space between us. "Take out what you can." He stroked my chin with his fingertips. "I'll get the rest somehow."

I pulled myself back together, starting with the breath he'd stolen. "You sure?"

"I'm sure." He gave me a sly, crooked grin. "You want to go to a party at Birch Hill with me tomorrow night?"

"Seriously? Yes!" I flushed with pleasure. Jonathan Webb had just asked me out. Me. Roswell Hart. Not Missy Cervano. Not one of the gorgeously available senior girls, but me. And to Birch Hill! A campground outside the city limits that was mostly deserted from September to May. The parties there were legendary — and exclusive. I'd never been last year. Even Missy had gone only once. I couldn't believe I was going to go, and with Jonathan Webb!

"Cool." He nodded toward the door. "Get what you can. We gotta get back."

"Don't worry. I'll take out eighty." What was eighty dollars anyway? I could come up with a lie, tell Mom I bought organic veggies or something. It was better than making Jonathan come up with it. It wasn't his problem. I'd brought him into this.

Thirty minutes after leaving, we slipped back into the side entrance of the school and hurried to the handicapped bathroom.

"Got it?" Tricia snapped.

"Chill!" Jonathan bit back. "Give me 'til lunch."

Tricia's cold eyes met Jonathan's. After a brief standoff, she said, "Rodney sent Ruth in here."

"Ruth?" I said. *Great, we're busted.* "Does Dellian know — ?"

Tricia's head whipped back in my direction. "That you two were screwing 'round in Jonathan's car?"

I glared at her. "We were —"

Jonathan put his hand on my arm. "Relax. Ruth won't tell, but D's suspicious." He turned back to Tricia. "Convince him!"

Tricia slowly pulled herself up and sauntered out of the bathroom.

I trailed behind her, paranoia mounting. I'd stuck my butt out for this ungrateful witch? And now, in her drug-withdrawn, maniacal state, she was supposed to convince Dellian all was cool? I couldn't afford more trouble, not with Dellian.

Tricia started flailing her arms as if some invisible entity were attacking her. "Let me go!" Her right arm smacked me hard on the head.

"Knock it off!" I shoved her arm away.

Tricia's lip curled into a snarl. "Grab my arm, you idiot!"

"We can't get her down there," Jonathan yelled as Dellian flew into the hallway.

Dellian grabbed Tricia's elbow and guided her toward class while I watched, bewildered. The way Tricia morphed so easily from on-the-edge drug addict to insubordinate SPED student, convincing Dellian as Jonathan had directed, playing him like a well-used guitar — I couldn't help wondering. Had I just been played too?

"Shut up!" Heather stopped stabbing her french fry in ketchup and stared at me. "Zeus put his arm around you? During class?"

Telling her we were in his car getting money for a drug deal would've killed the hype. I rubbed at an imaginary blemish on my apple. "We were on an errand for our teacher."

"That is so awesome! Hey, Stanford!" she said as Greg joined Fritz and Ricky on the other side of the table.

"Stanford?" Ricky repeated and looked at Greg.

"'Cause he's so Ivy League with his collared shirts and academic pursuits," Heather explained.

"Actually," Greg said, "Stanford isn't an Ivy League school. It's in California."

"Precisely." Heather grinned.

Greg seemed unsure whether he'd been insulted or not. I wasn't sure myself.

Behind me someone began singing "Copacabana."

"'She would merengue and do the cha-cha . . .'"

Heather, her fry midway to her mouth, peered over my shoulder. "Oh. My. God." A blob of ketchup fell to the table. "What is she on?"

"Dude!" Fritz said. "She must be buzzin' hard!"

I could see only movement above the crowd. "Is she standing on a table?"

"Yeah," Greg said. He turned back around, ignoring the spectacle behind him.

The rest of us kept watching.

Ricky whistled. "Now she's *dancing* on the table."

"What a slut!" Heather said. "You see how short that skirt is?"

"Ooh!" Fritz and Ricky both yelled as the girl did something.

"What?" I asked. "Who is it?"

"She's crawling across the table on her hands and knees. All seductress-like," Heather said. "It's that nut job who always wears the cape. She's got it draped like a boa around her neck."

"Great," I muttered, a sick feeling creeping into my stomach.

"I see her at my apartment building a lot," Heather continued. "She stays with this guy, brings a baby with her too. A new baby, only a few months old."

"A baby?" "Mother" was not a label I'd ever think to give Tricia.

"Oh, my God!" Heather giggled, as more than just Fritz and Ricky whooped around us. "I think she might start stripping."

I'd heard enough. I flew to the table. So did Dellian and two lunch monitors.

"We got her," Dellian told them. He and I each grabbed an arm and pulled her off the table. Despite some uncooperative squirming, we carry-walked her toward the exit.

Tricia turned her head to Mr. Dellian. "Rodney," she cooed, her voice whispery light. She nuzzled his neck.

He shrugged her off, letting her head fly violently to the other side. "To the nurse's office," he commanded.

We dragged Tricia to one of the two beds in the empty nurse's office. "T.," Mr. Dellian whispered, so softly I wasn't sure he'd said it. "What have you done? I thought you were past this?" He examined each arm, running a finger slowly up and down the veins, then ripped her shoes off and looked between her toes.

She giggled, muttered something, and giggled again. Her head lolled, her eyes rolling to the back of her head.

"Don't just stand there! Go find the nurse!" He slammed his fingers on Tricia's wrists. "And call 911!"

I scurried to the main office and came back with the nurse and a few bystanders. "Ambulance is on the way," the nurse said and pushed Mr. Dellian's fingers out of the way to take Tricia's pulse herself. "What did she take?"

"I don't know," he said. "She went through rehab a few months ago for heroin addiction. But there are no fresh tracks anywhere, not even between her toes."

"I . . . I think she was smoking pot," I offered.

"This isn't pot," Mr. Dellian snarled. Sirens wailed in the distance. "I'm meeting them at the door." Dellian picked Tricia up, cradling her like an infant. "I'll call her foster parents," he yelled from the hall. "I've got them on speed dial."

I stared after them. This was my fault. *What if she dies?*

"Are you close with her?" the nurse asked.

"No, I just met her." *I should've told Dellian what was up when I found her in the bathroom. God, what has happened?*

"But you were with her when she did this?" she asked. "You brought her here?"

"I helped Mr. Dellian bring her." *If this wasn't pot, then Tricia must've shot up with that needle. But Jonathan had taken it away. We should've searched her.* "Will she be okay?"

"I think so. Anytime drugs are involved, though, you can't be too careful." She smiled and handed me a pass. "Lunch is over. You should get to class."

"No tracks" meant no needle marks. If it wasn't pot, and she didn't shoot up, what was she on? Could something have been wrong with the pot? I needed to find Jonathan.

I was heading outside to leave a note on his windshield when he and another guy came in carrying fast-food bags. "Jonathan!"

"Later, Ethan," Jonathan said with a nod. "Hey, Beautiful, what's up?"

"Did you get Tricia the pot? 'Cause —"

He covered my mouth. "Shhh, not so loud."

"Dellian took her to the hospital," I whispered. "Did you give the needle back?"

"Tossed that." He led me from the entrance. "What happened?"

"She was dancing on the lunch tables." I liked being close to him, having a secret only we shared. It made me feel important. "Did you get her the pot?"

"Ethan said he'd take care of it. I'm sure he did."

"You didn't ask? That was a lot of money! *My* money. How could you not—" The image of Tricia cradled in Dellian's arms made me shut up. "I hope she's okay."

"Relax. Tricia's always pulling crap like this." He gave me a soft smile that made my heart somersault in my chest. "I'll ask Ethan, okay?"

"Hey!" Heather yelled behind me as I walked away. "Geez! Didn't you see me? I kept waving at you. You mad or something?"

"No! I just . . . sorry. What's up? I gotta get to class," I said.

"Just wondering what happened? Copacabana's boyfriend take her home?"

"Her boyfriend?" I asked.

"Yeah, the guy who helped get her down. He lives in my apartment building."

"Dellian?" I stared at her. "He's the guy Tricia visits with the baby?"

Heather nodded. "The very one."

Twenty-eight days before

Saturday night, Jonathan parked in an isolated campsite by the river at the bottom of Birch Hill. "Easier to sneak out if the cops come," he explained as he pulled into some bushes, out of view.

"Cops?" After Tricia yesterday, I didn't need more adrenaline pumping through my veins. Then again, running from the police with Jonathan by my side could be exciting.

Jonathan waved his hand. "Don't worry. Ethan's been sneaking the key from his dad for years, and we've never been caught. We're too far out of town for them to care."

The party was in the lodge used by Scout troops during the summer, but there were plenty of people outside too, huddled around bonfires. One large group called out to Jonathan as we came up, all football players and cheerleaders still in uniform from the game earlier in the day.

"Hey!" Jonathan said to a few of them. The group quickly engulfed him, and I was left standing outside the circle, feeling embarrassed and unsure of what to do.

"Roz?" a voice said.

My eyes flicked to the red and black Chance High Ravens jersey and then to the mop of curls. "You play football?" I said in surprise.

"I wouldn't say 'play.' I'm barely tolerable," Greg said with a laugh. "It's my first—"

"Hey, Roseanna," someone yelled. "Roseanna!"

"I think he's talking to you," Greg muttered.

My face began to burn as I turned to see Jonathan waving at me. "Come on. Let's go inside."

"You're with him?" An accusation, not a question. "He doesn't even know your name!"

I walked away without replying. "It's Roz," I whispered as I rejoined Jonathan. "Not Roseanna."

"I knew that!" He put his hand on the small of my back and led me toward the lodge. His touch made me feel confident, and I forgot his mistake as he guided me past girl after girl after girl, his hand leaving my back only to pull a keg donation from the wad of cash in his wallet.

Music poured from the walls. It filled the outside air with guitar riffs and bass that thumped through me like an additional heartbeat. This was my element. My body thrived on it. Made me giddy. Alive.

Once we were inside, though, the music deafened me and my mood began to change. Without my hearing to guide me, I felt out of it. Isolated. Unsure. An alien in someone else's world. I faked smiles and gave false nods when Jonathan's friends talked to me, all the while straining to hear, trying to read their gestures, desperate to know what they were saying or doing or laughing about. My earlier confidence drained away. Jonathan brought me a plastic cup of beer. Grateful for the distraction, I gulped the bitter liquid down. With a grin, Jonathan handed me another. I gulped it too, a little more slowly this time. The alcohol traveled through me. My muscles tingled, warm and relaxed. Soon I forgot about pretending. With a swig of beer, I belonged again.

Ethan said something. I leaned into him and giggled. "What?"

He laughed and handed me another cup of beer.

I'd just taken a big drink of it when Jonathan swooped it from me. "You don't need that," he whispered. His warm breath on my ear made me dizzy.

I snuggled closer to him.

His fingers played with my hair, stroked my neck, my ear. "Are you messed up?"

"Maybe," I whispered. His touch felt too amazing for me to concentrate on anything else.

He pulled me closer, muttered something. The words were muffled, simply sounds strung together. But his body against mine made me shiver. I moved my cheek closer to his mouth, breathing in his musky scent. His lips brushed my chin, my lips.

He was more intoxicating than the beer. I lost awareness of everything around me as I kissed him back.

Gently, he released me, grasped my hand, and led me away from the crowd. I stumbled along with him through the blurry fog of faces and bodies, up a flight of stairs to the loft. He stretched out on a reclining chair and pulled me down with him.

My world spun, my stomach flip-flopped. I was falling, spinning into a void. I leaned up to steady myself.

"You okay?" Jonathan asked. He seemed far away, too far away to catch me.

I tried to speak, but my mouth wouldn't work. My limbs felt like concrete. Light collapsed in on me, and then . . . darkness.

Twenty-seven days before

Flat black eyes stared at me. I blinked my contacts clear and stared back at the tiny moose faces on the upholstered chair. Peeling my cheek off the seat, I pushed myself up to a sitting position.

Bigger, blacker eyes greeted me. Satan herself. "Morning, bitch."

"It's morning?" I shot a look around me. Still in the loft. Music blaring. Sounds of people partying, though quieter now. Fewer people were down there.

"Two a.m.," Tricia said. "Shouldn't you be home with Mommy?"

"What do you want?" How was it so late? *Oooh*. My head pounded. I let it fall back against the chair. "Where's Jonathan?"

"Not here." Tricia pulled a cigarette from her cloak and lit it.

The smell gagged me. "Oh God. I think I'm —"

Tricia shoved a small plastic trash can under me, catching the vomit as it spilled from my lips. "I'm really sick of cleaning up your puke."

I snatched the trash can from her hand. "Then leave! I don't remember asking you to be here."

"I'm sure you don't remember much of anything," Tricia snapped. "You were passed out."

"I remember your strip routine in the cafeteria. Do you?" I meant this to sting, but the effort was too much. It came out in a dry whisper.

"Yeah." Tricia's voice softened. "That's why I'm babysitting your ass."

"I don't need a babysitter." I needed water. I tried to stand. My legs wobbled and the room spun. I sat back down.

"No? You wanted to be gang-raped then?"

The air left my lungs. I stared at Tricia's ear.

A wicked smile crossed her lips as she took a drag from her cigarette. "Could've happened, though, if I hadn't been watching. Don't you know not to pass out at parties?"

"It's not as if I knew I was going to pass out!"

"You're right. You don't know." She took another drag. "This isn't your scene. You don't belong here."

"Oh, but you do?" I said. "You think a . . . wastoid freak like you belongs here?" Instantly I regretted the words. I tensed, ready for retaliation.

She merely raised her eyebrows at me. "Wastoid freak?" She shrugged. "Yeah, that's me. I live in this wasteland. *You* don't have to."

I wasn't ready for us to be friendly; it was too weird and awkward. I redirected the conversation. "What happened at the hospital?"

"I slept it off." She took another drag. "Rodney overreacted."

Footsteps fell on the stairs. Tricia put the cigarette out on her palm and stood. "Come on. I'll get you home."

"Hey, Beautiful." Jonathan stepped into the loft. "Didn't know you were such a lightweight. How you feelin'?"

"Okay." I tried to stand. Tricia held out her cloaked arm and I clutched it.

"I'm taking her home," Tricia said.

"I got her." Jonathan put his arm around my waist. "You don't have wheels."

"I have access to wheels." Tricia pulled out her cell.

"She doesn't want to wait," he said. "Do you, Beautiful?"

And he was right. I didn't want to wait. I wanted to go home and lie down, snug in my bed, and sleep. "Thanks, Tricia, but Jonathan can drive me. I came with him."

"Suit yourself." She ripped her arm from me, unsteadying me for a split second before Jonathan gripped me tighter. Tricia glared at him and hissed, "Be more careful next time," then disappeared in a swirl of brown.

"Don't worry." Jonathan guided me toward the stairs. "Next time I won't let you drink them so fast."

Next time? Despite my concrete limbs and pounding head, I felt awesome. As I floated on Jonathan's arm through the minefield of discarded cups, spilled beer, and wasted bodies, I realized that somehow I'd done it. Somehow I'd crawled from the heap of rejects into the Land of the Chosen and found Normal.

It's not as if Jonathan said we were boyfriend and girlfriend; I don't think people really do that anyway, not like in the movies. It was just, you know, understood. He was always around and his attention made me feel beautiful and wanted. He made me belong. Nothing Dellian said or did now in class could change how people saw me. I was Zeus's girl. I must be normal.

This must've annoyed Dellian because a few weeks after Jonathan and I started dating, Dellian went for what he could still affect — my AP grade. As he handed out progress reports that Friday, he announced that a full grade of extra credit would be given to anyone who attended and wrote a paper on the Salem witch trials exhibit at the university museum. "However, it ends tomorrow. Given the long drive, you'll likely be forfeiting your plans for Saturday evening." There was a groan from the class. "I thought some of you would feel that way." He slapped my report down in front of me.

I stared in horror at the large C- on my report. I'd got As on the few assignments we'd had, but he'd been giving me zero after zero for participation.

"Of course" — Dellian looked right at me — "some of you who need the credit won't be going because you don't have a vehicle."

It was a challenge, plain and simple. Maybe he knew Mom worked weekends at the makeup counter and couldn't take me. Maybe he knew Jonathan would never miss a Saturday night with his friends to take me. Maybe he assumed I was too stupid or too chicken to use public transportation. Whatever it was he thought he knew, he was confident I wouldn't go. So he'd made sure I would need the credit.

"Ethan's having a party out at the Hill, Beautiful," Jonathan said when I asked him after school if he could take me. He cradled my face and kissed my nose. "How about Sunday?"

"Saturday's the only day. You two are going out tonight. Go with me? Please?"

"Miss the party for some museum? No way! Everyone expects me to be there."

I gave him a good pout face. "Don't have too much fun without me, 'kay?"

He pulled away from me. "You're not going with me?"

"I told you, I have to go to the exhibit."

"You're blowing me off? For a stupid museum?"

"I'm not blowing you off." I reached for his arm. He shrugged me away and left. "Jonathan!" I yelled after him.

Heather walked up. "He mad 'cause you dissed him earlier?"

"What?" I frowned at her. "When?"

"After lunch," Heather said. "He was talking to Liz Cobler and a bunch of others — you walked by him and didn't even smile."

"I did? He didn't say anything." I thought back to lunch. I had passed by so many groups, though, he could've been anywhere and I wouldn't have seen him.

"No? Liz even gave him crap about it. So why is he mad then?"

"Because I can't go to Ethan's party tomorrow. I have to see a museum exhibit for History." I looked at her hopefully. "Come with me? We could take the bus —"

"Are you crazy?" Heather said. "I finally got invited to one of Ethan's parties; I am *not* missing it."

Seven days before

"Rozzy," Mom yelled from the garage Saturday morning. "You going?"

Going crazy, yes. Jonathan wouldn't answer my calls, and I was questioning whether or not the extra credit was worth a fight with him.

But I knew it was. This was about more than a stupid grade. It was about standing up to Dellian. I grabbed my jacket and climbed in the back of Mom's bright orange hybrid.

"What is this thing you're doing in the city?" she asked.

"An exhibit on the Salem witch trials."

"Witchcraft? You know there's no such thing?" She clicked her tongue, shaking her head. "You're too much like your father."

"It's on the witch *trials,* Mom, not about witchcraft. And it's for class." I decided not to mention the exhibit *We Are Not Alone!* that I also hoped to visit while there.

"I'm just saying there's no such thing, okay? So don't get it in your head to start tracking down witches."

I rolled my eyes and stared out at the sun just starting to wake up on the horizon. The days were already so dark; winter would be here soon.

She dropped me at the bus station, and I sauntered inside to buy a round-trip ticket. The place was deserted, which was good. Three hours was a long time to ride in a crowded bus. "What time does the bus arrive back here tonight?" I asked, taking the tickets from the clerk.

"You're starin' right at the schedule," he said, and pointed behind him.

Actually, I was looking at *him* — or trying to — and I couldn't see the schedule. Which is why I had asked. "Sorry," I said, my cheeks getting hot. "I can't read that."

"They don't teach you kids to read no more? Nine . . . oh . . . two." He emphasized each number as if I were an idiot.

I ignored him and turned away. "Hey," I said on Jonathan's voice mail as I walked back outside to wait for the bus. "I can make the party after nine. Call me back."

A purple car with huge windows and a rounded back end pulled up in front of me. It looked more alien than automotive. Fingers emerged from the passenger window. "Roz!"

The sound of my name startled me. I bent down to look through the open window, half expecting a spindly gray creature with enormous eyes at the steering wheel. The fingers waved. "It's Greg. You're going into the city for the exhibit, aren't you? You need a ride?"

"Oh, hey!" I said. Of course he was going. What would that give him? An A++ in the class? The bus pulled up behind him and honked. "Thanks, but I already bought my ticket. Besides, I like taking the bus." The bus honked again, the driver really laying on the horn this time. I stepped back. "You'd better move before he drives over you! See you there."

I settled into a seat near the back. I'd spent most of last night making a playlist for this trip: *D. Can't Mess with Me*. It had a rather catchy title, I thought. Most of the tunes had bring-it-on lyrics, but I'd thrown a few love tracks on there too, to remind me of Jonathan. I had just pushed "play" when an all-too-familiar scent filled the air above me. I plucked the earphones from my ears. "What are you doing?"

"You won't ride with me, so I'll ride with you." Greg plopped down next to me.

A man wearing an oil-stained bomber jacket shuffled by. The smell of dehydrated onions and body odor lingered in the aisle.

Greg covered his nose. "You prefer this over my car?"

I laughed. "Watermelon bubblegum runs a close second to city bus smell."

"You don't like watermelon gum?"

"Actually, I do now. I used to think it was a bit strong, but . . ." I didn't finish. It would've sounded a bit come-on-ish if I'd said, "Now it reminds me of you."

He whipped the green pack of gum from his pocket and offered me a piece.

"Thanks." I took a square out and popped it in my mouth.

Loud voices came from up front. I heard the driver tell someone to get off the bus. As hostile words and obscenities flew, I felt Greg's body stiffen next to me.

I caught the smell of dryer sheets as I leaned in to Greg and whispered, "The company's much more appealing too," to distract him.

It worked. He put a hand on his heart. "I'm insulted."

"You should be."

A security guard jumped on and escorted someone off. Greg relaxed against the seat and grinned at me. "I think you were just chicken to drive in my hovercraft."

"Hovercraft!" I grinned at this. "It does have that otherworldly look to it. I bet even E.T. would hesitate to climb in for a ride."

His hand grabbed his chest again. "You're killing me! I'll have you know, it belonged to my grandmother. It's a 1980 Pacer, but in mint condition. Well, as mint as any decades-old car with an infinite number of miles on it can be."

"I stand corrected."

The bus lurched forward, jostling us against each other. One of my ear phones fell on Greg's shoulder.

"'Without music, life would be an error.' Nietzsche. So what are we listening to?" He held it up to his ear and then gave a thumbs-up. "Nine Inch Nails!"

I arched an eyebrow in surprise. I had him pegged as a Mozart or Bach guy; maybe B. B. King or Joe Satriani, if he was feeling dangerous, but Nine Inch Nails? Definitely would never have guessed that.

"One of my favorite bands," he said. "Nothing like screaming to 'Head Like a Hole' when things aren't going my way, you know?"

"Yeah," I said, grinning, because I *did* know, all too well. I pushed the "shuffle" button. "How about this?"

"I like that. Who is it?"

"Shinedown." I shuffled the player again. "How about this one?"

He beamed at me. "Godsmack."

No way! I squinted at the player. With my playlists memorized, I simply had to decipher a letter or two to "see" the bands. "How about—"

Greg laughed. "Is this a test? Because if it is"—he reached into his jacket pocket—"I have my own artillery. Care to play?" He handed me an earphone.

"Try me." I listened for a second, and then with smug certainty said, "Van Halen. Hagar, not Roth."

He shrugged. "Beginner's luck. You'll never get this one."

I let the music flood my ears. The voice sounded familiar. The lyrics I didn't recognize. "Is it Buckcherry?"

"Ha! I knew I'd baffle you!" He shook his head. "Tesla, although I will admit Buckcherry sounds a little like Tesla to the unfamiliar listener." He pulled a notebook from his pocket. "Let's keep track. The person with the most correct artists wins."

We spent the rest of the trip trying to stump each other. It was the most fun I'd had on a road trip. Ever.

"I didn't realize the characters in *The Crucible* were real people," I said. Greg was reading a list of those executed during the 1692 Salem witch trials out loud to me.

"You've read the play?"

"Movie," I said. "I don't read that much outside of school."

"You should. Movies are never like the books. *The Crucible* is one of the High School Hundred."

"High School Hundred?" I pulled out my cell phone. No call from Jonathan.

"One hundred literary works college-bound students should read before they graduate. That's why I read it."

"Oh." I put away my phone. "I watched the movie because I thought it was about witchcraft."

"And let me guess," he said with a laugh. "You were disappointed?"

"It was good, but some witchy, voodooish stuff would've made it better." We reached the end of the exhibit. "But that was the point, right? They weren't witches. Lies just spiraled out of control. So now what?" I wanted to suggest the planetarium exhibit. The bus wouldn't be leaving for four hours. We had time. But I was too afraid he'd laugh at the idea.

"Let's go eat," he said.

"So," Greg said after we'd bought a couple of hot dogs and sodas, "why don't you like to read?"

"It's not that I don't like to," I said. We sat down on the edge of a fountain in the center of campus. "It's just really frustrating sometimes. The print is usually too small and it takes too much effort." I shrugged.

"Most books come out on audio now. Or you could get yourself one of those readers like the one my grandmother has. It scans a book within minutes and reads it aloud."

It was one thing hearing this stuff from Dellian. But Greg? I breathed in the late September air. It smelled damp. "I think it might rain," I said.

We both looked up at the sky. The once-green leaves, now brilliant shades of orange and gold, created a striking contrast with its clear, cloudless blue.

Greg shook his head. "Too clear."

"Smells like rain." I sniffed the air again. "And fall. I love that smell."

"Decomposing foliage?" Greg shoved a bite of bun into his mouth. "Me too," he said over the mouthful. "It's actually methane and carbon dioxide released from rotting plants. The dead foliage feeds the fungi and bacteria living around it." He finished his last bite. "Fall's my favorite season."

He certainly had an endless supply of information. I finished eating my hot dog. "Winter's my favorite season. Not the cold. I hate the ice fog and the below-zero weather. But I like how the world gets quiet and the snow covers everything with a soft white blanket that tricks you. It hides things, making even a dirty, cluttered dump beautiful."

"Like T. S. Eliot. 'Winter kept us warm, covering Earth in forgetful snow.'"

"The Hundred list again?" I opened my soda.

He nodded. "*The Waste Land*. It's a poem."

Tricia had mentioned a wasteland when I called her a wastoid freak. I thought she was being clever with her word choice; maybe under that cloak Tricia was a scholar?

"We know I need the credit," I said after a while. "But why'd you come?"

"The way Mr. Dellian has been lately? I figured a few extra points couldn't hurt." He held his can up, examining it. "Truth? I also figured you might like the company."

"How did you even know I'd go?"

"I knew Roswell Hart wouldn't back out of a challenge, especially one issued by Mr. Dellian."

"Really?" I was flattered. And embarrassed. And a little annoyed. "You think you know me that well?"

"Well enough." A smile played at the corner of his mouth. "When Heather said you'd be taking the bus by yourself, I thought—"

And there it was. The real reason he'd come. "You thought you'd make sure the poor 'impaired' girl didn't get lost? So this was what, a charity event?"

"No!" He frowned. "It wasn't like that at all! I didn't come to assist you, just to hang out with you. I only asked Heather to make sure that, you know, Jonathan wasn't going. Because I didn't want to hang out with him. Just you."

Embarrassment replaced my anger. "Sorry. I get defensive sometimes."

"Apology accepted." He set his soda can on the edge of the fountain. "Think we have time for the planetarium? I've been dying to see their *We Are Not Alone!* exhibit."

I choked on my soda. "Seriously? I've been dying to see that too."

A toothy grin spread across his face. "Then let's stop killing ourselves and go."

The rain started on our way back to the bus station. It was sprinkling at first; then, in a sudden gust of cold air, huge pellets of hail began to fall. "You said it smelled like rain, not hail!" Greg joked as we ran the last two blocks, jackets over our heads.

I rubbed at my arms when we'd finally made it inside. Even with my sweatshirt on, the tiny shards of ice managed to sting my skin. The terminal announced that departure would be delayed due to the weather. While Greg called his mom, I called Jonathan. Voice mail. He hadn't returned any of my calls. I was beginning to think it wouldn't matter what time I arrived. He wasn't going to be there.

"So." Greg shoved his phone into his pocket. "What's your theory on alien existence?"

"My theory?" I shrugged. "I don't have one."

"Sure you do." He sat down, looked up at me, and waited.

"Okay. Actually?" I sat down next to him. "The idea really freaks me out. But believing there are others out there somewhere, as if it's a given or a truth . . ." I started to feel stupid. I stared down at the wet patches the hail had left on my jeans. "I don't know. It makes it less frightening somehow."

"Believing takes the unknown element away, to avoid being blindsided later on?" Greg nodded. "That makes sense. My theory's based on science. It takes the right conditions to support life. We're pretty arrogant, though, if we believe those conditions occurred only on Earth. So our life forms can't live on those other planets. There are microbes that can survive in toxic environments here on Earth. Why not intelligent life forms somewhere else? Man is so egocentric; we think we know everything. Arrogance, no, pride." He stomped in frustration. "What is that quote?"

I laughed. "I don't know. Does it matter?"

"Yeah, it's a good one about arrogance being man's downfall."

"You like quotes?" I pulled out my music. "I'll find you a good one. Lyrics are full of them."

He gave a snort. "It's not the same. My quotes come from world-renowned authors, philosophers, the Bible."

"Now who's being arrogant?" I began scanning my playlists. "Come on, I bet I can find a lyric worth quoting."

We started listening to each other's music in search of wisdom. By the time we boarded the bus, the game had mutated into "Name That Tune" or, as Greg called it, "Try to Stump Roz" — because he rarely could.

The temperature yo-yoed the whole way home, causing downpours of alternating rain and hail. The road was a mess, keeping traffic at a crawl. It was well after ten o'clock when we arrived at the Birch bus terminal. "Is your mom picking you up?" Greg asked. "I can give you a ride."

I flipped open my phone. Still no call. What the hell? The damp cold bit through me. I shivered and hugged my jacket close. Should I call him again or just forget it?

"That is, if you can brave it," Greg said. "I've heard E.T. wouldn't."

Jonathan was probably too drunk to drive anyway. I grinned at Greg. "I think I can handle it."

He opened the passenger door. I scooted in and buckled up. The interior of his car was spotless. Only the outlandish amount of room and the dashboard with its knobs, push buttons, and large gauges gave away its age. Everything else was in perfect condition. No rips or tears in the upholstery. No door handles falling off. It even had a new-car smell.

"I think it's going to snow soon — the pond by my house has already started to freeze over," Greg said, cranking up the heat. "I'm not looking forward to playing football once that happens."

"Maybe it will hold off at least until homecoming. Did you nominate people for royalty in homeroom yesterday?" I slid my cell phone out again. Still nothing.

"Is someone calling you? You keep looking at that thing."

I snapped the phone shut. "I thought Jonathan might. There was this party tonight." I shook my head. "Doesn't matter."

"I can give you a ride to Ethan's party, if that's where you want to be."

"I don't. I just want Jonathan to call me back. He was mad that I went to the museum."

"Mad? Doesn't he realize you need the credit?"

I shrugged. "I canceled our plans. He thought I was blowing him off."

"Well, I'm glad you did. I had fun today." He smiled over at me.

"Me too." I smiled back at him — okay, at his ear. He tried to catch my eye, so I looked away. "My house is on the next street."

"Do I make you uncomfortable?" he asked. "You never make

eye contact with me. You look at my ear or my shoulder, but never my face."

"No!" He'd caught me off-guard. "To see your eyes, I have to look at your ear." I gave a nervous laugh. "Weird, I know, but dots block things straight on, so I focus on something else and use my peripheral vision. Missy was always so creeped out by it — I figured she told you."

"She only said you have a vision problem. Is it like a sunspot I'd have to blink to see around?"

I laughed in surprise. "Yeah! That's exactly what it's like." That was the first time someone had ever understood my explanation. It felt — I don't know — freeing?

He pulled into my driveway and parked. "I don't think anyone's home."

"Never is." I started fishing through my purse for my keys.

He flipped on the interior light. "How come you haven't talked to Ratner yet about Dellian?"

I sighed and looked up from my bag. "I thought it would get better."

"Well, it hasn't. You should talk to him or sit in the back and let me take notes for you. I'm thorough. I record the lectures with my MP3 player for backup."

My fingers found the jagged edges of my keys. "I'd like that, actually. The notes." Dellian had started writing very small on the board. Even though I was sitting up front, it was hard to decipher them. "I'm not moving to the back, though." I opened the car door and lingered. I wasn't ready to say goodbye. The day had been too much fun. "You want to come in? I have some photos I think you'd like."

"If you don't think your mom will mind."

"She won't mind." I unlocked the door. "The photos are downstairs, on my bedroom ceiling."

Greg kicked his shoes off and jumped up on my bed, standing on his tippy toes to examine each of the UFO photographs plastered on my ceiling. "These are amazing. Where'd you get them?"

"My dad." I leaned back against my headboard. "He sends them in lieu of child support. Mom tried to sell one on eBay once, but no one bid. So she lets me have them."

"How does he find all these?"

"People give them to him. He's a . . . ufologist."

"Ufologist? Is that a real job?" He looked down at me. "He gets paid to study UFOs?"

I laughed. "Don't be too impressed. Mom made the same mistake — she heard the 'ologist' and saw dollar signs. Not sure if it's a legit title. But I know he doesn't make money doing it, just a grant here and there." I pulled my cell phone out. It was a habit by now. I didn't want to talk to Jonathan or go to the party anymore — I simply wanted to see if he'd called. So I could ignore it. "What's your verdict? Do aliens exist?" I turned my eyes back up to Greg.

He was watching me. "Did he call?" There was a tinge of annoyance in his voice.

"No, just . . . checking."

His hands left the ceiling. "Well, some of these probably are overexposure or sunspots. I'd have to look at where each was taken, the circumstances surrounding each incident, that sort of thing. They're definitely awesome." He stepped off the bed and leaned in an awkward pose against the dresser. "Your name, Roswell, makes sense now. I always wondered."

"My dad's idea. He said it was a family name. Mom says if she'd known it was a town in New Mexico, she never would've agreed." I fiddled with the phone in my hand.

"I should get going." He slipped his shoes back on and headed up the stairs.

"I had fun today," I said when we reached the door.

"Did you?" He turned around. "You seem really eager to call him."

"No! I mean, yes, I had fun. A lot of fun." I tried to give him a reassuring smile. "I'm not eager. I just" — I rubbed my thumb across the face of my phone — "wanted to see if he'd called, if he was" — I shrugged — "missing me."

"Roz, why—" Greg paused. "Never mind." He pushed the screen door open. "I'll get those notes to you Monday."

An insane desperation came over me on Sunday. I called Jonathan's cell every half hour. I walked by his house. I became the stalker I'd accused Greg of being. My heart pounded; my body shook. I could focus on nothing but making things right with him. I had to know that he still wanted me. That I was still beautiful.

Monday morning, he didn't pick me up. I called him every three minutes until finally, out of time, I had to wake Mom up to drive me and then I beelined to Life Skills. I flew past Tricia spinning in the hallway and ran into the classroom.

Tricia followed. "Can't say hi?"

"Leave me alone." I surveyed the classroom. He wasn't there yet. I threw my books down next to my desk and trotted back into the hallway.

Tricia trailed behind. "You know your name spelled backwards is Llew-sor?"

Clever. I made a mental scan of her name backwards, but got nothing. "You spend all weekend coming up with that?" The first bell rang. No Jonathan. I moved to the end of the hall, searching in both directions.

"Trouble in paradise?" Tricia said.

"No!" I snapped. "He's just late."

"Or off playing with his new toy."

"Shouldn't you be shooting whipped cream somewhere right now?"

"And miss this? Not a chance."

"There is no *this*. I'm just waiting for my boyfriend."

"Girls." Mr. Dellian motioned into the room with his head.

Tricia leaned forward after he'd gone back inside. "Boyfriend? I saw him at Ethan's Saturday, all wrapped up with his new doll — he's done playing with you." Tricia smiled her wicked smile and turned away.

I yanked her backwards by the hood of her cloak. "What are you talking about?"

"Watch it!" She examined her hood for a second, and then gave me an exaggerated look of sympathy. "Oh, you thought he really *liked* you? You were the payoff in my drug deal. Nothing more."

"You're sick."

"Am I? I had no money, remember? He took you as collateral. But I've got my own payment plan now. Your services are no longer required."

I hated her. "You self-absorbed witch. This has nothing to do with you."

"I thought there was no 'this'?"

"He asked me out." I seethed. "We were dating. *Are* dating." My voice got louder, angrier. "He's mad because I couldn't go out Saturday. Would he have got mad if I was just your — your —"

"Crack whore?" Tricia offered.

"Screw you," I said, and left Tricia laughing in the hallway.

I couldn't concentrate on anything, not even the chocolate éclairs Ruth had brought. I was too consumed by anger. And panic. What if he really had hooked up with someone else at Ethan's party?

I tried to find him after class.

Again before third and fourth.

Left messages. Texts.

At lunch, I ran outside to the seniors' parking lot. I got there just in time to see a brown blur getting into a shiny red blob a few yards away. The loud engine and boom of the base as it sped out of the school lot sent jealous waves through me. Tricia? What the hell was he doing with Tricia? I ripped out my phone as I came back inside.

"Hi," Greg said, walking up. "I'm still working on your notes. Tomorrow okay?"

"Fine," I mumbled. I called Jonathan. He wouldn't answer. Why wouldn't he answer? Where were they going? I turned back to the door and stared out the window.

"You waiting for someone?" Greg asked.

"No, just—" I turned around and headed to the cafeteria. I needed to talk to Heather. Maybe she'd seen something at Ethan's party. Heard something.

Heather wasn't there yet. I sat down at our table to wait.

"I wrote my paper for Dellian." Greg sat next to me. "The extra-credit one? Could you look it over?" He held it out to me. "Hope the font is large enough for you."

He had nothing to do with my foul mood. But I was angry and frustrated and he was there, annoying me with petty things like notes and extra-credit papers — and the large-font comment put me over the top. I ripped a red pen from my purse and raged through his paper, slashing words at random, then threw it back at him.

"What is this?" Greg cried. "Why did you mark all over my paper?"

"Because it's wrong!"

He rubbed at the red markings with his eraser, but couldn't remove them. I don't use erasable ink. "You didn't even read it! How do you know it's wrong?"

"Because you're wrong!" Tears sprang to my eyes.

Greg stared at me. "About what?"

I turned away from him.

He leaned forward. "Look at me," he whispered. When I wouldn't, he stretched his body across the table until his face was directly in front of mine. "What's wrong, Roz? Why are you upset with me?"

On the other side of the room I heard Missy laughing with her cronies. Her cackle made me realize Greg was not the enemy. "It's not you." I swiped at a tear before it could escape my eyelid. "Sorry about your paper." I focused my eyes on the renegade curl that had fallen across his left eye. "Jonathan won't talk to me."

"Oh." Greg recoiled, his eyes falling on the ink-riddled paper.

"I saw him leaving, with Tricia of all people. Why would he be with her? And she said he was with someone at Ethan's. I thought she was just trying to get at me like she always does, but she was with him just now! I saw them!"

Greg stood up. "Maybe you should let sleeping dogs lie." He picked up his essay and untouched lunch. "I have to go."

"Whatever!" I muttered as he walked away. I snatched up my own untouched lunch and retreated to my locker.

Minutes later, while I slammed books around on the shelf, Jonathan slipped his arms around my waist. "Hey, Beautiful."

"Jonathan!" I turned and hugged him hard. "Where've you been?"

"Around." He nuzzled my neck. "You still mad at me?"

"I never was! You were mad at me because I went to the museum."

"Yeah, I heard you went with some loser. What's up with that?"

"You mean Greg?" I inhaled his musky smell. Relished the warmth of his arms around me. "I didn't go *with* him. We were both there, so we hung out. Seriously, Greg's just a . . ." What? A friend? Friends don't ditch each other the way he had just ditched me in the cafeteria. "A classmate."

Jonathan pulled me close. "Bet he wants to be more." He kissed my chin.

I pushed away slightly. "Were you with Tricia at lunch?"

"Tricia? Nah." He kissed my ear. "I just got here."

"I saw her get into your car, Jonathan. I saw you two leaving." I tried to stay focused, to stand my ground. My body was melting into his touch, though, losing the battle.

"You sure it was my car, Beautiful? You know you don't see that well."

"I thought it was your car," I mumbled as his lips caressed my neck again. But I was already starting to doubt myself. I hadn't actually seen *his* car, had I? Just a *red* car.

"Nah, wasn't me." He pulled me in tighter. "You know I'm up for King." His lips brushed mine. "Be my homecoming date?"

My body surged as he kissed me again. "Yes!" I breathed.

He gently pulled away and slipped his hand in mine. "Come on, let's get out of here."

Hours later, while we were snuggling on my living room couch (I was too embarrassed by my UFO pictures to bring Jonathan into my room) and I was listening to Jonathan complain about Dellian's attempts to get him off the hockey team, the doorbell rang.

"Shit," he said. We scrambled to untangle our bodies. "Is that your mom?" He'd parked at his house and walked over in case she came home early, but still, we hadn't really thought she would.

I shoved his jacket at him and flew over to the living room curtains. Greg's purple hovercraft sat in the driveway. "Why's he here?"

Jonathan looked over my shoulder. "What the hell kind of car is that? Is that that loser?" He flew downstairs and ripped the door open. "What do you want?"

I could hear Greg's awkward surprise. "I . . . need to talk to Roz."

"Well, she doesn't want to talk to you," Jonathan said.

I felt embarrassed for Greg standing there, all uncomfortable. But I was annoyed at him for spouting that ridiculous quote and ditching me in the cafeteria. I stepped up to the door and looped my arm in Jonathan's. "I'm busy, Greg." I focused my dots on his face to fake eye contact so he'd know I meant it.

"That means get lost," Jonathan added.

Greg shoved a stack of papers at me. "If you don't show for class, the deal's off."

"What deal?" Jonathan asked, slamming the door shut.

"Class notes." I flipped through the notes as we walked back upstairs. Every single day was in there. Dated, categorized by topic. Typed. Large font. Bold.

This had taken time, effort. All for me. And I was a total bitch to him.

Suddenly I didn't want Jonathan there anymore.

I just wanted to be alone.

The next morning, my Life Skills class headed to the Division of Vocational Rehabilitation, the first step toward Dellian's job program. Everyone was excited. Ruth even brought croissants for the road. But I was distracted. Yesterday I'd been so quick to skip with Jonathan. The sight of Dellian, however, reminded me that he'd be asking for a pass in sixth hour.

"In the van, Miss Hart," Dellian said to me, and then to everyone, "Sit with your partners, please."

"But I always sit in the front," Jeffrey said. "I have to sit in the front."

"Not today, Jeffrey. Go sit in the middle bench with JJ."

"No! I. Sit. In. The. Front."

I ignored Jeffrey's outburst — it was pretty much routine anytime something was out of order or not what he expected — and headed to the back, where Tricia sat sprawled across the bench, spraying whipped cream on her croissant and licking it off. I flung her cloak off the corner of the seat and sat down.

Tricia clutched the material to her body. "You rip it, I kill you."

"Why do you wear that stupid thing anyway?" I said. "You attend a lot of impromptu Star Wars conventions?"

"Star Wars conventions?" Jeffrey said. He dropped his battle with Dellian and climbed into the middle seat. "Where?"

"Go away!" we yelled in unison. He turned back around.

"My mom made this." Tricia smoothed her cloak. "Before she went to prison."

"Prison?" I echoed, sure this was yet another lie to get a reaction from me.

Tricia squirted another blob of Insta-Whip from the canister, pushed the cap on, and shoved it in her pocket. "For killing her dealer."

"Lovely," I said.

"It was. All that blood on her Tahitian-brown satin sheets." Tricia's eyes glossed over. "Spreading out like petals on a flower."

"You saw it happen?" I still wasn't buying this. Tricia loved drama.

"Yeah." She breathed on the window until a little circle of fog formed. Slowly, she traced her finger through it, forming a smiley face. "Wayne was on top of me when she stabbed him."

"Jesus, Tricia!" My stomach wrenched. "That's, that's—"

She whirled around. "That's what?"

I stared back, at a loss for words. "That's . . . awful." There was nothing else to say. Whether true or another one of her lies, it was awful.

"So's your breath." She turned back to making smiley faces on the window.

Maybe it was the sickening revelation that drugs weren't Tricia's only demons; maybe it was shame over the notes Greg had painstakingly typed out for me; or maybe it was simply selfish fear because I didn't have an excuse for missing class the day before. Whatever nudged me, I decided right before lunch that it was time to talk to the principal.

"Mr. Dellian has been marking me absent —" I began.

"Yes." Principal Ratner leaned back in his chair. "Mr. Dellian informed me of this situation. Our tardy policy is clear. If you're more than fifteen minutes late, you're marked absent, whether you eventually make it to class or not."

Wait, what? "No, see, I was never tardy!"

"You've never been tardy?"

"No." I shook my head. "Well, yeah, I was late the first day because I got lost . . ." And I flat out skipped yesterday. "For most of those absences, I was there the whole time. He's lying."

"Roswell, when someone won't even make eye contact with me, it usually means *she* is lying."

"But I'm not!" This was not going well. "My eyesight —"

"Mr. Dellian said you'd try to use your disability to get out of this. Let me guess. He's not accommodating your IEP?"

My mouth dropped open.

"He said you'd say that too." He gave me a look of pity. "Mr. Dellian knows his students very well, Roswell, including you. He thinks you may be feeling overwhelmed with the AP class but are afraid to admit it. No one will think any less of you if you transfer out, okay? But skipping or arriving unacceptably late, that's a disruption and not fair to the rest of the class."

My mouth was still open. Dellian had thought of everything. It was all twisted, distorted. "You don't understand —"

"I do understand. And if I had my way, you'd be suspended for these absences, but Mr. Dellian requested that nothing be done at this time. He's given you a second chance, Roswell. Use it wisely." As I stood up to go, he added, "If you need to get out of that AP class, I can send you to the counselor right now."

I didn't answer — my body was caught between crying and screaming, and I really wasn't sure what would've come out of my mouth if I had answered. I left, feeling powerless and trapped, and desperate to talk to Greg. He was the only person who seemed to understand. Maybe he'd have an idea of what to do next.

If he'd talk to me.

I hurried toward Heather and Greg at our usual lunch table. "Greg—"

"Hey, Roz!" Fritz said as my face began to burn. I'd mistaken him and Ricky for Greg and Heather. It would have been comical if it hadn't been so embarrassing. "Heather sick again?"

I frowned, disoriented by my mistake. "Not sure," I said, searching now for Greg. "Is she at *Grease* tryouts?"

Fritz shook his head. "Those aren't until Thursday."

"Oh." I hadn't spoken to her since Friday. *Was* she sick? Or was skipping two days in a row normal for her? "Have you seen Greg Martin anywhere?"

Fritz pointed to the far corner of the cafeteria. "Tell Heather I said hey."

"Thanks. I will." I made my way to where Greg sat studying. "I talked to Ratner just now," I said, sitting down. "Dellian sold him some story about my being supertardy every day because I can't hack an AP class."

"That's too bad," Greg mumbled without looking up.

Not the response I'd hoped for. "Thanks for the notes. They're very thorough and neat and . . . thanks."

Greg gave a half nod, still not looking at me.

"I won't miss class again," I continued. "Jonathan and I—"

"I don't want to hear about him."

"'Kay." I shrugged. "I won't talk about him."

"Good." He pretended to read his notebook.

I stared at his ear. "I know you're not reading," I said. "I'm the queen of fake reading. The trick is to move your head a teensy bit from left to right to look legit. And turn the page in a timely fashion. That's a must."

"I'm studying. I don't need to turn the page."

"Oh. Are you studying the same word over and over? 'Cause you're not moving your eyes that I can see. That could be because I can't see . . . " I was making a fool of myself. I just wanted to apologize. I ripped the notebook from under his nose, ignoring his outcry, flipped to a clean page, scribbled "I'm sorry," and shoved it back at him.

He shrugged and gave me a blank stare.

I rolled my eyes. Of course he wasn't going to make this easy. "I was a bitch yesterday. Forgive me?" I wrote.

He took the pen from me: "Yes. I'm sorry too for being a jerk."

"You weren't a jerk. I was," I said.

"We both were." He smiled. "It would've been difficult ignoring you during our presentation."

"What presentation?"

"That's what I wanted to tell you last night. Dellian said we have to present what we learned at the exhibit to the class today if we want our extra credit."

"Why does he want me to fail so badly?" I said, my voice catching.

Greg shook his head. "He tried to get me to present yesterday. I'm sure because you weren't there. I lied and said you had all our notes." He tapped his notebook. "I made us bullet points."

I imagined him in class freaking out, stressing, lying. Meanwhile, where was I? At home with Jonathan's tongue down my throat? "Sorry you had to lie." I sighed, feeling defeated and deflated. Everything had spun so out of control. "Maybe I should just sit in that back seat, huh?"

Greg sighed too. "It might be the only way to stay above water at this point."

"I guess he wins."

"No," Greg said softly, "he hasn't, Roz. We'll find another way to win."

I hated taking that seat, and the way Dellian gloated over my sudden compliance made me sick. He noted my presence with a loud "Hart, present!," gave Greg and me an enthusiastic "Well done!" after our presentation, and remained uncharacteristically upbeat throughout his lecture.

"Miss Hart?" he said after class ended. "Now that you are sitting where you belong, are there any accommodations I can provide you? Prewritten notes perhaps?"

"Whatever." I started to leave.

"One more thing." He picked up his attendance book. "With the number of absences, yesterday's puts you at risk of suspension. Do you have a note excusing you?"

"Suspended? That's the first time I've missed!"

"I'm not going to discuss the number of days you have or have not missed, Miss Hart. Do you have an excuse for yesterday?"

"No." I didn't know how to fight anymore. *Go ahead,* I thought, *I give up.*

Mr. Dellian leaned back in his chair. "Were you by any chance with Ms. Torres?"

"Ms. Torres? You mean Heather? How do you . . . ? You don't—"

"No, I don't have her in any classes, if that's what you're asking, but I am aware that she has been absent these past two days and that you two are friends. How is she?"

"She's . . . hanging in there?" Why was *he* asking about Heather? Had something happened to her?

"Please tell her I asked about her. I'll erase this absence for now, but if you miss again without an excuse, you'll be suspended. Understood?"

"Yes." He was erasing it? That didn't make sense. None of this made sense. I yanked my cell phone out and dialed Heather's cell as I left the room.

Greg was waiting. "What happened?"

The call went straight to voice mail. "Heather, this is Roz. Call me." I shut the phone and looked at Greg. "I need to find Heather's address."

"Is something wrong?"

"Maybe. I need a phone book." We walked down to the main office and borrowed the white pages. "What's her dad's name?" Greg asked. "There are tons of Torreses."

Crud. I had no idea. "Wait!" I said as he closed the book. "Look up Dellian!"

"Mr. Dellian? I thought you wanted—"

"He lives below her! Find his address and we can—"

"Find hers," Greg finished, his head already scanning the book again. "Got it, and"—he flipped back to the *T* section—"got it. Let's go!"

When we'd pulled onto the highway, Greg asked, "So why the urgency?"

"Mr. Dellian asked if I was with Heather when I skipped class yesterday."

"Reasonable assumption—you were both absent, and you're friends."

"You don't understand. She doesn't have him for any classes. She didn't even know he was a teacher. She thought he was Tricia's boyfriend because Tricia's there all the time."

"At his apartment? Yuck!"

"I know. Anyway, Dellian told me to tell Heather he'd asked about her."

"So he's being neighborly."

"No!" I cried. "She doesn't know him. She doesn't talk to him. How would he know she was sick if she isn't in any of his classes and she doesn't talk to him?"

"Okay." Greg nodded. "That is a little weird."

"More than a little." I tried Heather's cell phone. Again it went to voice mail. I dialed the home number Greg had copied from the phone book. It rang and rang.

"When was the last time you talked to her?" Greg asked.

"Friday afternoon. I asked her to go to the museum with me."

"You haven't talked to her since Friday?" Greg glanced at me. "And you're just now getting worried?"

"I've been busy!" I said. "And I don't know her *that* well. I thought maybe skipping was routine for her." But his question shamed me. I was a lousy friend. "I'm worried now, though. *Really* worried."

We climbed the stairs to Heather's third-floor apartment and knocked. No answer.

I put my ear near the door and listened. "She's in there."

Greg pushed his head up against the door and listened. "I don't hear anything."

"Well, I do. I have sonic ears; trust me. She's on the other side of the door. Heather?" I said into the door. "Come on, open up. It's Roz."

The chain clanked. Heather slowly opened the door. Dark half-moons covered the skin below her eyes, rubbed mascara maybe, or lack of sleep, or both. Her hair was tangled and matted.

"Hey." She stiffened when she saw Greg. "What's he doing here?"

"I drove," Greg explained. "But I don't have to stay."

"Okay," Heather said.

Greg shrugged at me. "I guess I'm going. Call when you're ready to go home."

"You have football practice, right? I'll take the bus."

"No, call me." He took my cell and began pushing buttons. "I'm programming me into your speed dial." He handed it back. "Number 2 for my cell, number 3 for my home."

"Only number 2?" I asked. "Why not number 1?"

"One's voice mail." He paused. "You were being sarcastic. I can take my numbers out if you don't want them."

"No, I want them." I brought my hand up just as he went to grab the phone back. Our fingers tangled. For a startled second, his eyes caught mine.

I pulled free and looked away as Greg shoved his hand in his pocket.

Heather grunted and shuffled back into the dark apartment, letting go of the door.

I stuck my foot between the door and the frame to keep it open. "I should go. Thanks, Greg."

"Promise you'll call." Something in the soft way he said it made my stomach flutter. An uncomfortable flutter I didn't want to have. Not for Greg. I nodded and walked into the apartment, but I knew I wouldn't call him.

The thick drapes that hung over the sliding glass doors were drawn closed, making it seem much later than it was. I wrinkled my nose at the smell of bleach-masked vomit in the air. "Is your dad home?"

Heather sat on the couch and hugged a pillow to her chest. "He's in South America until next week."

I sat on the edge of a recliner. "You're sick, huh?"

"I was. Saturday night."

"So how come you missed school?" I asked.

"Avoiding humiliation."

That didn't sound good. "Does Dellian have anything to do with that?" Her head shot up and I knew he did. "He asked how you were today."

"Oh God!" Heather threw the pillow over her head. "I can't go back to school."

I moved to the sofa next to her. "What happened?"

"Drank too much at Ethan's. I woke up in the stairwell downstairs. That teacher and Copacabana were trying to help me up the stairs. I was covered in puke."

"Eew!" I said, imagining Tricia and Dellian hanging on each other as they walked into the building. Stopping when they saw Heather. "I mean the two of them together, not the puke — well, I guess that's gross too."

Heather kept her head buried in the pillow.

"Doubt they'd say anything about it. They'd have to fess up to being together, right?" I offered.

Heather pulled the pillow from her face. "I'm not worried about them." She sighed. "I made a fool of myself! And I puked in" — she glanced over at me — "some guy's car. It's fifth grade all over again. I can't face school."

"Fifth grade?" I asked.

"You don't remember?" She snorted. "You're probably the only person in the whole state of Alaska who doesn't remember." Heather rolled off the couch and padded into the kitchen. "You want a pop?" she asked, holding open the refrigerator.

"No, thanks."

Heather opened a can and took a drink. "Remember that end-of-the-year dance to celebrate our promotion to middle school, graduation from fifth grade, all that garbage?"

"Something happened at the dance, right?"

"Mm-hmm, my mom happened. She chaperoned. Spent the entire night dancing with our English teacher—"

"Ms. Brody!" I finished her sentence. "I forgot about that!"

"Well, I didn't. Now they share a condo across town." Heather took a final swallow and walked back to the couch. "That's when I found out Mom's gay. Unfortunately, so did everyone else. The stuff people said. Especially Rona."

"Rona's a bitch," I said.

"Yeah, well, at least that humiliation wasn't my fault. This time . . . God!" She buried her face in the sofa.

"By next weekend, no one will even remember."

"Maybe." She rolled onto her side. "So, you and Stanford?"

"No!" I blinked at her. "I'm with Jonathan."

Heather flicked something off her sweatshirt. "I thought he was mad at you."

"Not anymore." I grinned. "He asked me to homecoming yesterday."

"Oh," she murmured. "Then why are you with Stanford?"

"I'm not *with* him. I freaked when Dellian asked about you, and Greg was there."

"He's always there, Roz."

"I'm with Jonathan, okay? Greg's nice and all, but, as you said, he's no Zeus."

"No," Heather said. "He's not."

Wednesday morning Jonathan called at the last minute and said he wasn't going to school. I had to wake Mom for a ride and got there late. I fully expected another lecture from Dellian, but he wasn't there yet. I slipped into my seat, grateful for the break. In most classes, a teacher's absence triggers out-of-control chatter. Not in Life Skills. No one spoke or studied. We just sat staring at our desks or our feet, or, in Tricia's case, the back of our eyelids.

As the silent seconds ticked on, I became disturbingly aware of Tricia's breathing. "Hey, guys —" I said.

"Shhh!" Jeffrey hissed. "Not supposed to talk when Mr. Dellian isn't here."

I sighed. "Okay, but" — the sound was too much to stay quiet, though — "don't you hear Tricia, Jeffrey? She sounds as if she can't breathe. Does she have asthma?"

This caught his — and everyone else's — attention. "Wake her up," Ruth said, coming over.

JJ drove up alongside and carefully moved Tricia's stringy blond hair to peer down at her face. "Yeah, we should totally wake her up." Even Bart, who seemed to be disconnected from the rest of us most of the time, made his way to Tricia's desk.

"Tricia. Wake up," we called in unison. JJ gave her a gentle shake. "Tricia!"

Still she wheezed on, unaware of the circus ring around her.

I filled a cup with water and brought it back to Tricia's desk. Bart's eyes got big. Jeffrey covered his mouth in horror. But they all watched in perverted glee as I pulled Tricia's head up by the hair and threw the water in her face.

"What—the—" Tricia leaped out of her chair, demon possessed.

Everyone scattered.

"Roz did it!" JJ tattled as he zoomed out of the line of fire.

"Morning, Sunshine," I said, handing Tricia a paper towel. "You've got a whole tube of mascara running down your face."

Tricia glared at me. "What's your problem, bitch?"

"My problem? Your wheezing. I didn't want you dying in your sleep."

Tricia snatched the paper towel from me. "I don't wheeze."

"Yes, you do," Jeffrey said.

"Did I ask you?"

"Leave him alone. Come on, I'll help you clean up. Jeffrey, tell Mr. Dellian I took Tricia to the bathroom."

"I hate you," Tricia said.

"The feeling's mutual."

I held open the bathroom door. Tricia walked into a stall and locked it behind her.

I was rubbing liquid soap onto a paper towel when a sickly sweet smell, like burned sugar, reached me. "Are you smoking something?" I dropped to my hands and knees and crawled across the crusty tiled floor into the stall. Tricia was propped up in her usual place, smoking from a green glass pipe. "What is that?" I demanded. "Weed?"

"You're not afraid of me," Tricia said, ignoring my question. "So why don't you ever look me in the eye?"

"I . . ." I shrugged. I wasn't going to discuss my eyesight with her.

She took another hit off the pipe. "That's how animals show submission, you know. They avoid eye contact." She held the pipe out. "Want some?"

"No." I shoved it away.

"Yeah, you don't need this. You're tough." She slipped the pipe into her pocket, her fingers lingering on the soft brown material of her cloak. "My mom made this so I could be tough and no one would hurt me again." She'd morphed into a little girl, sad and vulnerable.

"Hurt you? Like Wayne did?" I asked.

She brushed a long strand of blond hair from her face. "He said I could help pay the money she owed him." A sad grin crossed her lips. "But she made *him* pay."

"Tricia? Does Dellian . . . ?" I took a deep breath. My heart pounded in my chest. "I mean Rodney. Does he —"

"I wanna dance!" She leaped onto the toilet seat, teetering off balance as her spiked heels straddled the seat.

"Not up there." I tried to steady her with my hands while I coaxed her down. "Come on, you can dance in class."

She tugged her arms free but jumped to the ground. As soon as she landed, she began singing some crazy lyrics I didn't know.

Flashbacks of "Copacabana" flooded my brain. Should I take her to the nurse? She'd slept it off last time, right? Dellian had over-reacted? I decided to guide her back to the classroom.

"Tricia's . . . not well," I told Dellian as we walked in. Tricia was singing some hip-hop song now while flopping her arms around like a hysterical rag doll. "Should I take her to the nurse?"

"Oh." He looked around the room. Everyone was watching him. "No, thank you, Miss Hart. She can stay here today until she feels better." As he said this, he gave me a look. A look that said . . . what? The way he was focused so fully on me, I knew that look had a ton of meaning. Unfortunately, I was clear across the room, so I couldn't see his eyes or his facial expression, and his silent message was lost on me. But I got the feeling he was hiding something. Something maybe . . . he was afraid I knew?

At lunch, I decided to see if Tricia was still sleeping it off in Life Skills. I found her leaning against the wall just outside the classroom door, squirting Insta-Whip in her mouth, while the distinct voices of Jonathan and Dellian argued inside.

"What's going on?" I moved to the door to listen.

She grabbed my arm. "We need to talk." I followed her into the bathroom, and she locked the door behind us. "Swear you won't tell Rodney about today."

"You mean that you were smoking crack?" I smiled at her look of surprise. "You think I don't know the difference between a crack pipe and a peace pipe?" When she folded her arms across her chest, I shrugged. "So I guessed. It didn't smell like pot."

"I'm not addicted, okay? It's not like the heroin. I can stop any-time. But if Rodney finds out —"

"You think he couldn't tell? He's not an idiot, Tricia."

"Just swear you won't tell him."

"I'll swear," I said, "if you tell me the real deal between you two."

Her jaw tightened. "I can't talk about that."

"Then I can't swear."

"People could get in trouble, okay?"

"Who? Dellian? Maybe it's time you protected yourself for a change."

"As if you care! You only want to nail Dellian to get him off your ass!"

"Maybe." I unlocked the stall door. "But at least he's not nailing my ass."

"Screw you!" Her voice trembled. "You don't know anything!"

"I know he's using you. I think I'll bypass Dellian and go straight to Ratner with all of this." I stepped out into the hall. And stopped. Wasn't I using her too? I didn't care if she got hurt; as she said, I only wanted to get at Dellian. I ducked my head back in the door. "Okay, I promise not to tell if you promise that whatever's going on, you'll find a way to stop it. You deserve better."

Mascara and tears streaked her face; she wiped her nose. "I . . . I will. Monday, okay?" She pulled out her green pipe and stepped back into the stall. "Just let me get through homecoming."

Hours before

I skipped the homecoming game Friday night. Last year I froze my butt off while people like Missy paraded around on the field during halftime to make sure everyone knew they had been nominated for homecoming royalty. I didn't see the need to watch a repeat. Besides, Jonathan told me he couldn't hang out with me anyway — too much "homecoming stuff" to do.

"Hey, Beautiful," Jonathan said when he called Saturday morning. "I can't pick you up tonight. Homecoming stuff, you know? Can you meet me at the dance?"

"I guess so." I rolled my eyes. What "stuff" could he possibly have to do that meant he couldn't pick me up? I was his date!

He launched into his usual rant about the scouts who would be watching him play hockey this year and how Dellian was going to mess it up because he was trying to have Jonathan benched for grades. I'd given up trying to interject my own Dellian woes long ago. Jonathan never listened.

I hung up and called Heather. Ever since Ethan's party, she'd been on the fence about going to the homecoming dance. Now that I wasn't driving with Jonathan, I figured I could talk her into coming with me. "Sorry," Heather said. "Stanford made reservations for us at Café de Paris before the dance."

"What?" I wasn't sure I'd heard right. "You're going with Greg?"

"Stanford didn't tell you?"

"His name's Greg! And no, neither of you told me. Last time we talked, you just went on and on about the paradise-themed dress code. You never said anything!" It shouldn't have bothered me so much. But it did. "I gotta go. I'll meet you there."

"Remember to dress tiki!" Heather yelled as I hung up.

I didn't dress tiki. Besides the fact that I was in a foul mood, I really didn't think that many people would. Nobody but cheerleaders and drama club members ever participated in themed events like pajama day or Halloween. I figured this would be the same. I mean, it was homecoming! Who dressed in beachwear for homecoming? So Mom helped me pick out a little black dress from her closet — classic, knee-length, spaghetti strap — and dropped me off at school.

Decorations had transformed the gym into a tropical paradise. Grass skirts and bamboo lanterns dressed the tables. Lights that filtered through a special lens created green and orange palm trees on the floor. Flowers floated in the punch bowl, and little umbrellas stood in each cup. Everyone wore gardenias in their hair and leis of fresh flowers around their neck to accessorize their paradise-themed attire. Everyone, that is, except me.

"I told you to dress tiki!" Heather said when she saw me. She wore a flamingo-pink beach cover-up with a matching bikini top and flip-flops. She'd even braided her raven-blue hair into faux dreads with little fuchsia beads on each end. "When I give you fashion advice, listen. Greg did. Doesn't he look adorable?"

I took in Greg's fluorescent-orange eyesore of a shirt patterned with turquoise surfboards and neon-green palm trees. "Yes, very . . . tropical."

"I think you mean obnoxious," he muttered.

"Not obnoxious, more like"—I grinned—"an overzealous Jimmy Buffet fan."

"I'll take Buffet. I was shooting for a ninety-year-old Miami tourist, though."

"You almost nailed it, except"—I leaned forward and sniffed, ignoring how his watermelon smell made my heart pound a little faster—"you should've gone with a lime-doused mothball scent; watermelon screams amateur."

We laughed, and I found myself wishing I could joke like that with Jonathan. "I should probably go find my date. You guys seen Jonathan anywhere?"

Greg's smile fell away. He and Heather exchanged a look I couldn't see well enough to read.

"What?"

"It's nothing, okay?" Heather said.

"Tell me!" My stomach turned. I knew I wasn't going to like whatever it was.

"I saw Jonathan's car at Missy's last night," Greg said. "After the game."

"Missy?" My heartbeat quickened as jealousy pumped through my veins. "He was with Missy last night?"

"He could've just been giving her a ride home," Greg said.

"Or not. If I were you, I'd go confront him." Heather frowned at Greg. "What?"

"You should just forget him," Greg said. "Come sit with us."

"He's her date," Heather argued. "He at least owes her an explanation."

Yes. He did. I looked around. "Where is he?"

"Whatever." Greg sighed. "You two go search for Zeus, the king of all that is deceptive and fake. I'm going to get a table. Try Mount Olympus," he yelled as he left, "or the Underworld, with Hades."

"I don't see him; try the hallway." Heather hurried after Greg. "Greg, wait!"

I stood in front of the trophy case facing the gym's double doors. I thought it would be the best vantage point to find Jonathan, but it was too crowded. In a crowd, it's impossible for me to focus my dots on anything long enough to identify someone.

I moved toward the main foyer and found couples waiting in a long line. When I followed it to the front, I discovered the yearbook staff photographing the homecoming nominees. Jonathan stood front and center, looking fantastic in white shorts and an island-blue, Hawaiian-print button-up. Girls flanked him on either side, but after years of practice, my eyes were quick to spot one in particular. Long blond hair. Doe eyes. Island-blue bikini top. Island-blue skirt that tied at the hip. *Island blue.*

I flicked back to Jonathan. He and Missy matched. A little too perfectly. As if they'd coordinated their outfits. Missy stood below him, head tilted up, skin glowing as though she'd just stepped off the beach, while he smiled down, eyes locked on hers, hand brushing her hair from her face.

That familiar ache of envy caught my breath.

"Have you been to a beach before?" Tricia was pulling her cloak off a few feet away. She handed it to the coat check girl and walked over to me. "Only losers wear black." Grass skirt. Bikini top. Even Tricia blended in tonight.

I wasn't in the mood for her insults. I shoved past her and into the bathroom. I tried to tell myself it didn't matter. Jonathan didn't matter. I didn't like him that much anyway, right? I winced at my reflection. I looked like Rob Zombie at a luau. Who was I kidding? It *did* matter. Jonathan liked me. He called me Beautiful. He made me feel important, as if I belonged. And *I* was his date, not Missy. I headed back out to claim him.

"Hey, it's about time!" Jonathan said when I walked out. He was standing with Liz Cobler and some others. "You have to pee so badly you couldn't say hi?"

"Oh . . ." He was copping attitude with *me?* He was the one drooling all over Miss Island Blue! "I didn't think you saw me—"

"You were looking right at us," Liz said.

"Sorry, I was . . . distracted . . . by Tricia."

"That freak!" Liz snorted. "God, did she wear her cape?"

"See?" Jonathan slipped his arm around me before I could respond to Liz. "I knew she wouldn't dis me." He kissed me—in front of them all—and then gave me that brilliant smile of his. "So, where's your bikini, Beautiful?"

The way he kissed me, the way he stood up for me, telling them he knew me — he made me feel wanted and liked and . . . I couldn't ruin that. I couldn't ask about Missy. "Too cold for swimsuits." I kissed him back. "Can we go dance?"

"Sure." He led me inside the gym, but stopped at the refreshment table. "Hold on, I gotta talk to someone." He disappeared into the mass of bodies.

I watched the gobs of faces, waiting for Jonathan to pop into my visual range again. When he didn't, my eyes wandered over to the dance floor. Everyone was bouncing to a lot of bass. A flash of bright orange caught in my peripheral vision. Maybe it was because Greg was having fun while I wasn't, or maybe it was because he was having fun with someone other than me. Whatever the reason, I suddenly felt envious.

I looked back at the refreshment table, this time focusing on clothes. I spotted Tricia's grass skirt next to Jonathan's island-blue shirt at the punch bowl. Eyes on Jonathan, I tried to push through the crowd toward them. But when I focus too hard on one thing, I miss what's going on around me. Just as I was about to reach Jonathan, I tripped on someone's foot.

"Sorry," I said to the jeans and floral-print shirt — nowhere near as gaudy as Greg's.

"It's rather crowded, Miss Hart. Commandeering a glass of punch?"

"What?" I frowned, my concentration broken. I'd lost sight of Jonathan.

Mr. Dellian said louder, "Punch?" As he handed me a cup, Tricia appeared.

"Don't forget your umbrella!" She dunked one into Dellian's punch.

I looked behind her for Jonathan. He wasn't there. Was he *trying* to ditch me?

"Do you have an umbrella for Miss Hart?" When Tricia said nothing, Dellian held his cup out to me. "You can have mine."

"No!" Tricia slapped his hand away. "I'll get her one." She reached through the mob for an umbrella and threw one at me.

I took the tiny toothpick umbrella and clomped over to an empty table, my back to the dancers. What the hell was I doing here? Homecoming was supposed to be fun! I glared down at the umbrella. The thin paper had caved in on one side, crushed, no doubt, by Tricia's violent handling. I poked at the paper to pop it back out. It didn't work. The fragile item was broken. I abandoned trying to fix it and instead twirled its wooden toothpick shaft between my fingers, mesmerized by how beautifully the colors swirled together the faster I twirled it, despite it being broken.

The tempo changed to a soft slow dance. The DJ announced that the homecoming nominees would lead everyone in the first slow dance of the night. Bodies scurried by in search of dance partners. I slumped in my chair, aware that Jonathan would now surface, but he'd be dancing with a future queen, not me.

"Can I sit with you?" a familiar voice said behind me. "Or are you and that umbrella too engrossed in conversation for company?"

"We *are* having a pretty heavy conversation, but I don't think he'll mind. Where's Heather?" I asked after Greg sat down.

"Bathroom." He peered over at me. "You don't look as though you're having fun."

His soft tone made my throat catch. I waved my hand. "I'm fine. Just bored. You want to dance?"

He shook his head. "No, I—"

"Right, you and Heather. Say no more."

"No, that's definitely not what I was going to say." He leaned forward. "Why did you want me to come with her?"

What was he talking about? "I wanted you to come with Heather?"

"That's what she said when she asked me."

I started to protest—to say I didn't suggest it, never would, not in a million years—but that would've opened up another conversation. One I wasn't quite ready to have. "I . . . just did."

"Just did?" He acted as if I'd spoken in tongues.

"I thought you'd have . . . fun together. You're a lot alike." The words sounded false, and I knew he didn't believe me. *I* didn't believe me. They were nothing alike.

"Are we?" His voice dropped to a whisper. "I thought you and I . . ." He leaned in really close. So close I could see his face, his expression, his eyes. "Roz—"

"Hey, Beautiful," Jonathan said somewhere behind me.

I whirled around, feeling guilty. Caught. But Jonathan wasn't there. I frowned back at Greg.

He sat back in his chair, arms crossed against his chest, now too far for me to see his face, his expression, his eyes. But I didn't need to. I heard it all in his voice. The disgust. The pity. "Over there," Greg snapped. "Dancing with Missy."

I didn't need this humiliation. I fished my cell out of my clutch purse and headed to the coat check.

"Where're you going?" Heather asked as I was putting on my jacket.

"Home." I dialed Mom's number. No answer.

"They haven't even announced the royalty yet!"

"Jonathan . . ." My voice cracked. I tried Mom again, and then slammed the phone shut. "My mom isn't answering."

"I'll take you." Greg came up behind Heather.

"But you can't come back in once you leave," Heather said.

"She's right. Stay. I'll call a cab," I said to one of the neon-green trees on his shirt. I couldn't look at him.

"I don't want to stay," Greg said. "Heather, I'll pick you up after the dance."

"No!" Heather glared at me, and then spotted Jonathan. "Zeus!"

Greg and I both grabbed at her arm. "Heather, don't."

She ignored us. "Roz wants to go home."

"Home? Why?" He slipped his arm around my waist. When I pulled away from him, he frowned. "What's wrong?"

Heather pulled a reluctant Greg away as I whirled on my date. "If you weren't going to acknowledge my existence at this dance, why'd you even ask me?" I demanded.

"I'm ack-whatevering you right now, aren't I?" He leaned in, smiling that all-too-brilliant smile. "You look beautiful in that dress, by the way." He tried to shimmy my jacket off my shoulders.

"As if you mean that." I yanked my jacket back up. "I heard you call Missy Beautiful too."

He cocked his head. "Well, she *is* beautiful. Can't I give a girl props?" He put his palms on my hips and tried to pull me into him. "That doesn't mean you aren't beautiful."

I stood sideways, unfaltering. "I know you were with her last night! Greg saw you!" I meant to be firm, strong, but I sounded whiny and childish and . . . pitiful.

"Yeah, he saw me give her a ride home." His fingers traced a gentle path along my neck to my jaw line. "Come on, don't be like this." He carefully turned my face up to his. "Please?" He kissed my chin.

I felt myself weakening, and hated it. I balled my hands into fists, but still my head did not turn away from his touch. My anger seemed stupid now; somehow he'd made my body forget what my brain had been so sure of a second ago.

"Hey." He pulled me toward him again, as if he knew my body was giving in and wouldn't resist him this time. He brushed a strand of hair from my face. "You're . . ."

His words were lost in a jumble of voices and shouts behind us.

"Can we go talk somewhere else?" I asked.

"After the dance we can head to the party, hang in the loft. I'll tell everyone to leave us alone."

"Can we just go now?"

"Now? They haven't crowned me king yet." The commotion behind us became really loud. We both turned to look.

"What's going on?" Jonathan yelled.

"Mr. Dellian puked all over the place!"

"He . . . puked?" Jonathan echoed.

A teacher exited the gym with Mr. Dellian, a wastebasket clutched in his arms. "Go home, don't worry about a thing," the teacher was saying.

Dellian vomited into the trash can with such force, he couldn't respond.

The teacher grimaced and eyeballed everyone standing around. "Someone go find the janitor, please. Who can drive Mr. Dellian home? He" — the wrenching sound of another round of puke interrupted her — "really shouldn't be driving."

"I will." Tricia stepped through the crowd, brown cloak already on, ready to leave. "I know how to drive his stick."

A few people snickered. The teacher stared at Tricia. "His what?"

"His Toyota's a manual — you know, transmission?" Jonathan said with a grin. "Don't worry, Miss Kelly. I'll follow to make sure she gets home okay."

"Thank you, Jonathan. That would be wonderful."

I stared after them, stunned. He couldn't leave with me because he hadn't received his precious crown, but he could leave for Tricia? What the heck was going on? Okay, yeah, Dellian was sick, but Jonathan hated Dellian. Why would he miss out on his crown for him?

"Move along now! The dance is over!" Miss Kelly yelled at the bottleneck of students now forming in front of me. "We're evacuating the gym."

Evacuating? Liz Cobler gagged by me. I asked her what was going on.

"Mr. Dellian," she said, eyes watering. "It really reeks in there."

"Roz!" Heather called from the exit. "Greg's taking me home. Unless you have a better idea?"

"There's a party at Birch Hill," I offered reluctantly. Like Greg, a part of me wanted to go home and just be done with the evening. Another part of me was obsessed with getting Jonathan alone. If we could talk the way Greg and I always seemed to, about nothing and everything, maybe that would somehow make things right between us.

"The dance got shut down," I said to Jonathan's voice mail. "Meet me at the party?"

Heather frowned. "Zeus left already?"

"He took Dellian home."

"He drove a puking teacher in his precious Corvette?" Heather snorted.

Her attitude annoyed me. Everything about this night annoyed me. "Tricia's driving Dellian in his truck. Jonathan's following so Tricia has a ride home."

"Why would she need a ride? She lives there," Heather said.

"Maybe back to the dance?" I said, but she was right. It didn't make sense. What was going on with those two? I had to talk to Jonathan. "Are you guys going to the party?" I asked. "I need a ride up there."

Heather rubbed her hand on Greg's arm. "Are we, Greg? It could be fun."

"Why would you want to?" Greg's scowl was directed at me. But before I could say "None of your business," he turned to

Heather and said, "You got so wasted last time, you were ashamed to come back to school."

Ouch.

Heather dropped her hand and stared at the floor.

"Geez, you can be such a jerk!" I looped my arm in Heather's. "Come on, Heather. I'm sure we can find a ride." We turned to merge into the crowd.

"Wait." Greg grabbed my elbow. "I'll take you. Sorry. I shouldn't have said that, Heather."

Heather shrugged. "It's the truth. I'm not drinking anything tonight."

"Me neither," Greg said.

"That makes three of us." I needed to be in charge of my senses with Jonathan tonight. Speaking to him was hard enough when sober.

The weather had gone from bitterly breezy with a few flakes of snow to wickedly windy with an onslaught of slush. Cars were spinning out all along the road. Greg parked at the bottom of the hill without even trying to drive up closer. "If you don't want to walk in your heels," he said, "we could leave."

I knew that was what he wanted, but I was determined at this point to talk to Jonathan — even if it was simply to break up with him — and Heather was dead set on doing anything but going home. So we crouched over like little old grannies, clutching each other's coat sleeves, and walked sideways up the hill to the lodge.

It was too cold for bonfires, and everyone was crammed wall-to-wall in the lodge. I left Heather and Greg huddled near the entrance and shoved my way through the throng of partyers in search of Jonathan. Realizing I'd never find him in this crowd, I changed direction and headed to the keg to find Ethan and a much-needed pocket of air.

"Have you seen Jonathan?" I screamed over the music.

"Who?"

"Jonathan?"

He stopped pumping beer and held his hand up to his ear.

"Zeus!" I screamed.

He shook his head and handed me a cup.

I pushed it away and pointed upstairs. "Tell Zeus I'm up there!" I moved through the knots of bodies to the loft. There were a few couples up there already, including Heather and Greg. "Hope I'm not interrupting anything."

"As if," Heather snorted. "You find Zeus?"

I shook my head. "Probably on his way."

"Probably stuck at the bottom of the hill," Greg muttered.

"Such a pleasure, isn't he?" Heather looked at Greg. "Why are you so grumpy?"

Greg sighed. "I'm hungry. Why don't we forget this party and go get some food?"

"I could use some fries, or pancakes. Mmmm," Heather said. "You in, Roz?"

Just then, the crowd roared "Zeus!" downstairs, and I rushed to the banister.

"I'll take that as a no." Greg stood. "Let's go before I lose my appetite."

I peered over the balcony. Too many bodies, but I knew he was down there somewhere. "Jonathan!" I screamed blindly into the crowd. "Zeus!"

"Hey, Beautiful!" came the response, and I spotted him near the stairs, shoving by Greg and Heather as they made their way to the door. His hands started groping for me before he'd even sat down.

I shoved him away. "There are people —"

"Out," he said. Just like that, everyone went downstairs. He grabbed for me again.

"Wait!" I threw his hands back to his side. "I thought we were going to talk."

"This is more fun." He covered my mouth with his. His hand slid under my dress, up my thigh.

"Stop!" I yanked his hand away.

He smoothed his hair. "What's your problem?"

"You ignored me all night!"

"Well I'm not now, am I?" He reached for me.

I pulled away and stood up. "Only because you want to mess around. That's all you ever want to do."

"Yeah." He sat back against the chair. "That's the point of having a girlfriend."

"That is *not* the point of having a girlfriend!" *What an ignorant* — "Ugh!" I stormed downstairs, almost tripping over Tricia's cloak, which was splayed across the bottom step where she sat, head against the wall. "Damn it, Tricia! Move your shit!"

She looked up at me, tired, pale, sickly.

I stopped midrage. "You okay?"

"Zeus up there?"

"His name's Jonathan! Why does everyone think he deserves a god's name?"

A weak smile crossed her face. "You finally cut the cord? 'Bout time. He didn't deserve you."

"No, he didn't." I slid down next to her. "What was I thinking?"

"That you were a loser. He's a user; users look for losers. It's what they do." She rubbed at her face with a shaky hand and then turned her weary, kohl-rimmed eyes to me. "You're not a loser, Roz."

I blinked, shocked by the compliment. "Thanks." I wanted to say something else. Something nice. Nothing came to mind. "You're not either," I said finally.

She snort-laughed and gave me a sarcastic smile. "I'm as loser as they come." Her mood darkened. "Go away." She leaned her head against the wall again.

"Tricia—"

"Go!" she screamed.

Whatever. Sick of the nut jobs and jerks, I just wanted to go home, where there was no one but me to figure out. Crawl into bed. Hide from "civilization." I tore through the mob to the exit. When I stepped into the frigid air, it hit me.

I had no way of going home.

"Damn it!" I screamed into the dark night. A group slipping up the path to the door fell on each other, erupting into giggles. I knew there'd be no answer, but I tried Mom's cell again anyway, hanging up when her voice mail answered. My finger hovered over Greg's speed-dial button before I shoved my phone back in my pocket. If I called, there'd be an I-told-you-so from him—not to mention the wrath of Heather—and I was in no mood for either.

After the hell this night had been, Jonathan owed me a ride home. I fought my way back through the crowd. Ethan held a cup out as I thundered past, and I took a huge mouthful as I stomped toward the loft. The stairs, now empty of Tricia and her cloak, hit my feet too quickly. Beer sloshed out onto my dress.

I wiped at the spill with my bare hand, but it only made it worse, spreading the wet stain across my stomach. *Great. If I ruined this dress,* I thought, reaching the top of the stairs—

I heard a moan and looked up.

Jonathan sat on the couch, a brown blanket draped across his lap.

But no. The blanket moved, bobbed.

Stringy blond hair fell across his jeans.

It took a second for my brain to piece it together.

Only a second.

"Oh!" I gasped.

The stringy blond hair whipped around. "Roz!" Tricia fell backwards. She tried to scramble to her feet. "It's not—" She stumbled forward and reached for me. "I needed—"

"Get away from me!" My vision blurred. I felt out of breath, dizzy.

"Wait!" Tricia grabbed at me again. My shove sent her sprawling across the floor.

Jonathan touched my shoulder. "She just climbed on me—"

I shrugged him off. The dots blocking my central vision

increased suddenly like a head rush. I couldn't see straight. Couldn't think straight. I tripped toward the stairs. What was wrong with me? I staggered down the steps, barely aware of the crowd that had gathered.

"Let's go talk. How you wanted." Jonathan's voice seemed far away.

"I wanna go home," I mumbled, holding on to the wall.

"Sure, Beautiful. Anything you want."

My legs wouldn't work right. Confusion set in. I let Jonathan hold me up. Lead me out. Something cold hit my face. And twigs. Sharp twigs.

The rest of the night was a mere montage of quick images and fleeting snapshots, like tiny remnants of a dream that didn't make sense. Jonathan's body against mine . . . arms . . . and Mr. Dellian's face.

It's always darkest before the dawn.

— Proverbs

Missing

Day 1

I woke up in the living room, covered with the ratty orange throw that had resided on the back of the couch since dinosaurs roamed the earth. "I must've been really out of it to use this thing last night." I tossed it aside and sat up. "Why did I sleep here?"

I tried to remember. Beyond the nasty scene in the loft and walking through the cabin with Jonathan, I had nothing. No, not nothing. There were glimpses, fragments of memories. I remembered Jonathan next to me and being cold, really cold, and there'd been arms everywhere; and —

"Dellian?" That wasn't right. Dellian wasn't there. Was he?

The more I tried to remember, the less I knew. A cement wall blocked me and wouldn't let me pass. I had hardly had any beer. Why couldn't I remember?

Maybe seeing Tricia and Jonathan had just shut the rest of me down? I'd seen it happen in the movies. Something unbearable occurs, like an alien abduction, and people get amnesia because they can't deal with the truth. It seemed as plausible as any theory, so I chalked my memory loss up to self-preservation and moved on to hiding from the world.

I spent the day in my room, ignoring the thirty million phone calls from Heather and Greg. They'd left before the Incident, but there were plenty of people around who had seen what happened. I couldn't bear to talk about it yet.

Not with Heather. Definitely not with Greg.

Day 2

My stomach ached on the way to Life Skills on Monday. I planned to tear Tricia apart, guilt-trip her with her betrayal, and then finish her off by telling Ratner about her and Dellian, her drug habit, everything. So what if Ratner didn't believe me? At least I'd feel better, and Tricia would feel betrayed. She'd know I stabbed her in the back the way she'd stabbed me.

But she wasn't twirling in her usual spot. I paused, unsure about how to proceed. The scene I'd planned ended with me bounding off to the office. I hadn't intended to go into class, where I'd have to face Jonathan. The tardy bell rang. Mr. Villanari popped his head out. "Roz? Come on in."

My eyes darted to Jonathan's chair, then Tricia's. Both empty.

"Mr. Dellian is out sick. I'll be his substitute."

Dellian's name triggered my bizarre recollection of Saturday night. He'd been sick at the dance. Gone home. Obviously was still sick. No way was he at Birch Hill. That meant the image I had of him was simply a mistake, some weird dream.

Wish I could have said the same for the rest of it.

•   •   •

"Ohmygodohmygodohmygod!" Heather screamed at me on my way to second hour. "Can you believe it? Isn't it awful?"

Awful. Too awful to discuss in front of everyone. "Gotta get to class, okay?" I kept walking.

"See you at lunch!" she yelled after me.

Right. Lunch. I couldn't wait. I ducked into class, prepared for comments about Saturday night's "event." No one said anything, though. "Zeus cheating on Roz with the lunatic fringe" had been trumped by some wannabe X-Games skateboarder who'd almost died.

I'd planned to skip lunch, skip Heather, skip Tricia, Jonathan, Missy, the whole scene. Unfortunately Greg intercepted me at my locker. The soft smile he gave me said he knew — and felt sorry for me. I fumbled for an excuse to escape him but didn't get one out before Heather found us.

"There you are!" She hooked her arm in mine and led me toward the lunchroom. "I've been dying to talk to you since I found out on Sunday. Is your phone broken? I kept calling you."

"I forgot to charge it," I said lamely. I stole a glance at Greg as we sat down. His eyes tried to meet mine, and I had to look away.

"Just a stupid rumor," Heather was saying, "by people who don't know him. I mean, don't gossip unless you have the facts, you know?"

I stared into my lunch bag. I didn't feel like eating. Not even the extra-large brownie I'd packed as comfort food. "The rumor's true."

"What?" Heather grabbed my arms to turn me toward her.

"When did you hear that? I talked to Ricky in third hour. He said he's *not* in a coma!" She looked around the cafeteria. "Where's Ricky?"

"Coma?" I stared at the back of her raven-blue hair as she frantically scoured the room. "What are you talking about?"

"Heather, relax," Greg said. "Mom said he's not in a coma. He may be paralyzed, though." He turned to me. "Fritz almost died Saturday. He's in ICU at Memorial."

"What happened?" Then it clicked. "Wait, that was Fritz who took a header off the stadium bleachers on his skateboard? The X-Games guy?"

"He's not in the X Games," Heather snapped. "That's another one of those stupid rumors by people who don't know what they're talking about."

"He and Ricky were simulating X-Game jumps," Greg explained. "Ricky thinks Fritz hit black ice —"

Heather put her hand on her heart. "He fell almost two stories down and smacked his head on the edge of a step. If you'd answered your phone messages, you'd know this!"

"Hey, Helen Keller!" Rona yelled from across the cafeteria. "Lose Zeus somewhere? Have you checked under the *cape?*" Her table erupted into giggles.

Heather yammered on about hospital visiting hours and ICUs as if she hadn't heard, but Greg gave me a somber look. He knew. He definitely knew.

Which made me dread sixth hour. A substitute for Dellian meant library time or some other form of emancipation. Given the opportunity, Greg would corner me, ask how I was doing, sympathize with me — and I couldn't handle sympathy from Greg. So after fifth hour, I detoured to my locker, gathered my things, and boarded the city bus home.

Thirty minutes later, even though school wasn't out yet, Greg showed up on my doorstep. I knew what it cost him to skip a class. And he'd done it for me. Still. "Sorry, Greg," I whispered as I moved away from the window without answering the door. "I can't talk to you, not about this."

I sat at the kitchen table eating a turkey sandwich while Greg rang the doorbell incessantly. After fifteen minutes, the ringing stopped. I plopped down on the couch and had just closed my eyes when the doorbell rang again.

"Geez, he is relentless!" I flung the curtain back. Greg's purple beast wasn't in my driveway. A green truck was. I peered through the peephole. "Mr. Dellian?" I said as I opened the door.

"Miss Hart, I'm trying to locate Miss Farni. Have you heard from her?"

"Tricia?" I shook my head. "Why would I? We aren't exactly friends."

"Yes, well after Saturday evening's . . . *altercation,* she said she wanted to make things right with you. She didn't contact you?"

I was still stuck on "altercation." She *told* him? How sick was that! And now he was trying to find her? Her confession must've caused a pretty brutal fight.

"Miss Hart, please? Did she contact you?"

"No, she didn't."

Mr. Dellian sighed. "If she does, please let me know right away. We need to know she's okay."

We? Himself and the baby? For a brief second, the image of a helpless baby crying for his mother gave me a twinge of concern. But then I remembered Tricia's head in Jonathan's lap, and that twinge of concern turned into disgust.

Day 3

Snow fell all night. By morning, there was almost two feet on the ground, and nothing was moving. Including my bus. I'd waited forty-five minutes in the freezing cold and was contemplating waking my mom, when a very old, very noisy, very rusted-out plow truck pulled up.

Greg stepped down from the driver's side wearing a fur hat with floppy earflaps and gigantic white bunny boots that made his scrawny legs look like pencils stuck in marshmallows. "Can I give you a ride?" He extended a gloved hand.

I shook my head. "The bus should be here any minute."

Greg shook his head, his earflaps slapping his cheeks. "No, it won't. I passed it in the ditch a few miles up the road. Come on. I promise not to talk about you-know-who, okay?" He took a step toward me, hand still extended.

I chewed on my inner cheek, deliberating. If the bus was stuck, I'd for sure have to wake Mom. And Mom hated the first snow-falls of winter. "Too many idiots who forget how to drive in snow out on the roads," she'd say.

"Promise?" I said. "No lectures, no discussion?"

"Promise." He helped me through the snow to the passenger's side. "Someone coming to plow your driveway?"

"Yeah, me and my good friend Shovel. I figure I'll wait until after it stops snowing."

"I'll save you the energy." Greg had it plowed in less than three minutes.

"So, is your hovercraft grounded?"

He grinned. "This tank works a bit better in freshly fallen snow." He nodded out the window, slowing down. "And it comes in handy for scenes like this one."

One of my neighbors was spinning her wheels at the end of the road. Greg plowed the snow out of her way, and then pulled over, grabbed a chain from the back, and hooked it to her bumper.

"Are you always such a good Samaritan?" I joked when we were back on our way.

"'What do we live for; if it is not to make life less difficult to each other?' George Eliot."

I grinned. Greg could be so . . . Greg . . . sometimes. A flash of red in the snowbank up ahead caught in my peripheral vision. "Oh God," I muttered, barely audible over Greg's "Idiot! Who drives a Corvette in this weather?"

Drive on by, drive on by, drive on by, I pleaded in my head.

But, as I knew he would, Greg slowed and pulled over. He stepped out of the truck, and my bad dream turned into a nightmare. Missy popped into view.

It was only Tuesday! Tricia on Saturday and now Missy?

I watched the scene unfolding outside. Jonathan squatted alongside the Corvette, poking at the snow underneath with a snow brush, while Missy stood next to him, huddled under a blanket.

Greg approached with his chain. Jonathan jumped up, shook his head, and waved his hands emphatically. Greg shrugged and then pointed at the Corvette. Jonathan's waving hands slid down on top of his head. He walked over to where Greg had pointed, while Greg walked back to the truck.

"He doesn't want me to touch his precious car," he said as he opened my door. "He's high-centered anyway. A tow is liable to rip everything off the underside. We need to chop away as much snow as we can, then push it out. I have another shovel if you want to help." He gave me that soft smile. "I understand if you'd rather not."

I glanced at Princess Missy shivering on the side of the road. "I'll help," I said. "Let's just make it quick." I climbed out and took a shovel from Greg.

Jonathan looked over in surprise. "Hey, Beautiful. What're you doing here?"

I stared at the ground. Watching him from behind the protection of the glass had been fine, but out here I felt exposed. I went to the other side of the car with Greg and began chopping at the clumps.

Greg let the metal tip of his shovel "accidentally" hit the car.

"Watch it!" Jonathan yelled.

I let my shovel slip too.

"Hey! Come on!" Jonathan bellowed.

"Sorry!" we yelled, grinning at each other.

Once the snow was cleared on the left side of the car, Greg

went around to the other side to help Jonathan. I stepped back behind the car, sharing the same space with Missy without acknowledging her. Thankfully, she did the same.

"You do realize the right front tire is completely flat?" Greg said. "You drove over that piece of plywood with the nails sticking out."

Jonathan stomped to the front of the car. "Screw it!" he yelled, flinging his shovel down on the ground.

Missy and I flinched, but Greg didn't miss a beat. "I'd rather just help you change it. You have a jack?"

"Yes." Jonathan seethed from the snow pile he was carefully disassembling, looking for more nail-ridden plywood. "In my trunk."

"I'll get it," I said. The jack was wedged underneath the spare tire. I had to lift the tire up to free it. It was heavy and hard to do while holding the jack in the other hand, but I managed to yank the jack free. I set it aside and tried to lift the tire out as well.

It was too heavy. I let it fall back on the brown cloth it had been resting on. "I can't get the tire out," I called and picked the jack back up.

"Don't need it yet," Jonathan said in my ear. He reached around me and slammed the trunk shut.

I shoved the jack at him and stepped backwards, hating how, despite everything, he still made my heart pummel madly in my chest. I climbed back into Greg's truck and waited for them to finish.

"What does everyone see in him?" Greg said when we were

finally on our way to school. "He's so . . . ugh! Forget him. He's not worth it."

"I know. I want to. It's just" — I shrugged — "hard." We should've been at school by then, but traffic was moving at a snail's pace. Unfortunate. I could feel a lecture coming, one he'd promised not to give.

"Okay, I get that he hurt you, but did you really expect anything less from a guy everyone calls Zeus? Just move on." He shrugged. "Get over it."

"Get over it?" I said. "I found him with someone I never in a million years thought he'd be with. Someone I thought, for some sick reason, was my friend. And now he's moved on to yet another girl who was also once my friend. It hurts, Greg. I can't just get over that!" I sighed. "You can't just get over love —"

"*Love?*" Greg cried. "You *love* him? You dated only a few weeks!"

"No, I meant love in general. Your love life. People who break your heart. And it was a month, Greg. We dated a month." I wanted him to understand this wasn't about Jonathan and what I'd seen in him; it was about what I thought Jonathan had seen in *me*. "I thought he liked me, okay?"

"He's scum," he said with disgust.

"Yeah, he's scum. I'm an idiot. I get it." Whatever. I stared out at the cars in ditches that we were passing. Where was Mr. Good Samaritan now? Busy being Mr. Holier Than Thou, that's where. "Life isn't perfect, Greg. Sometimes we fall for the wrong person. Even you did. For someone who'll never like you back." It was a low blow, bringing up Missy. But he had started it — after he had promised not to. "Have you *moved on?* Did you just *get over —*"

The sudden acceleration as he screeched into the school parking lot cut me off. He slid to a stop and slammed into "park." "You think he loves you? He doesn't even respect you." He flung the door open and stepped out into the cold October day. "And yeah, I fell for the wrong person, but I have definitely moved on!"

"Greg, wait." I scrambled out of the truck to catch him. "I'm sorry!" Even with his long legs stuck in those bulky bunny boots, my canvas sneakers were no match. He was gone before I had reached the hallway.

"Have you heard from Miss Farni?" Dellian asked when I walked into class.

"I . . ." It took me a second to remember Tricia was missing. I was still thinking about Greg and how to apologize. "No, and I'm sure I won't." I started toward my desk.

He stopped me. "There's a Detective King waiting to speak with you in the counseling office."

"Speak to *me?*" I noticed then. There was a somberness hovering in my classmates' silence. "Why? What happened?"

"Miss Farni happened, remember? You were one of the last to see her Saturday."

I was? "Wait, she disappeared Saturday night?"

Dellian nodded. "Yes, right after the . . . altercation."

"No. That doesn't make sense," I said. "She told you — I mean you talked to her —"

"Your classmate is missing," Mr. Dellian interrupted. "We'd all appreciate it if you'd think of someone else for a change and go speak with the detective."

Once again, he'd twisted everything around, made things my fault, made me look bad. The entire class was staring, judging me. It was Dellian they should've been judging.

"And Miss Hart?" Dellian said as I walked to the door. "Try to look Detective King in the eye when you speak with her. You have a tendency to look elsewhere when you're conversing. It makes you appear dishonest."

He was giving me advice on how to speak to the police now? "That's the only way I *can* look her in the eye. If I focus on her face, I won't see her at all!"

"It's not always about *your* comfort level, Miss Hart. Police officers are trained to read people. Eye contact is the first thing they use to sum up a person. Don't let your eyesight be your demise."

"My demise?" I stared at him. "I didn't do anything!"

"I'm aware of that. Detective King isn't."

Dellian's words had me on edge when I entered the counseling office.

Principal Ratner had assumed I was lying because I wasn't looking directly at him. What if the detective did too? I had nothing to hide, though. Nothing to lie about.

Detective King was a tiny woman, younger than my mom, with long brown hair, not at all like the buff, brutish image I had conjured up in my mind. "Roswell Hart?" She ushered me into a counselor's office. "I understand you and Tricia Farni are friends?"

"We're partners in class." I tried to look her in the eye. My dots blocked out her entire face and neck. I leaned forward. The shorter distance helped a little, but the detective's eyes and nose were still missing. "We aren't friends." But that was a lie, wasn't it? I had started to consider her a friend, sort of.

"Oh?" Detective King said. "Her sister, Abbey, said Tricia talks of you often."

The way she said "Oh?" worried me. Could she tell I wasn't being truthful? Without seeing her entire face, I couldn't read her expression. I darted my eyes to her ear for a quick look.

She was watching me, closely.

"Well, we are friends in class." I flicked my eyes back to hers to make fake eye contact. "We never speak outside of school." Except at Birch Hill. The thought of her with Jonathan in the loft made me cringe automatically — and then I grimaced because I'd cringed. Crud! I was making myself look guilty. Why did I let Dellian freak me out like this?

My eyes darted back to her ear to see if she'd seen the face I'd made. She was staring at me. "Has she been staying with you, Roswell?"

"No, I haven't seen her since Saturday." I blocked out Detective King's face so it would look as if I were looking her in the eye again. It struck me as ironic how looking at her ear rather than her eyes — for me — meant I was making eye contact and therefore telling the truth. But to her, it meant I wasn't making eye contact and therefore could be lying.

Ironic and very disconcerting.

"Let's talk about Saturday night. You were at a party with her at Birch Hill?"

"Not *with* her, no. I was with my boyfriend." I involuntarily grimaced again. "Tricia was there too."

"A few students told me there was a fight of some sort? Between you and Tricia and your boyfriend?"

"Not with fists and all. We just argued."

"After this argument, what happened?" Detective King looked down and began writing in a little notebook after she asked this. Thank God. It was the one question I was dreading. I had no idea what happened afterward.

"My . . ." He was *not* my boyfriend anymore. "Jonathan Webb drove me home."

"And Tricia?" She looked up from the notebook. "Where'd she go?"

Back with the eye contact. I hated this. "I have no idea. We left before she did." At least I thought we did. What if we hadn't? Was unintentionally lying a crime?

"Okay." Detective King nodded. "How about before Saturday night. Had she ever stayed with you, maybe crashed on your couch a few nights?"

"No." The thought of Tricia and I having a slumber party was mildly amusing.

"Did she ever mention where she was living?"

The eyes' back-and-forth thing was making my head hurt. My stomach too. "We weren't that close."

"Her sister reported her missing, but—" Detective King sighed and put her pen down on the desk. I let my eyes fall to my lap. "Her foster family admitted they kicked Tricia out over eight months ago. We need to find out where she's been staying to proceed. She could simply be skipping school."

I looked up in surprise. "Mr. Dellian probably knows." More than probably.

"He's got no idea." Detective King handed me a business card. "Thank you, Roswell. Let me know if you hear from her."

Dellian had no idea? I stared at the card as I stood, wondering if I should say something. But what did I really know? And what if she *was* simply skipping? Or took off to get away from Dellian? She had said to give her until Monday to end whatever it was. Maybe taking off was how she'd meant to do that.

I shoved the card in my pocket and walked out just as Jonathan came into the counseling office. I pretended not to see him.

"Hey," he whispered and followed me out. "You talk to that cop?"

I nodded. How could he just waltz up and talk to me as if we were friends? I tried to will my heart out of its frenzy.

"Where do you think Tricia is?" he asked.

"Run off someplace?" I shrugged and stared down at my shoes. This was harder than I thought. Just the smell of him made my pulse react, whether I wanted it to or not.

"Probably." He nodded. "You didn't tell the cop about that stupid fight, did you?"

"Stupid fight? That's what you call it?" I glared at his ear. "No. I didn't give details about our 'stupid fight.' I said there was an argument, and that Tricia was still there when you took me home."

"You told the cop we argued, and" — he paused — "I took you home?"

"Don't sound so shocked. I didn't do it for you." What had I ever seen in him? "I'd rather not relive that moment if I can help it."

"So," he said. "That's what you want me to say too?"

"I don't care what you say. Just stay away from me."

"Why didn't you tell me?" Heather had finally heard about the Incident. "And now Copacabana is MIA? You can't even hate on her in class? How lame is that?"

"I had to talk to a detective. Are you sure it's Tricia you see at Dellian's?"

"Not too many freaks wearing brown capes in this town."

"Maybe you should tell the police. They're trying to find out where she's been staying." I looked around for Greg's familiar outline. I needed to apologize for this morning. "You see Greg anywhere?"

She shook her head, mouth full of fries. "At some study thing. Oh!" She looked around now too. "I need to tell Ricky, Greg can take us to see Fritz after school."

I raised my eyebrows. "You talked to Greg today?"

"At my locker after class." She grinned. "He didn't want me to worry about him during lunch, I guess. Isn't that cute? Speaking of cute." She pulled an envelope from her binder and slid it to me. "FYI? Never have yearbook take your homecoming pictures. There's a hair in every photo. Mr. Dellian is yearbook advisor, isn't he? Tell him to clean the lens."

I pulled each glossy sheet out, but barely looked. There was a lump in my throat I couldn't quite defuse. Greg was seeking Heather out now? Instead of me?

Desperate to apologize to Greg, I almost sat in that front desk again. But as I approached, Dellian looked up. "Miss Hart? Everything go well this morning?"

So, I muttered, "Fine," and went to the back. I stared at Greg's head the entire period, willing him to turn around, look my way. But he didn't.

After class, he tore out ahead of me.

"Greg!" I screamed as I ran after him. "Greg Martin!" I found him waiting a few yards from my locker, arms folded against his chest.

"What do you want? I need to go. I'm taking Ricky and Heather—"

"To the hospital, I know. I wanted to talk before we went, though."

"We? No. You aren't going." He looked at the wall instead of me.

"Greg, I'm sorry about this morning. You promised no lectures, so I got defensive." A blue smudge lined his chin. "You and your ink." I reached up to rub it off.

He slapped my hand away. "Is that what matters to you? Looks?"

"What? No!" I reached for his arm. "Greg—"

"Don't." He brought his hands up. "Just don't. I can't do this anymore."

"Do what anymore?"

He looked away. "You'd better go. You'll miss your bus."

"I don't care about my bus," I said as he walked away. "Greg, wait!" But he just waved his hand and kept walking.

No one talked about Tricia much. Her disappearance was a mere afterthought, an "oh, by the way"— more intriguing than disconcerting. Like a UFO spotting or a ghost story, her whereabouts fueled speculative conversations around lunch tables or on Saturday nights while people passed around a bottle of Schnapps and a bong in a borrowed SUV.

It was the mystery, the unknown, that everyone found exciting and newsworthy, not Tricia herself. After all, Tricia had been a freak, an alien among them. No one cared where she was when there was more pressing gossip, like how Gina Preston was slipped something at a party, or how Zeus and Missy were now dating "exclusively." And I was just as guilty as anyone. I was more concerned about the love life she'd wrecked and the one blooming between Heather and Greg than I was about Tricia.

Except in Life Skills. Although none of us there talked about her either — not directly — she became the invisible string that connected us. Her absence was something we shared, her empty desk a solemn reminder that all was not right in our world. And sad as it sounds, that mutual element made me regard my classmates differently. They seemed more real now; not just people in a class, but individuals, like me.

Every morning Ruth brought in whipped cream–filled pastries and served the first one to Tricia's empty desk. It was always gone the next day, eaten perhaps by some clueless sap in another Life Skills class or by Bart, who was sentenced to that room all day, or maybe it was just the janitor, simply doing his job. Wherever the pastry was ending up each day didn't matter. It was a symbol, an unspoken reverie in her honor, our collective prayer for her safe return.

Her disappearance had the opposite effect on Dellian and Jonathan, severing the string once attaching them. Her absence polarized the two of them, and it all came to a head the Friday after she went missing.

"You are skating on some mighty thin ice, Mr. Webb!" Dellian snapped when Jonathan wandered into class long after the tardy bell had rung.

"You sure about that?" Jonathan flopped into his chair. "I think you're the one on thin ice."

He may as well have pulled a gun. Mr. Dellian went ballistic. He flew over the desk and snatched Jonathan out of his chair by the collar.

"Miss Hart!" He yanked Jonathan out the door. "You're in charge!"

I sat stunned. The two had been fighting all week, but physical aggression? That was new. I considered following them. Despite my own dislike for Jonathan, I was concerned he wouldn't make it to Principal Ratner's office uninjured. I looked at my classmates to see if they had the same thoughts.

They were all looking at me.

"Wow," I said. "That was scary."

"Why are you in charge?" Jeffrey said. "Ruth's older."

He had a point. I was the newbie and the youngest.

"Well?" Jeffrey challenged. "You're in charge. What do we do?"

"I don't know." Since Tricia had disappeared, we really hadn't been doing much of anything in class. "Study?"

"No!" Jeffrey said. "You have to look in his book to see what to do."

"He said I'm in *charge*; he didn't say teach the class."

"Look in the book," Jeffrey insisted.

"Fine!" I made my way to the front.

Why did everything always have to be so exact with Jeffrey? I thought as I shuffled things around on Dellian's desk. Always by the book. A slight deviation from the norm and he got so testy. "Where would it be?" I asked after a few frustrated seconds of searching.

"Try his drawer," Ruth said.

The first drawer was locked. The others weren't. I rifled through miscellaneous office supplies, files, and papers before finding his brown planning book. "Okay . . ." I flipped it open. Taped to the back inner flap was a small brown envelope. I peeked inside.

A tiny key.

Interesting. Only one drawer was locked. The items I'd expected to be locked up — the files with personal info, grades, and

142

so on — were sitting in the unlocked drawers. What could he possibly have locked away in that skinny little top drawer?

I carefully fingered the key out of the envelope.

"Well?" Jeffrey said. "What does it say? Do you need your magnifying glass?"

"No!" He could be so annoying when he was focused on something. Like a pit bull, once he latched on, he wouldn't let it go. I scanned today's date. Blank. "Nothing. Guess we're studying again." I turned the key between my fingers. I really wanted to sneak a peek.

Jeffrey slumped in his chair. "When do we apply for jobs?"

"I'll look." I flipped through the pages, still distracted by the locked drawer. What would it hurt? One quick look? I glanced out at the class. They'd all slipped back into their catatonic states — except Jeffrey. He was still waiting for my reply.

I kept my blind spot on the book, pretending to read, while I pushed the key forward until it was between my thumb and finger. Feeling for the keyhole with my middle finger, I slid the key into the lock — a trick I'd mastered long ago. It's amazing how much you can "see" with your fingers.

The lock turned easily. I slid the drawer open and peeked over. It was empty except for a blank yellow notepad.

Lame.

"Sorry, Jeffrey, it doesn't say." We both sat back, disappointed. Why would Dellian lock up an unused pad of paper? Unless . . . the pad wasn't empty?

Jeffrey had gone back to staring at his desk. I took the pad out, fanning the pages in search of writing. Nothing. Totally clean.

I reached forward to put it back, then stopped. An eight-by-ten piece of photo paper was face-down on the bottom of the drawer.

I flipped it over. Although the images were slightly blurry and out of focus, I knew what I was looking at: Mr. Dellian on a couch in his jeans, eyes closed, shirt unbuttoned, with Tricia next to him in her bikini top and grass skirt, kissing his neck.

"Oh, my God!" I slapped the photo face-down into the drawer and threw the notebook back on top.

Everyone jerked their heads up. "What's wrong?" Ruth asked.

"Paper cut." I put the key back and sucked on my finger. "A really bad one"

"What a perv! I told you he was with her," Heather said at lunch.

"I guess I didn't believe it until now. I mean, he's a teacher!" I thought about the scene with Jonathan and Dellian that morning. Was she the friction between them? Had Tricia told Dellian about herself and Jonathan to make him jealous? Was that her plan? To use Jonathan to end it with Dellian?

"It was taken the night of the dance—she was in her grass skirt and Dellian had on his floral Hawaiian shirt—"

"He wasn't wearing a floral print," Heather interrupted. "His shirt had palm trees."

I frowned. "Are you sure? I could've sworn—"

"Positive," Heather said. "I remember wondering where he got it because it was so much better than the one I had found for Greg."

"Oh, well, whatever, she was in her grass skirt, so—" I paused.

"You think that's why she ran away? To get away from Dellian?" If it was true, *I* certainly wasn't going to help that sick jerk find her.

Heather shrugged. "I saw some other chick with the baby yesterday. At least I think it's the same baby. Babies always look alike to me."

I stole one of her fries. "Babysitter?"

"Hard to tell. Hey, you!" Heather smiled as Greg plopped a pile of notes in front of me and sat down next to her.

"Thanks." I smiled. He nodded without looking at me and began eating.

"Did you sign up for driver's ed yet?" Heather asked me.

My face began to burn. What part of "legally blind" didn't she get? "No."

"Well, don't bother. It's full. I'm so bummed. I wanted to start learning now." She slapped my hand away as I reached for another fry. "Get your own!"

"I'll teach you," Greg said.

"You will?" Heather smiled at him. "Can we start now? We still have fifteen minutes until lunch ends."

When he shrugged okay, Heather jumped up, clapping her hands like a little girl. "Here." She shoved her plate of fries at me. "Have the rest."

But I didn't want them anymore. I'd lost my appetite.

Day 9

"Jonathan Webb will no longer be our class aide," Mr. Dellian announced the following Monday as Life Skills ended. "Ruth and Roswell will now be partners."

"What about when Tricia comes back?" Ruth asked.

"We'll figure that out if" — Mr. Dellian paused — "*when* Miss Farni returns."

If? Was that simply a wrong word choice? Or did he know something the rest of us didn't?

"Miss Hart, I need to speak with you." Once everyone but Bart had left, Dellian said, "I removed Mr. Webb for your benefit. Being in class with him after what he did couldn't have been easy for you. Were you able to disclose everything to Detective King last week?"

Was I able to "disclose" everything? Why did he keep bringing that up? Did he like the fact that I'd been humiliated by Tricia and Jonathan? And for my benefit? Who was he kidding? It had nothing to do with me! "I'm sure it couldn't have been easy for you either, right?" My fists clenched tightly. "Were you able to 'disclose' everything to the detective also?"

I was standing about three yards away from him, too far to

read his expression. But I saw his body stiffen, felt the weight of his stare.

"Are you still on speaking terms with Mr. Webb?" It was more an accusation than a question. One I didn't think needed an answer.

"That's none of your business," I said and walked out.

I'd ended the conversation, but Dellian wanted the last word. Ever since I'd skipped AP History class that day, I'd been sitting in the back where Dellian wanted me to — yes, it was easier than battling Dellian, but it was also the only legitimate excuse I had to talk to Greg. As long as I was back there, he would take notes for me.

About five minutes into his lecture, Dellian suddenly stopped. "Mr. Martin, is that a music player on your desk?" He knew what it was. Greg had been using it since the first day of class.

"I'm recording the lecture for my notes," Greg said.

"Is it a music player?" Dellian asked again.

Greg's curls nodded yes.

"Music players are not allowed in this classroom. Put it away, or lose it."

I glared a black hole into Dellian's skull. Why did he bring Greg into this? This battle was between me and him. No one else. I could handle Dellian's crap, but Greg wasn't used to it. He was Mr. Straight and Narrow. The reprimand, being singled out in front of everyone — I knew Greg was humiliated.

"Greg," I said, catching up to him after class. "I'm really sorry about that. He got mad at me this morning and —"

He sort of half turned, keeping his body forward. "Just stay away from me, okay? I'm tired of being thrown into your messes."

"My messes?" I repeated, but he was already walking away.

A few minutes later, Heather texted to say she and Greg were going driving after school, and oh btw, they wouldn't be eating lunch with me for a while. Lunch was now their "driver's ed" time.

But I knew the real reason. Greg couldn't stand to be around me anymore.

"Yes!" JJ's wheelchair narrowly missed me as I entered the SPED hallway after Thanksgiving break. Another wheelchair flew by half a second later.

"You got more practice and a motor," the occupant of the other chair told JJ. "But I'm lifting weights. Motor or not, just wait, you'll be eating *my* dust soon."

I knew the voice. "Fritz?" I turned back around and hurried over to him. "Oh, my gosh! When did you get out of the hospital?" I gave him a big hug.

"A couple of weeks ago," Fritz said.

"A couple of weeks ago!" How had I not heard this? Heather had been keeping me up-to-date on his progress — or I thought she'd been. I'd just spent all afternoon and evening with her yesterday, and she hadn't said anything about his being out of the hospital.

He nodded. "So what brings you down this deserted hallway?"

"Going to class," I said. "You?"

"Besides racing?" He smirked and patted his legs. "Life Skills.

Gonna learn some mad skills for these bum legs."

"The only skill you'll learn in that class is how to be bored." Before he could ask, I added, "Bum eyes."

"Then we'll be bored together." We headed toward the room. "Missed you at my party Saturday." He cranked his wheels faster and faster, flew forward, and then screeched to a halt a few feet ahead of me.

"Party?" I hurried to catch up.

"Mr. Grandman, welcome!" Mr. Dellian said as he passed us. "Miss Hart."

"Hey, Mr. D.," Fritz said. He looked back at me. "The welcome-home party Greg threw for me. Heather said you were busy helping your mom?" He tried to make a sharp turn into the room and rammed the wall instead.

They had a party for Fritz and didn't invite me? I pulled Fritz's chair back so he could try it again. "Oh, right, taking inventory at the cosmetic counter she works at." So was Heather, *last night*. Saturday I'd done absolutely nothing.

"What's the scoop with Heather and Greg? Are they dating or just friends?" He wheeled backwards, realigned his wheels, and then sped forward again.

"Dating," I said.

"Really?" He careened through the door, made an abrupt left-hand turn to avoid colliding with a desk, and slammed to a halt with a grin on his face. "Always thought she'd go more for the daredevil type."

•   •   •

"I already have a partner!" Jeffrey said when Mr. Dellian told him he and JJ would be partners with Fritz. "'Partners' is two people, not three!"

"But we have an odd number of people, Jeffrey. The three of you will need to partner up."

"I can't push two wheelchairs!" Jeffrey screamed.

"No one said—"

"When have you ever had to push my wheelchair?" JJ interrupted. "I'm not a friggin' idiot! I can motor myself."

"Ditto for me, Dude," Fritz said. "I might be new to this thing, but I can handle it just fine."

But Jeffrey had already worked himself up, and that pit bull in him wouldn't let it go. "You said if your partner is having a bad day, you are having a bad day. That means I have to have double the bad days, and how am I supposed to get both of them in here if they are both gone? I can't! Their chairs are too heavy!"

"It's not as if you even have to!" JJ screamed right back. "When have we ever had to do anything as partners?"

Dellian put his hand on Jeffrey's back to calm him.

"Don't touch me!"

Dellian's hands flew up. "Okay, I won't touch you."

It was Ruth who came to the rescue. "Fritz can be our partner," she said in a calm, quiet voice. "We can handle three. Right, Roz? Until Tricia comes back?"

"It's been two months, Ruth," JJ muttered. "She's not coming back."

Jeffrey's outburst didn't surprise me, but I'd never seen JJ like that — first angry and now defeated. He was usually the quiet one who sat at his desk reading his comic books and bothering no one.

"She's coming back, JJ," I said. "She just needed some time away. Like when she left her foster family for eight months — they didn't know where she was, but she was around. Right, Mr. Dellian?"

I honestly said this only to reassure JJ. But the way Dellian stared me down, for what seemed an eternity, before moving on, gave me the feeling he thought I was throwing something in his face. And he didn't like it.

Day 86

I was grateful for Christmas break a few weeks later. Dellian had become obsessed with humiliating me. In Life Skills he'd call attention to my vision problem in front of Fritz by asking me where my magnifying glass was or telling me to sit up front. He even brought in a bunch of low-vision aids to demonstrate to the class — for "Miss Hart's benefit," he said.

In AP he was a bit more subtle. He started handwriting the quizzes and tests in the tiniest, most cryptic print he could make. He'd call on me to read aloud from the book or the board, then say, "Oh, I forgot. You *can't* read," then call on someone else.

But when school finally let out, I felt even more isolated. Mom spent the entire vacation either working or with Tony, her new boyfriend. Heather spent the first week with her mom, and when she went back to her dad's, she seemed to have something planned with Greg every time I called. So when Mom said I could have a few friends over for New Year's Eve while she was out of town with Tony, I jumped at it.

"How do I get Greg over there?" Heather said when I called. "I can't even get him to eat lunch with you. And don't say 'use my feminine ways.' He won't even kiss me!"

That news made me smile. "Tell him Fritz and Ricky are coming, and that I got two new UFO photos for Christmas."

"Photos? Wouldn't a keg be a better carrot?"

"With Greg?" She didn't know him at all. "Just tell him. It'll work. I promise."

Heather showed up with Greg in tow. She wore a silver sequined cami over leather leggings; they were so out of sync with Greg's casual jeans and green fleece, I almost laughed. Almost — if seeing them together hadn't made my heart ache so much.

The first few minutes were painful. Heather tried to overcompensate for the uncomfortable silence with stupid, brainless jokes and exaggerated laughter, while I shoveled food into my mouth and tried to ignore how lonely the two of them made me feel. I think we all breathed an inward sigh of relief when Fritz and Ricky showed up.

"Those stairs are gonna be a problem," Fritz said when I opened the front door.

Shoot. I hadn't even thought about my house being a split-level. Whether going up or down, he'd have to take on twelve stairs.

"Could we carry you?" Greg asked.

"Nah, man. I'm too heavy, and that's a lot of stairs."

"Go through the garage," I said. "There are only two steps leading into the den."

This worked but it meant moving the party downstairs. Heather and I relocated the food and punch from upstairs, while the boys muscled Fritz into the den. "Our movies are out. No television down here." I carried in several drawers full of CDs from my room. "But we've got music."

"Dang." Ricky flipped through the cases. "You have a little bit of everything, don't you? Marley, Morrissey, Mudvayne . . ."

I realized then that Greg wasn't in the den with us. I had a feeling I knew where he was — this was my chance to talk to him alone. "I have my dad's old record player and album collection too. I'll go get them." Just as I thought, Greg was standing on my bed, looking at the UFO photos.

I grinned. "I knew you'd be in here."

"Sorry." He started to climb down.

"No, stay, look at them. There're two new ones." I pointed to the photos Dad had sent for Christmas. "This one's kind of crappy — taken with a cell phone. The other one's awesome, though."

I carried a stack of records to the den and hurried back to my room. To Greg.

"Where was this taken? The noncrappy one?" Greg asked. "Hand me your magnifying glass for a second."

"Indiana." I handed him the magnifier. "A few months ago. It looks like a blimp or something thick; see how the lights appear to be above one another on the same side? But if you look closer —"

"The lights are spaced apart, not one above the other! It's definitely cylindrical in shape, isn't it?" He surveyed the other photos again, like a kid in a candy store, eagerly jumping from picture to picture with the magnifying glass. "Did he send you any other new ones?" he asked, finally stepping off the bed.

"Just a news article about a dead Big Foot found in the Alps.

You can read it if you want. The corpse looks like a deranged mountain man in his Halloween costume."

He grinned.

It had been so long since I'd seen him do that, I blurted out, "God, I've missed that smile," before I even knew what I was saying.

The smile froze on his face. "I should get back out there."

"Wait. Please?" My fingers clutched the fabric of his fleece. "I hate this. I miss laughing with you, and bitching about Dellian with you, and talking about aliens with you; I even miss how you have a quote for everything. I'm sorry I ruined that."

He didn't try to move away. I released the fabric and dropped my hand. "That day in your truck? I shouldn't have said that Missy will never like you. I honestly don't know if she does or doesn't. But it was mean to say it, and I'm sorry . . ."

His face took on a weird expression — one I couldn't read. Was he considering forgiveness or flight? I wasn't sure, but he *was* still here.

"Okay, for the record? It wasn't Jonathan I had to get over; it was the idea of him. You know, the popular guy liking the freak? The whole idea that he wanted me — it was so . . . like the first time you hear a dance song with a catchy beat. You know how it makes you just want to jump up and down and dance and sing. You can't get enough of it, right?"

He shrugged, that odd expression still on his face.

"Okay, but after listening a few times, the song with its nonsensical lyrics and shallow, meaningless rhyme written for rhyme's sake — it all just gets annoying. That was Jonathan. He made me feel good at first, but . . . he was just a great dance song with crappy lyrics."

"I hate dance songs with crappy lyrics," Greg said, a hint of a smirk on his lips.

"Me too." I grinned.

Heather bounced in. "Hey, what's the holdup on the record player? Fritz found a Nazareth *Hair of the Dog* album he wants to hear." She looked at me and then at Greg. "Come on, you two. It's New Year's Eve. Can't you put your stupid fight away for one night?"

"We're trying," I said.

Greg nodded. "Give us a minute?"

"I want smiles when you two come out." She unplugged the record player and scooped it into her arms. "Got that? Smiles!"

Greg shut the door behind her. "You're not a freak, Roz."

I shook my head. "That doesn't matter. Look, I just want you to understand that I got what you were saying that day. You were being a friend, and I wasn't one back. I am apologizing, or trying to, because I really, really miss my friend."

"Me too." He gave me a shy smile.

"Truce then? You'll acknowledge my existence now?"

The smile widened into that quirky, toothy Greg smile. "Acknowledge your existence? What are you, Sasquatch?"

"You know what I mean. Are we friends again? Will you stop ignoring me?"

"Friends again. You're really hard to ignore anyway, what with your big feet and all that fur . . ."

● ● ●

Our talk left me happy and giddy and high for most of the night. The five of us played round after round of Name That Tune, as Greg and I had done on the bus. Fritz and Greg were fierce competition for me, but in the end, I stumped them both with obscure songs from B sides.

Then Ricky and Fritz left. We moved upstairs to watch some new action thriller that Heather had brought. I'd planned to watch *Almost Famous* because Greg said he'd never seen it, but Heather insisted we watch her movie, since I owned *Almost Famous* and her movie was due back soon. Whatever. Half of it took place on a Russian ship, which meant it had subtitles I couldn't see. I sat on the couch with Heather between Greg and me, staring at the screen while she chatted at him the whole time. The sound of her voice annoyed me, and as I sat there, with Greg close by yet so very far away, the giddiness drained from me. I felt empty and hollow and alone.

I wanted to talk to Greg without Heather around. Over and over, I replayed the conversation we had in my room. I wished we'd never joined the others. I wished I'd invited only Greg or made up some lie so everyone but Greg had gone home.

"You want me to read those for you, Roz?" Greg said, cutting into my thoughts.

"What?" I said, realizing then that Heather had stopped talking.

"The subtitles. You want me to read them for you?" he said as I glanced over. Heather was asleep, her head resting on his shoulder.

The intense jealousy that ripped through me made my heart ache. "No, I'm not watching." I stood up. "I'm gonna watch the fireworks." I grabbed my jacket and headed outside.

It was well below freezing, minus-thirty degrees, and the blast of cold air slapped some sense back into me. Why shouldn't she have her head on his shoulder? They were dating. Still . . .

I sat on the porch swing and tried to calm the confusion churning inside me.

"They start yet?" Greg sat down at my side.

"A few more minutes." I stared at the star-speckled black sky, watching for the first signs of celebration. The fireworks in Birch, Alaska, were always huge. With full-time sunlight in the summer, we couldn't set off fireworks on the Fourth of July, so the city made the New Year's display spectacular.

"For the record," Greg said, "I never had a thing for Missy."

"Liar!" I said. "Yes, you did."

"No, seriously, I didn't."

"Dude, I should know. I had a killer crush on you until I realized you were all gaga for her."

"Killer crush?" He gave me a crooked smile. "On me?"

I waved him away, embarrassed. "Remember that Valentine's Day party Missy had at her house? I showed up early and you were already there, helping her decorate with roses *you* brought."

"That's your proof? That I helped her decorate for a party with roses my mom sent over?" He still had that silly grin on his face.

"Every time I came over to hang with Missy, you were there, and you wouldn't leave unless we kicked you out."

"That just proves my lack of social skills."

I rolled my eyes. "And anytime we went somewhere — the movies or the state fair — you begged to come with us."

"So I like movies and roller coasters; that doesn't prove I liked Missy."

"Okay. How about all of our softball games?"

He shook his head. "I stopped going after you quit."

"I didn't quit. Missy told Coach I was legally blind, and he decided I was a liability."

"That's why you two don't talk anymore?"

"Partly, yeah." I stared at the ice crystals sparkling in the snow. I couldn't tell him the rest — how she'd done that only in retaliation for what I'd done to her.

"Liability? Did he forget your double play that won the game that time?"

I stared at him. "When I was in fourth grade? You remember that?"

"Hard to forget that grin. You wore it for a week. There's a fallacy in your reasoning, Roz. You overlooked an important part of the equation." He looked up at the night sky. "You. It's always been you."

His words settled over me. The world hushed around us. The only movement, the telltale puffs of breath that lingered under our noses. Just as there are stars in the day sky that you can't see until nightfall, I realized there were things right there in front of me that I'd missed.

His gloved hand traveled across my lap and curled around

mine. Despite the layers of fleece, his touch sent my pulse racing faster than any skin-to-skin contact with Jonathan ever had. Our legs, jeans to jeans, barely touched, but I could feel the heat from his body. A searing warmth that stole my breath.

As if on cue, the fireworks started. We held hands in silence while the most magnificent displays of greens and blues and reds burst against the velvet-black sky.

The finale disintegrated and the night grew quiet again. "Happy New Year," Greg whispered and squeezed my hand.

A bubble of guilt caught in my throat. "What about Heather? She's not going to understand. When Jonathan cheated with Tricia—"

"Do *not* compare me to him," he said. "It's not the same. Heather and I aren't exclusive."

"How can you say that? She's the only girl you ever go out with!"

"I'm teaching her to drive! And okay, we go places together, but it's more hanging out than dating. We're just friends. I never said 'Be my girlfriend' or anything."

"Jonathan never said that to me either."

"Yeah, but come on. It was obvious; you were always—" He stopped.

"Together?" I asked. "Whether that's how it was or not, Greg, you two looked exclusive to everyone, especially to Heather."

His head fell back against the swing. "God, I am an *ass*." He rolled his head to the side to look at me. "This is your fault, you know."

"My fault?" I said. "How?"

But he was already shaking his head. "No, it's mine. But you got me so mad when you said I fell for the wrong person. I thought you meant you. I decided hanging out with Heather would show you how I'd *moved on*."

"You've been using her? Because of me? Greg, she thinks you like her!"

He gave me a pained look. "I swear that wasn't my intention."

"I know." I pushed a rebel curl from his eyes. I felt sick. This wasn't my intention either. To ruin things between them. Or was it? I hadn't told Heather to bring him just so we could be friends again, had I? Deep down, I'd been hoping for something more. Something like this. I *was* a lousy friend.

"I'll talk to her. I'll fix this," Greg said.

"Just" — I chewed on my lip — "don't make it about me. That would kill her."

The screen door slammed behind us. We jumped apart. "There you guys are! What are you doing out here?"

"Fireworks." I motioned at the empty black sky. "You fell asleep, so —" I stopped midsentence. The way she was staring, I didn't need to see her face to know. She knew we'd rekindled more than just our friendship.

I stayed on the porch swing after they'd gone, letting the cold breeze push me. If Jonathan was a dance song with crappy lyrics, Greg was that unreleased song on a favorite album that defines you. The one you discover sandwiched between two favorites; the one that keeps you listening to the album long after its time. Unfortunately, the album wasn't mine. It belonged to Heather.

An ache wrapped itself around my heart and squeezed the breath from me.

I knew the right thing to do was to leave Greg alone. Just walk away. But if that was the right thing, why did the very thought of that hurt so bad?

Day 93

I arrived at school the first day after break in a mixture of excitement and dread. I was excited to see Greg, but dreaded seeing Heather. Greg swore he didn't say anything about me when he told Heather they should see other people. The way Heather had been ignoring my calls and e-mails, though, I knew she had figured it out.

"Boy, is Heather pissed at you," Fritz said as he rolled up outside of Life Skills. "What the heck happened between you and Greg after I left your house?"

"Nothing!" I said. "I swear!" I glanced into the classroom while Fritz high-fived JJ in the doorway. Someone was sitting in Tricia's desk. *Oh, my gosh! She's back?* I thought, as I squeezed around the chairs to get to her.

But it wasn't Tricia.

It was Ruth. She looked up from Tricia's desk, her usual happy smile gone.

"Ruth?" I noticed a plate of brightly frosted Christmas cookies in front of her as I sat down. "What's wrong?"

"I thought she'd come back over break. For Christmas. She

loves Christmas." Ruth stared down at the cookies. "Why didn't she come back?"

"Maybe she did. The bell hasn't rung yet, maybe —"

But Ruth was shaking her head. "Mr. Dellian said she's never coming back."

"Why would you tell her Tricia's never coming back?" I snapped.

"No, no, no, Ruth. I said probably never coming back in *here*, this class." He turned to me. "And what I tell my pupils is none of your business, Miss Hart."

"I thought Tricia *was* my business," I said. "My *partner*."

"Yes, Miss Hart," he said in a cold, harsh tone, "I thought so too."

"Zeus got you diamond earrings? Let me see!" Rona screeched at Missy.

I ignored them and focused on the black blob sitting in Heather's spot at our lunch table. As I got within a few feet of it, I realized it was Heather, clad head to toe in black.

"As if Rona hasn't seen them eighty times already." I took in the hot-pink streaks in Heather's raven-blue hair as I slid in next to her. "That was totally for our benefit."

"More yours than mine," Heather said without looking up from the book in her hands. "How about you? Any diamonds for Christmas? From Greg maybe?"

"Heather, you know he didn't give me anything for Christmas."

"Do I?" She twirled a pink strand of hair between two fingers. "There seem to be a lot of things I don't know about you."

"I'm not going out with him. I won't even talk to him if that's what you want."

Heather shrugged, pretending to be engrossed in her novel.

I snatched it from her. "*Great Expectations*? I thought you read only the QuickNotes."

"And I thought you said you didn't like Greg." She swiped the book back from me. "I'm auditioning to be Miss Havisham. I have a lot in common with the old bat now that I'm destined to be a crazy spinster."

"Don't be ridiculous. You may look batty in that all-black getup, but you two have nothing in common. Miss Havisham never had pink hair."

Heather smacked me. "Don't make me laugh. I'm mad at you." Her voice dropped. "What happened at your party?"

"Nothing. I promise. Greg and I are just friends. Peace offering? Fries with all the ketchup you want?"

"Throw in double fudge brownies and I'll consider it."

Day 140

Greg and I thought avoiding each other until Heather cooled off would be easy. As weeks turned to months, however, and Heather continued to wear black and mope, the whole situation became impossible. Every day when I entered sixth hour, my nose zeroed in on watermelon gum and dryer sheets, sending my heart ricocheting out of control. I couldn't focus on Dellian's lectures, only on Greg. His tousled hair, his shirt, the way he bent over his desk . . . Note exchanges after class and virtual dates (watching shows together while on the phone) just weren't enough anymore. We wanted to be together.

"I'm going to the public library tomorrow to start on my AP paper," Greg said on the phone one Saturday night after we'd finished watching an *Alien Abductions* episode. "Come with me?"

"Greg —"

"She won't be there, Roz. She doesn't 'do' academics," he said. "Even if she were, it would look legitimate. Just two classmates finding research."

I bit my lip. I wanted desperately to go. Valentine's weekend had sucked. We'd spent all night on the phone instead of together. I wanted to sit next to him on my swing again. Our legs touching. His hand in mine. Just the thought of that night sent electric waves through me. I wanted to feel that way again.

But I'd promised Heather nothing was going on between us. "We can't."

"Roz, I really need to talk to you alone," he whispered. "Please?"

His plea made my heart ache. Heather had play practice and wouldn't be near the library. How could it hurt? "Okay, pick me up at noon?"

"I said noon!" I told Greg as he stepped out of his car at eleven thirty the next morning. "What if Heather drives by on her way to play practice?"

"It's nice to see you too," Greg said.

"Sorry." I looked at him then — jeans, the same green fleece he'd worn on New Year's Eve, the same watermelon bubblegum/dryer sheet smell that drove me mad — it *was* nice to see him. Nice and . . . awkward. I suddenly felt shy. "Hi," I said with a nervous glance at his ear.

His smile lit up his whole face. "Hi." He took my hands in his. "Sorry I'm early. I couldn't wait to see you. Heather won't be on this side of town, though. She's at her mom's this weekend."

"You . . . talked to her?" I hated how jealous I sounded, how jealous I felt.

"No!" He gave my hands a reassuring squeeze. "Every other week I picked her up at her mom's. You know, to teach her to drive?"

It was meant to reassure me. But the idea of Greg teaching Heather to drive — something he'd never teach me — made me only more jealous. I tugged my hands free and stepped away. "You ready to go?"

I saw his puzzled expression out of the corner of my eye, but I ignored it and walked around to the passenger door. A bunch of food wrappers fell out as I opened it.

"Sorry." He grabbed a handful of trash off the seat and threw it in the back. "Haven't had much time lately. My mom —"

"Driving lessons keeping you busy?" I interrupted. A messy car was out of character for him, and somehow I figured it must be Heather's fault.

"What? No!" He stared at me. "What's wrong?"

"Nothing! Let's just go before we run out of time."

"Right, I forgot. Our entire life is dictated by Heather Torres now." He slammed the gear into reverse and backed out.

I folded my arms across my chest and glared out the window. After all this time wanting to be alone with Greg, here we were and I was being jealous and stupid. An idiot. "What were you going to say about your mom?" I asked.

He shook his head. "Nothing. Never mind." He was mad.

"I'm sorry," I whispered. "I got jealous because . . ." And then I thought, *Why can't he teach me to drive? I can navigate through hallways and streets okay. As long as I'm somewhere clear of cars, why shouldn't I be able to drive?* "Teach me to drive?" I asked.

"What?" He frowned. "Are you serious?"

"The fairgrounds parking lot is huge and totally deserted at this time of year. There won't be anything for me to hit, and if there is, you could tell me. Be my eyes. Please?"

"I don't know—"

"Do you trust me, Greg?" When he nodded, I smiled. "It'll be fine. I promise."

I should've asked if *I* trusted me.

After an hour in first gear, driving around light posts and parking between lines, I'd finally mastered the clutch enough to try speeding up to fourth.

"Do you hear how it sounds as if it's working too hard?" Greg said as I accelerated. "That means you need to put it into third."

Keeping my right foot on the gas pedal, I pushed the clutch in with my left foot and put my hand on the gearshift. Greg helped me ease it into third.

"Perfect," Greg said. "Now speed up some more so you can get it into fourth."

We were approaching the longer end of the L-shaped lot. I would have to turn right, travel the shorter length of the lot, then make a U-turn and come back up. "Shouldn't I stay in third until after I turn?" I knew I wasn't going that fast, but I felt a bit out of control.

"No, you're fine. Bring it up to at least forty so you can shift into fourth."

I squinted at the odometer. Too small. I leaned forward to get a closer look and the wheel swerved right. "Whoa," I said, frantically recorrecting to the left.

"You're okay; just realign. You see that post, right?"

We'd been using the lampposts as lane dividers. I looked up.

There was a post now centered with the car, rather than on my left. "Yeah, I see it," I said. The post was still a ways ahead. I had time. I began gradually turning the wheel right.

"Roz! The post!" Greg grabbed the steering wheel.

Too late.

The car slammed into the post. We were flung forward and then ripped backwards as the car stopped on impact.

"Oh, my God!" The lamppost I hadn't seen was clearly visible now. I looked over at Greg. He was staring at the lamppost too, his mouth wide open. "Greg, are you okay?"

He nodded, still stunned. "Are you?"

"Oh God, Greg!" I said, the realization that I'd wrecked his car settling over me. "I am *so* sorry. I didn't see it."

Someone tapped on my window. "Are you kids okay?"

"Great," Greg groaned.

Detective King opened my door. "Roswell Hart, right? You two okay? I was driving by. I saw you heading straight for that lamp. Did you even brake, hon?"

The whole thing was a nightmare. I got ticketed for driving without a license or permit. Greg got a ticket for letting an unlicensed driver drive his vehicle, and, Detective King informed him, his insurance most likely wouldn't pay for the damages because of that fact. The good news? The car still drove. We didn't need to call a tow truck or Greg's parents.

"Mom can't handle this right now," Greg said when Detective King finally let us leave. "Dad's going to be so mad."

"I'll pay, okay?" I said. "It's my fault."

He just shook his head. "Probably nothing to pay for, Roz. This is an old car. I'll be lucky if I find a replacement grille or hood."

"So you're stuck with it looking like this?" I asked.

"They may be able to hammer the hood dents out, but there'll always be damage."

"I'm so sorry," I groaned as another thought occurred to me. "If you can't fix it, people will ask. What if Heather finds out I was with you?"

He glared over at me. "Are you serious?"

"I'm not saying I don't care that I just trashed your car or anything! I just —" I shrugged. "She's my friend. I don't want to hurt her."

"You think Heather would do the same? Avoid a guy she likes for you?" He didn't let me answer. "She wouldn't. I know that for a fact."

"What's that supposed to mean?"

"It means" — he sighed — "you say you're friends, but *are* you? I bet you don't know who else she's dated this year, do you? Or what her dad does for a living? When her birthday is?"

"You're right. I don't know her birthday and she didn't know mine was over Christmas break. Guess you and I can go out after all!" I rolled my eyes. "What, you're friends only if you know someone's birthday?"

"No! I meant" — he took a breath and let it out — "I meant . . . I mean . . . you barely know her, Roz. Is she really" — his voice got quiet — "more important than me?"

"Oh, Greg, no! Of course not! I'm not choosing one of you over the other. Don't you understand? You two were dating. I know how much it hurt when Jonathan —"

"Him again! Is this even about Heather? Or is it just an excuse because I'm not cool enough? Not popular enough? Do you even *want* to go out with me?"

"How can you ask that? Of course I do! Would I be sneaking around with you if I didn't?"

He pulled into my driveway. "I don't know. Would you be sneaking around with me if you really wanted to be loyal to Heather?"

My mouth dropped. "Do *you* not want to be with me? Is that what this is all about? Are you breaking up with me?"

"How can we break up, Roz? Our only dates have been virtual. I might as well be dating an avatar!"

"You think I want it this way? I don't. I want it to be normal too. I want to go to the movies, parties, dances; I want to hang out with you! But" — I shrugged — "'you can't always get what you want.'"

"The Stones? You're quoting the Stones? How philosophical of you." He gave a condescending snort that made my blood boil.

"What? Mick Jagger not intellectual enough for you?" I flung the door open and stumbled out. "I'll be sure to quote T. S. Eliot next time." I headed toward my door.

"Don't bother!" Greg yelled over the clanky chugging noise his mangled purple beast was now making. "There won't be a next time!"

Day 157

"No, Greg's not like that," Fritz said in Life Skills approximately two weeks later. He was trying to convince me that Greg wasn't being vindictive when he had Missy deliver my AP notes. "They're neighbors, right? He probably had something to do and asked her for a favor."

"Three times, though?" And the last time, Jonathan had been in tow. Whether Greg meant it to be or not, it was humiliating. More than that, it hurt. I sighed and took a bite of my *beignet*. Ruth had made the sugar-coated French pastries to celebrate — everyone but Fritz and I was applying for jobs today. "And now Heather's not speaking to me either. I think Greg told her I was the one who wrecked his car."

"No, he didn't." Fritz hung his head. "That was me. It slipped out that you were driving." He looked up through his long bangs like a dog begging for forgiveness. "Sorry?"

I laughed and grabbed a second pastry from Ruth. "I should've worn sweats today. These are good."

Fritz licked sugar off his fingers. "If they don't hire you at that fancy French restaurant downtown, you can cook for me, Ruth. I'll take these over frosted flakes any day."

"Lookin' spiffy, JJ," Fritz said as JJ rolled up in a suit and a grin a mile long.

Mr. Dellian came in behind him. "Yes, JJ, you do look nice. Thank you for taking this job application process seriously." He looked at Fritz as he said this.

Fritz glanced down at his dark green oversize suit jacket and *Dead Zombies* T-shirt. "What? It's not as if I'm applying!"

"It's important that we all make a good first impression." Mr. Dellian set a paper down on an empty desk. "I'm going to check on the van. Look this list over and decide which positions you'd like. Except the Birch Hotel position. That's for Bart."

Everyone but me swarmed the paper. One by one, shoulders slumped. The mood in the room went from giddy to glum. Something wasn't right.

Fritz was the first to speak. "What the hell is this?"

"What's it say?" I asked.

JJ began reading aloud. "ShopCo — Customer Greeter. Responsibilities: Greet customers in courteous, friendly manner; collect shopping carts; assist customers as needed. Pay — voluntary, no wages. Birch Hotel — Housekeeping Assistant. Responsibilities: Sort and fold laundered towels. Pay — voluntary, no wages. Riverside Veterinary Hospital — Kennel Cleaner. Responsibilities: Clean and maintain pet kennels. Pay — voluntary, no wages."

Ruth frowned. "Does this mean I can't apply at Café de Paris?"

Jeffrey's eyes flew to me. "I thought we got to choose where to apply?"

"I thought so too," I said. Dellian was such an ass. How could he do this to them?

"All that crap about ADA equalizing the job market. What a crock!" Fritz said. "These businesses just want free labor! I bet they'll pat themselves on the back for hiring the handicapped too. This is bullshit."

"I can't work at Café de Paris?" Tears fell from Ruth's almond-shaped eyes.

My anger boiled to the surface. With the exception of Bart, none of us had a disability that kept us from interacting in society. Sure, we had our quirks, our obstacles, but doesn't everybody? I was so sick of being told what I could and couldn't do because someone put a label on me. "Ruth, this doesn't mean anything. This class, Dellian, it's all nothing. It's *your* life; Dellian has no say in that. You can apply at Café de Paris, or anywhere you want, and no one can stop you."

Ruth wiped her eyes. "Right now?"

I glanced at Fritz. "Why not?" I said, a smile playing on my lips. "You in?"

"Oh yeah!" He grinned. "Let's do this!"

"We need bus fare," I said. "Everyone empty your pockets."

"Got it covered." Fritz pulled a ton of quarters from his jacket pocket. "JJ, you wanted to apply at that hobby shop down the street from the café, didn't you?"

JJ nodded, his chair zooming to the door.

"The movie theater is one block over," Jeffrey said as he snatched his Indiana Jones hat off his desk.

I heard Dellian's shoes squeaking in the hall. "We gotta go. Bart?"

He started to rock back and forth.

"Okay, you stay, Bart, but shhh!" Fritz put his finger to his lip. "Don't tell."

Single file, we moved out the door. "We're going to the van," I told Dellian as we passed him in the hall.

"It's nice to see initiative, Miss Hart," Mr. Dellian replied. "I'll get Bart."

When we rounded the corner, we raced out the back doors toward the city bus stop. "Hurry, Ruth!" Jeffrey called. "We'll get caught if you don't hurry."

But Ruth's short legs couldn't keep up with us. Fritz stopped wheeling and motioned to her to hop on his lap. Her squeals of laughter followed us all the way to the bus stop.

"This is something Tricia would've done," Ruth said with a smirk as we sat down on the bus. "What do you think she's doing right now?"

Doing? Drugs and dudes, what else? I shrugged. "I don't know."

"I think she's taking care of people, maybe kids," Ruth said. "That's what she does best, you know. She takes care of people."

We arrived back at school during lunch. The hall monitor immediately apprehended Fritz and me and ushered us into Ratner's office, where Dellian was waiting.

"What kind of asinine stunt was that? You had no right taking those kids out of school without permission! I should charge you both with kidnapping!"

"Nobody was kidnapped!" Fritz said. "We went of our own free will."

"And we had permission. You sent it home last week, remember?" I said.

Mr. Dellian glared at me. "They had permission to apply for jobs, not —"

"That's what we did," I said. "Well, JJ, Ruth, and Jeffrey did. For *real* jobs, not faux jobs like the ones you set up. Ruth even got hired at Café de Paris to wash dishes."

"Wash dishes? How is that better than the positions I arranged?"

"Because *she* chose it, not you. In June she can work food prep too, like she wants."

"Yeah, for a real paycheck," Fritz added. "None of that tax write-off bullshit you were pushing."

Mr. Dellian almost exploded. "You two don't know what you're doing! Those kids can't handle the pressures of employment in the real world! I worked hard to set up safe environments for them to learn in, to avoid another situation like Renny's, and you two just waltz in and tear that down? You're both suspended!"

"No, they're not. Skipping a field trip is not acceptable, but it warrants only detention at this juncture — unless of course the others say they were forced to go."

"Then I want them out of that classroom. I've had it with their insubordination."

"Insubordination?" Fritz laughed. "What is this, the military?"

"That's enough, Fritz." Principal Ratner frowned at Dellian. "That class is now a requirement in their IEPs, remember? I understand your frustration, but you were the one who implemented this new policy change, Rodney, so that no kid with a disability slipped through the cracks."

"I know why I implemented it!" Mr. Dellian snapped.

"And it's a good policy. One we need to stick to, whether you like the students or not." Principal Ratner pursed his lips. "Why don't you head on back to class, Rodney. I'll handle it from here."

Ratner gave us detention for the rest of the week, but I didn't care. Detention couldn't erase the freedom I felt. Our rebellion was invigorating, empowering. For once, I felt in control of my life, and I didn't want it to end; I couldn't go back to being invisible. So . . . in sixth hour, I marched into AP History, smiled at Dellian, and plopped down at the forbidden front desk.

"Miss Hart!" Dellian hissed. "Absent!"

"Here we go again," Greg muttered next to me.

I took a deep breath, my smile unfaltering. "Yes," I said, loud and clear for the entire class to hear, "here we go again."

And this time? I wasn't backing down.

War broke out in Life Skills.

Dellian interrogated the others one by one, threatening detention unless they admitted we'd forced them off campus. When that didn't work, he told Ruth she should quit her job, that his jobs were more "conducive to her learning style" or some garbage like that. That made everyone only more defiant. Ruth's parents even called Ratner, questioning Dellian's qualifications on school-to-work issues.

It was beautiful. We were finally using some life skills in Life Skills. But Dellian blamed me, and although he doled out detentions as punishment, I knew that wouldn't be enough for him. Underneath that cool façade, he was raging, and he wouldn't stop until he'd had his revenge, especially now that I was back to "insubordination" in AP too.

It took about two weeks. And it came in the mail, right before Easter break.

"What is this?" Mom stormed into my room, waving a letter at me.

"I don't know. What is it?" I grabbed at the letter, but she snatched it away.

"It says if you skip one more AP class, they'll suspend you! Rozzy, what are you thinking? Is it that boy? The one with the Corvette? Is this his doing?"

I blinked at her. "Jonathan? Mom, we broke up in October! Don't you pay attention?" I sighed in frustration. "I told you about this at the beginning of the year. Dellian's marking me absent because I'm sitting in front."

She folded her arms across her chest. "Teachers don't mark kids absent for the hell of it, Rozzy."

I folded my arms too. "This one does."

"Oh yeah?" She postured, hands on her hips. "Then bring me proof. Otherwise, you're grounded."

"Proof?" I yelled as she left my room. "What do you want, a photo?"

But then a thought occurred to me. Maybe a photo was exactly the proof I needed.

And I knew just where to find one.

JJ and Fritz were doing wheelies in the SPED hallway when I got to school the next day. "Fritz, I need a favor."

Fritz spun over to me. "Shoot."

"Can you get Dellian out of the room for ten minutes?" I knelt next to his chair. "I have to find something in his desk."

"Ooh, I'm intrigued," he said. "A little CSI action?"

"More like 007." Blackmail wasn't really CSI's thing. "Are you up for it?"

Mr. Dellian rounded the corner. "Miss Hart, Mr. Grandman, if you're not inside in thirty seconds, you'll have another detention."

"Are you a good actor?" I whispered. "Tantrums work well in this class."

The words were barely out of my mouth when Fritz shoved me backwards. "Get off me!"

"Fritz?" JJ gawked from the classroom door.

"Leave me alone!" Fritz screamed.

Dellian turned around.

I stifled my smile. "Fritz? What —"

"I said *get away!*" Even though I knew he was acting, I jumped.

Fritz whipped his chair around and began wheeling down the hall, away from the classroom, still yelling.

Dellian sprinted after him, trying to hush him as students and teachers came running from all directions.

"What's wrong with him?" JJ asked. "What did you say?"

"Nothing." The rest of the class had come out. They were all looking at me.

"You told him Heather won't go out with him, didn't you?" JJ said.

"Heather?" I said. "Heather Torres?"

"The girl with the pink hair," Ruth said.

"She doesn't like him?" Jeffrey asked.

"What? No . . . I mean . . ." How did they know that? Now that I thought about it, yeah, it made sense. How had I missed that?

It didn't matter. I had a job to do. Fritz's love life would have to wait. "I'll fix things with Heather, okay? Just not right now." I hurried over to Dellian's desk.

I'd just pulled the key from the back of his planning book when Jeffrey asked, "What are you doing?"

"Seeing what's on the agenda for today," I said.

"You can't. He didn't put you in charge."

Typical Jeffrey. I didn't have time to come up with a lie. I needed to find that damn photo before Dellian came back. "Look, Dellian's trying to suspend me. There's something in here that can stop him. Fritz is helping me. He freaked to get Dellian out."

The room was deathly still. Great. I should've lied. "If you need to tell Dellian, I understand," I said. "But I'm running out of time, so —"

Jeffrey walked to the door.

It figured. Now I really had to hurry. My fingers fumbled with the key in the lock.

"I'll whistle when he's coming," Jeffrey said.

"And I'll stall him in the hall if you need more time," JJ said.

"Me too," Ruth added.

"Thanks." I smiled briefly and then returned my focus to the drawer.

There were files inside that hadn't been there before.

I took them out in one big stack. Then the yellow paper pad. Then . . . nothing. *Where'd it go?*

I went through the files, page by page, in case the photo had slipped in between.

It hadn't. It wasn't there. He'd taken the photo. My only leverage.

When I walked into the nurse's office after class, Fritz was parked next to the bed I'd brought Tricia to so very long ago.

"Hey! You get that *assignment* done?" he asked with a sly grin.

"Couldn't find it. Hi, Mrs. Martin," I said to her baggy nurse's smock. She looked a lot thinner than I remembered. "Can he leave now?"

"If he's ready. He had a panic attack," she said. "It happens. I've had a few myself lately."

"It's the chair's fault," Fritz said. "It makes me crazy sometimes."

"Oh? I heard it was Heather," I teased. "How come you haven't asked her out?"

Fritz shrugged. "I guess I was afraid she'd say no."

"She'll say yes." I pushed Fritz to the door. "Her wardrobe is less black lately; she's done mourning Greg." I blushed. I'd forgotten Greg's mom was there.

"I didn't hear that." She laughed. "If you need help again, I'm here. You too, Roz."

"Actually," I turned back, "I'm having a problem in AP. Maybe you could help?"

My heart was hammering its way out of my chest by the time I entered AP. My legs shook as I sat in the no-sit zone and waited for the bombs to fly.

The bell rang. I focused on the chalkboard behind Dellian.

He was peering over the podium at me, an impish grin on his face. He grabbed his roll book and lifted his red pen dramatically in the air. "Roswell Hart."

"Excuse me, Mr. Dellian?" Mrs. Martin tapped on the open door.

Mr. Dellian flinched in surprise. "Yes?"

"I was hoping to observe today. May I?"

"Of course." He gestured for her to enter.

She walked past me to the back row and stopped at my "assigned" desk. "Is this seat okay, or is it taken?"

The class knew what was up. We held our collective breath.

"That's fine," Dellian said with a thin, polite smile.

"Thank you." She sat down. "Please, continue. I believe you were on Roswell?"

A manic giggle rippled through me. I had to clench my lower lip between my teeth to keep the laugh from escaping.

"Right, yes. Roswell Hart." Dellian had to physically force the word out of his mouth. "Present."

The class breathed again. I stared down at my notebook, biting my lip until it bled and digging my nails into my palms, but it was no use. A smile spilled across my face.

I flew out the door when class ended to avoid a confrontation with Dellian. Greg found me at my locker, books clutched to his chest. "That was awesome, what you did, telling my mom."

Dryer sheets. Watermelon. My smile slipped away. It hurt too much to stand there and pretend we were friends. "I gotta go," I said, and walked away.

Heather was waiting at my locker the next morning. I could tell by her bright spring colors that life was good. "Let me guess," I said as I pulled my locker open. "Fritz asked you out?"

"You knew?" She slapped my arm. "Why didn't you tell me?"

"It took a while to convince him you'd say yes. I thought he might chicken out."

We headed toward our classes. "He told me what you did in History yesterday; pretty gutsy. Are you worried about class this morning?"

"Am I! I'm about to puke, but what can Dellian do? Mrs. Martin knows the whole story." I sighed. "Still, Dellian's sneaky. I know this isn't over."

"Oh, my God!" Heather stopped so abruptly, I ran into her.

"What?" I stepped around her to look. My heart leaped into my throat. My lungs failed.

Greg was at his locker, his arms around Missy.

No, that's not Greg, I thought. *My eyes are mistaken.* But I knew this time they weren't. Heather had seen it too. I slunk closer to the couple in question. Closer to that outline I'd grown so good at identifying. Closer to the carefully ironed khakis. The curly mess of hair.

Too close.

The nastiest odor I'd ever smelled — lavender and vanilla mixed with watermelon bubblegum and dryer sheets — hit me with an acrid slap. Greg wasn't just hugging Missy. He was *comforting* her, *holding* her, while she cried on his shoulder.

I ran. Through people. Down hallways. Into the handicapped bathroom. I wanted to scream, cry, tear the walls down around me. But the hurt was too intense. I could only rock back and forth like Bart, hugging myself.

"Roz? You okay?" Heather tapped on the stall door. I unlatched it. "I didn't realize you liked him that much," she said, coming inside.

"Me neither," I managed to whisper before a lump squeezed my throat shut.

"Maybe it's not what it looked like." Heather pulled a bag of M&M's from her pocket and poured me some. "Jonathan's been hooking up with Jenny Rinker behind Missy's back." She poured the rest of the bag into her palm. "I bet she just found out."

"And ran to Greg for comfort?" I said. "Great."

Heather stared at the candy in her palm. "Roz, I'm sorry I was such a bitch about you two." She flicked a green M&M with her fingernail. It skipped across the tile and disappeared under the stall. "I thought it was, you know . . . payback for me and Jonathan."

I wasn't following. "What do you mean?"

"At Ethan's?" Heather shoved the rest of the candy into her mouth. "The night Dellian and Copacabana found me?"

"Wait, what?" It took a second. "You and Jonathan? While we were dating?"

"I thought you knew," Heather said. "Greg didn't tell you?"

"You . . . and Greg knew?" I felt as if I'd been stabbed in the back, and then in the gut, and then in the back again. So much betrayal. I couldn't catch my breath.

Heather slumped back against the wall. "You and Jonathan were in that fight and I was really drunk . . . things just happened, okay?"

"Things just happened?" I said. "You guilt-tripped me over and over about Greg, and you'd screwed Jonathan behind my back?" I clawed at the door latch.

"I didn't screw him!" Heather said. "Where are you going?"

I was through trusting people. I hated everyone. I flung the stall door open and let it smash against Heather.

"You're not going to do anything with Fritz, right?" Heather cried after me. "To get back at me? We're even, okay?"

Even.

I would've laughed if I wasn't about to cry. That's all we were.

Not friends. Just even.

I didn't bother going back to my locker. I ran past Principal Ratner and a hall monitor, out the front doors, past the city bus stop, and the next bus stop, and the next. I didn't stop running until I'd run the three miles home.

I sequestered myself in my room, under my UFO sky, turned

on AM 760 so I wouldn't hear any songs that reminded me of all the backstabbers in my life, and willed the world away.

But I couldn't will the world away.

The broadcast played less than seventy-two hours later.

The body of seventeen-year-old Tricia Farni was pulled from the Birch River Friday night . . .

Three things cannot be long hidden:
The sun, the moon, and the truth.
— Buddha

Discovery

One day after

Dead.

Tricia was *dead.* Not shacking up with some drug dealer or hooking her way across Alaska — but dead. How could that be?

She'd said to give her until homecoming to end whatever sick thing was going on between her and Dellian, and yeah, it ended all right. But *who* ended it? Dellian had seen her that night, talked to her. He had said so himself when he came looking for her — what if that had been a ruse? A ploy to make it look as if she'd run off? To keep everyone from learning the truth about what had happened to Tricia that night?

My heart ached to think about Tricia, frozen in that river all winter, alone and voiceless, while I was oblivious, barely giving her a thought, hating her all the while. Why hadn't I asked questions? Why hadn't I looked for her?

Because I was a bitch. I didn't care. But not anymore. I was going to find out what had happened. I was going to give Tricia a voice.

But how? God, if only I could remember that night! All the time I spent trying to forget what I *did* remember — Jonathan and

Tricia in the loft — and as sick as *that* was, I had an even sicker feeling now about the things I *couldn't* remember.

I had to find out what happened that night, to fill in the gaps I was missing, and there was only one person I knew for sure who could do that for me: Jonathan. As much as I hated him for hurting me, I hated Dellian more for hurting Tricia. Whether her death was suicide, accident, or murder, I believed Dellian was involved. I believed it like I believed in extraterrestrial life — a gut feeling with no proof. To get proof, I had to start filling in the blanks, and like it or not, that meant talking to Jonathan.

Early Easter Monday, I pulled on my jacket and walked to Jonathan's house. As I walked up his driveway, he stepped out of his car. My heart started to pound. Although I'd seen him plenty of times around school, we hadn't spoken since that day outside the counseling office. The day the detective came asking about Tricia. *I feel nothing,* I reminded myself. *He's just a guy I need information from.*

"Hey, Beautiful! Can you believe this shit?" he said. "Tricia's dead!"

"No, I can't believe it." I kicked at a small mound of snow underneath his mailbox. "Jonathan, what happened with Tricia that night?"

"You know. She just attacked —"

I winced. "Not that. After. What happened *after?*"

Jonathan shook his head. "I don't know."

My head swung up and my mouth dropped. "You don't remember either?"

"Of course I—" He frowned. "What do you mean? What don't you remember?"

A gust of wind blew through the trees. I pulled my jacket tighter around me. "That night. I remember the loft, *obviously*." I tried to sound nonchalant as I looked back down and kicked at the snow some more. "And I remember walking through the party with you to leave. The rest is a blur of random things." I paused. "Was Dellian there? I remember him, but . . . he was sick, right? Tricia took him home from the dance."

He stared at me. "You seriously don't remember?"

"Seriously," I said. "No."

"Ooh." Or was that "Ugh"? A cross between a sigh and a groan—either way, it didn't sound good. "I get it now." He rubbed his face with his hands. "Shit."

My stomach twisted. "Get what? What aren't you telling me?" I said, training my dots on his ear, desperate to see his facial expression now.

"When you said to tell the cop we'd argued and I took you home, I thought you were, you know, keeping our stories straight. I didn't know—" He cursed again and looked down the street. "We shouldn't talk out here." He nodded at his car. "Come on."

I obeyed, too afraid now to breathe.

"Look." He rubbed his forehead before continuing. "I'll tell you about that night, but if that cop comes nosing around again, stick to what we said before, okay? She'll think we're frickin' guilty if you change your story."

"Change my story? Jonathan," I said, panic rising, "what happened?"

"You were wasted. I was letting you chill in my car until you felt better, in case you puked, you know? Then Tricia comes screaming all sorts of crazy shit. She dragged you out of the Vette."

My mouth fell open. "Oh, my God! I fought — I fought with her? Is that how she —"

It was too horrific for words.

"Died? No. No way. I got you away from her before any damage could be done. That's when Dellian showed."

"So he *was* there!" It was slightly comforting knowing my memory wasn't a total bust.

"Yeah, she called him when we left the loft."

It was starting to make sense now. All the hands I remembered, Dellian's face. "What happened after that?"

"Like I said, I got you away and back in the Vette. But then she jumps me and is totally wailing on me when Dellian shows. Then *he* starts wailing on me! As if he could take me." He slammed the steering wheel with his fists. "I should've pummeled his ass!"

"Jonathan!" I said. "What happened then? What about Tricia?"

"She took off, still screaming crap, totally messed up."

"But was she okay? Was she bleeding or anything?" A physical fight with her. Now I understood why he thought I wanted him to lie. We totally looked guilty.

"I don't know. It was dark and I was still dealing with that dickhead —"

"But did I fight with her again?"

He shrugged. "Not that I saw."

Somehow that didn't feel reassuring. "Why can't I remember? I only had a sip of beer. How could I have been wasted?"

"Maybe someone slipped you something. It happens."

I stared out at the gray day, gloomy and cold like I felt. I had answers now, but they raised only more questions. Could Tricia have hit her head during that fight? A concussion that made her fall in the water? Or did something happen after Jonathan and I left? Maybe between her and Dellian?

"When Detective King talked to you after Tricia went missing, did you get the feeling that she knew Dellian was there that night?" I asked.

"Nope. And I was pretty damn relieved because when you asked me to lie —"

"I *didn't* ask you to lie," I corrected. "I thought it was the truth."

"Whatever. I'm just saying that I was pretty freaked, and when the cop didn't mention D., I was glad." He raised his eyebrows at me. "It kind of makes you wonder, huh? Now that we know Tricia's dead."

I nodded. "You know, they were living together. Tricia and Dellian."

"Did she tell you that?"

"No, my friend Heather —" I stopped. My friend, please; apparently Jonathan knew her better than I did. "Plus I found a pretty telling photo in Dellian's desk. I think it was taken the same night." He didn't say "Whoa!" or "No way!" or anything — just nodded. "You knew?" I asked.

He shrugged. "Pretty frickin' obvious."

My fists balled up in anger. "Why didn't you tell Detective King?"

"Why didn't you?" he snapped back.

He was right. I'd failed Tricia as much as he had. "So, what do we do now? Tell Detective King what really happened?"

"No!" Jonathan said. "We stick to our story. She can't think we're lying."

"But what if Dellian killed Tricia? If we don't say he was there, he gets away with it. I'm sick of him getting away with everything."

"He's not getting away with anything." He cocked his head and gave me the sweetest, most sincere smile. I almost forgot he'd ever betrayed me. Almost. "I got your back, okay? We stick together, we'll be fine. Trust me."

"That's just it, Jonathan. I don't trust you. I didn't lie on purpose. If I tell the police now, tell them I was mistaken, it should be okay. But if I lie again —"

"Look, you've got every reason not to trust me, but, Beautiful, who else can you trust? We're both in the same boat here because you told me to lie! If you talk, and it turns out Tricia was killed, you think they'll look at Dellian? No, they'll look at us, to the kids who fought with her that night and lied about it."

I hated to admit it, but he was right. I'd set the lie up — and whether I meant to or not, I'd gotten him to lie too. I couldn't tell the truth now and get us both in trouble, not while we still didn't know what had happened to her that night. "Okay," I said as I got out of the car. "I won't say anything. I have your back. You have mine, right?"

I was so caught up in my thoughts as I walked home that I didn't hear the police cruiser until it was beside me. "Roswell?" Detective King said from the window. "Can I give you a lift?"

Great. What was she doing here? "I'm only a block from home."

"I know. I was coming to see you. We can talk as I drive." It wasn't a suggestion. "Sorry, you'll have to climb in the back. We can't have civilians up front."

I looked at the cage separating the front seat from the back. Already I felt guilty, and I hadn't been asked any questions yet. At least sitting behind steel bars meant I didn't have to make eye contact.

"I'm sure you heard Tricia Farni's body was found?" She turned her head sideways, talking over her shoulder to me.

"Was it suicide?" Tricia had said that once—that she'd kill herself before she went back to rehab. Maybe Dellian had threatened to send her there after he found out about her and Jonathan?

"We don't know yet. But the medical examiner thinks she drowned, and a preliminary tox screen found alcohol, crack, and GHB in her system. We usually don't even screen for GHB, but we've had reports recently."

"GHB?" I couldn't help feeling relieved. She had drowned high and drunk, not because of an injury from a fight.

"It's a recreational drug that's sometimes used in date rape."

"Date rape? Was she—" My throat went dry.

"We don't think so," Detective King said. "But that doesn't mean the intent wasn't there. She could've been incapacitated when she hit the water, so how she got in the water doesn't matter as much as how she came by those drugs." Detective King turned and looked at me. "Do you understand what I'm saying, Roswell?"

"Yes," I whispered. "You're saying Tricia might have been murdered."

Everything was much more official this time around. Once inside my house, Detective King pulled out a tape recorder instead of a pocket notebook, and then asked if I wanted to have my mom present for our interview.

I didn't "want." But getting Mom out of bed and cleaned up after her evening of partying would take a little time. Time that I needed. I was torn between telling Detective King everything, telling her nothing, and telling her a hybrid of truth and half-truths. I desperately wanted to call Jonathan. That would send alarm bells off in Detective King's head, though. I couldn't risk it.

I woke Mom, and then hurried into the kitchen to make coffee while I waited for her. Anything to look busy.

Mom stumbled out fifteen minutes later, wearing the Johnny Cash "Ring of Fire" T-shirt she'd stolen from an ex-boyfriend. Her too-blond hair was tangled in a hair-spray nest, and her mascara was smeared under her eyes. "I wasn't expecting company," she said, sinking into the recliner. "I had a rough night. Tony and I broke up." She looked at Detective King then — really looked at her — and sat straight up in the chair. "What've you done, Rozzy?"

"She's done nothing, Mrs. Hart. We're here about her friend Tricia."

"Priscilla," Mom said, "and it's Braylor. I haven't been Mrs. Hart in years." She looked at me. "Who's Tricia?"

"A classmate, Mom. She's dead, Mom."

"Oh, dear Lord! What happened?"

"That's what we're trying to find out. Ready, Roz?" Detective King pushed "record" and set the recorder in front of me. "Earlier, you said you had an argument with Tricia the night of October sixth at a party out at Birch Hill. What was the fight about?"

My pulse began to race. "I walked in on her and my date, Jonathan Webb."

"Walked in on? Can you be more specific?"

I stared at a stain on the carpet. "She was kneeling, her head in his lap, and —"

"And?" Detective King repeated after a few seconds.

"Come on," Mom said. "I think you can fill in the blank."

"Was it an oral act?" Detective King asked.

"Yes."

Detective King continued. "Did it look consensual?"

"Yeah, one hundred percent consensual."

"How did Tricia seem to you?"

"I don't know." I shrugged. "Guilty?"

"Okay, what was her demeanor, though? Think, Roz. It's important. Did she appear drunk? High? Was she slurring her words? Stumbling?"

"We'd been talking on the stairs before that," I said. "She looked tired and pale, but our conversation was surprisingly sane, considering —" The second I said it, I regretted it.

Mom and Detective King looked at me. "Considering what?" the detective asked.

"Tricia was sort of . . ." What? Psychotic? Schizophrenic? I realized I had no idea what she was. I just knew she belonged in Life Skills. She had said "severely emotionally disturbed" once; was that the label that had earned her admission? "Tricia was always out there, you know? Usually high on pot or crack."

Detective King sat forward. "So you're saying that night she didn't seem high?" I nodded. "Okay," she continued. "After you walked in on them. You two fought?"

"Yes, she grabbed me to stop me from leaving. I pulled away and left." I felt sick to my stomach suddenly. If she asked about the fight outside, I wasn't sure I could lie. And I'd forgotten to make eye contact with her. *Crud.*

"And Jonathan? What did he do?"

"He took me home."

"You let him take you home?" Mom said. "After what he'd done with that girl?"

"Mom, stop! She's asking the questions, not you."

But she'd piqued Detective King's curiosity. "Why did you go with him?"

"I wanted to go home." I glared at the leather headrest behind Mom. "You didn't answer your phone, my friends had left already, and cabs won't come out that far."

"I understand Jonathan drove Tricia out there. How did she plan to get home?"

I was covering my butt and Jonathan's; I refused to cover Dellian's. "She called Dellian as we were leaving." So what if I hadn't heard her call him? Jonathan had.

The effect was instantaneous. "Rodney Dellian?" Detective King perked up. "You're sure?"

And then I knew how I could get her to investigate Dellian

without my confessing to the fight. "Positive." I nodded. "And when he came by here looking for her after she'd disappeared? He knew what had happened in the loft. How could he have known that unless he had talked to her?"

"How indeed," Detective King muttered. She flipped through her notebook, looking for something.

"This is your teacher we're talking about?" Mom said. "The one trying to have you suspended for skipping class? Why on earth would he be picking this girl up from parties?"

"Because Tricia was living with him." I looked at Detective King. "I wasn't sure when I talked to you before, and I have no proof. Heather Torres lives in the same apartment building, though. She's seen Tricia there a lot. With a baby. I found a photo when I was looking for something in Dellian's desk once. Right after she disappeared. Tricia and Dellian were kissing. I'm positive it was taken that night. Tricia wore the same grass skirt and bikini top from the dance, and Dellian had the same blue floral-print shirt" — I paused, remembering Heather's comment — "maybe it was palm trees. I don't know. I'm sure it's what he wore to the dance, though."

"You don't sound sure, Rozzy. Flowers don't look anything like palm trees —"

"Mom!" I snapped. "I'm sure, okay?"

"Well, all that can be verified with the photo." Detective King was studying me hard. Eye contact was critical. "Where is this photo now?"

I brought my eyes up to hers, letting my blind spot erase her face. "His desk? I left it there." I couldn't admit it wasn't there without admitting I'd gone back to steal it. She was the cop, though. Let her find it.

"I really wish you had contacted me with all of this earlier, but thank you for the information, Roswell." She stood. "If you think of anything else or learn something new, please, don't keep it to yourself, okay? Call me." She handed me a business card. "Thank you, Priscilla."

"Thank *you*," Mom said. "I'm calling the school and having that man fired! He's done nothing but make my daughter's life miserable all year long, and now he's a pervert too."

"Ma'am, please don't," the detective interrupted. "We don't know if any of this is true. If it is, though, we must tread carefully and make sure we have all our facts straight before doing anything. I promise I'll let you know what I find out."

"Do," Mom said. "I don't want that pervert near Rozzy anymore."

I called Jonathan minutes later while Mom was in the shower. "Detective King just left. She said Tricia drowned because of drugs."

"She drowned because of drugs?" Jonathan repeated.

"Too messed up to swim. She had a date-rape drug in her too. You said people sometimes slip stuff, that maybe that's why I don't remember—"

"You didn't tell the cop that, did you?"

"No, I was afraid to say much of anything. But if GHB is what was wrong with me—if someone gave it to me and Tricia— shouldn't we tell the police?"

"Not unless you want to go to jail! If they know you can't remember, our story gets shot to hell! We'll look guilty. Is that what you want?"

"Of course not! But she didn't die because I was fighting with her."

"It doesn't matter, Beautiful. If they know you can't remember, they will know we lied, and they won't believe anything we say. What if they find out we bought her pot? They'll spin it to make *us* look guilty."

The air went out of my lungs. He was right. The police were looking for whoever gave her drugs. It didn't matter if it was pot we'd helped her buy. Drugs were drugs. "God, Jonathan, I'm scared."

"Me too, Beautiful." There was a shuffling as he covered the phone. I heard him yell something to someone, and then he whispered, "Shit, the cop's here."

"Wait! I told her Tricia was living with Dellian and she called him from the loft. About the photo too." Dellian deserved to go down for this. We had to make sure the police arrested Dellian, not us. "Tell her anything you know about Dellian and Tricia, okay? They have to nail him for this."

Four days after

The day before Tricia's funeral, Fritz called. His friend had borrowed a van so that anyone from Life Skills who wanted to go could. Bart's parents didn't want him to go, but the rest of us did. Fritz hadn't known Tricia. It was pretty cool that he'd go out of his way to arrange things, and that he had friends who'd borrowed a van for us.

When I opened the door the next morning, I almost didn't recognize Greg in his black suit and tie. "What are you doing here?"

"Picking you up."

"*You* borrowed the van? Why? You didn't even know Tricia." I looked past him at the van. "Did you bring your girlfriend? This isn't a party, you know. It's a funeral for someone I cared about."

He kept his voice calm and even. "I know. That's why I offered to drive. I'm not sure what you mean by my girlfriend, but no, I didn't bring a date. It's not a party, it's a funeral." He opened the passenger side door for me. "Hope you won't mind sitting up front with me. The back's kind of full."

I glanced back as I grabbed my seat belt. Heather was seated directly behind me. Seeing her made me even madder. Since none of us drove, I could understand Greg, but Heather? Please!

She was just trying to score points with Fritz — or to make sure I didn't score points with him. Making sure I didn't get *even*.

"Hi, Roz." Ruth's sad tone brought me back to earth.

"Hi, Ruth," I said. "Hey, Jeffrey, JJ . . . *Fritz*." I turned back around without saying a word to Heather.

There were more pews than people at the funeral, but we sat smooshed together on the shortened handicapped bench so that both wheelchairs could be accommodated. Dellian sat directly in front of us, where he comforted a blond woman, who turned out to be Tricia's sister, Abbey. He had no handcuffs. No police escorts. Detective King was there, though, no doubt keeping an eye on him.

Greg's mom was the only other school personnel there. Ratner must've been too busy relaxing on his Easter break to make an appearance. Despite the hype the body had brought, only one photographer from the paper showed up. Jonathan didn't come either. Pathetic. So few seemed to care.

I'd never seen a dead body before, and I was nervous about seeing Tricia's. Somehow I thought seeing her body would give me answers. It wasn't as if I thought she'd sit up and speak — not exactly. But I sort of thought there'd be some divine intervention, like God or the Virgin Mary or Tricia's spirit giving me a sign, pointing something out — cuts, scratches, a knot on her forehead, the markings of a struggle — something that would illuminate the truth and tell me what had happened. I guess it was ridiculous and naive, but I honestly thought seeing her body would explain everything.

When the time came, fear took over. My hands shook; my legs wobbled. Greg silently slipped his suit jacket around my shoulders. The body heat he'd left behind settled around me, comforting me, giving me back my strength. I clutched the edges of the jacket and made my way to the open casket.

No bolt of lightning. No ghostly premonition. No haunting stare from Tricia's dead eyes. No blood or bruises or track marks. Just a sleeping beauty.

She looked nothing like Tricia. Navy blue dress with white piping on the collar. Blond hair combed smooth, cascading around her shoulders. Hint of pink on her lips. Beige eye shadow on her closed lids. She was beautiful. The perfect replica of a person at peace, with no trace of the hard-edged drug addict we'd all known.

Her appearance left me unsettled. Something wasn't right. As they carried her casket down the aisle, I realized what it was — not her perfect blue dress, her neatly combed hair, or even her tasteful makeup.

It was her cloak. It wasn't with her.

I understood wanting Tricia to look presentable, soft, peaceful — but that cloak *was* Tricia. It was a part of her. Surely Abbey would want Tricia to be buried with the one thing that connected her sister and their mother?

This nagged at me. Too much to let it go. After introducing myself to Abbey, I asked, "Why aren't you burying her with her cloak?"

"They never found it." Abbey's shoulders fell. "It makes me sick not to; she never went anywhere without it."

"Maybe they missed it along the bank somewhere?" I said. "We should look—"

"I'll drive you," Greg interrupted. Before I could respond, he looked around. "Anyone else want to go?"

Everyone did. Fritz wasn't sure he and JJ would be much help. It was breakup season. All the snow and ice on the ground was melting fast. Between the streams of water and yards of mud, neither chair would get very far. But they wanted to come along anyway for moral support.

We were loading JJ and his chair into the van when Jonathan's red Corvette pulled up. "How was it?" he asked.

I shrugged. "Horrible. They never found Tricia's cloak. We're going to go look for it. Want to come?"

Jonathan eyed Greg with a smirk. "Relax, Loser. I'm not going." He looked back at me. "You know you won't find it. It's probably stashed at his place."

"At whose place?" Greg asked.

I threw Jonathan a warning glance. "They pulled her from the river. That's the best place to look."

Jonathan leaned in to me. "Call me when you don't find it," he whispered. "I have a better plan."

Greg drove to the muddied dirt road leading to the Birch River. Large sheets of broken ice floated by, now the only evidence of the ice bridge. Piles of melting snow flanked the riverbank, blackened by the exhaust of the rescue vehicles that had worked to retrieve first the semi and then Tricia's body the week before.

Heather stayed in the van with Fritz and JJ while the rest of us climbed out. Jeffrey and Greg began searching near the rescue site, working their way downriver. Ruth and I wobbled along in our heels in the opposite direction. I was grateful for Greg's suit jacket, which I still wore. The spring air was numbing and cold.

There were plenty of objects peeking out of puddles and snow piles. Discarded chip bags, soda cans, water bottles, candy wrappers—but no cloak, not even a shred of material that would indicate it had been there. Disappointed, I pulled a soda can from a crystallized grave. A candy wrapper. A plastic bag.

Ruth began doing the same. Soon we were moving farther upriver, collecting trash in discarded grocery bags as we walked toward Birch Hill and the cabin where I'd last seen Tricia.

"Think they'll have a memorial at school?" I asked.

Ruth shook her head. "They didn't for Renny."

Renny. The boy whose suicide triggered the policy change that ruined my life this year. "What happened with Renny? Why'd he commit suicide?"

"I don't know. We were best friends. We did everything together. He never said he was sad." Ruth stopped. "Do you think I'll do that before graduation too?"

I stared at her. "God, no! Ruth, why would you say that? Are you . . . do you think about killing yourself?"

She shook her head. "But he had Down syndrome, like me."

"Ruth!" I put my arm around her shoulders and hugged her to me. "Down syndrome is just a stupid label, a category. It's not *you*. You're Ruth Paladeno, an awesome chef, a loyal friend, the girl with the kindest heart I know."

She hugged me back. "You too, Roz."

We looked out over the river, watching a chunk of ice slowly float by.

"Renny liked plaid," Ruth said, breaking the silence. "Tricia told us to wear plaid to graduation, for when they called his name, to remember him. They never did. You know what Tricia did? She spray-painted R-E-N-N-Y across the sidewalk in front of the school and on Ratner's car." Ruth smiled up at me. "That was really good."

I smiled too. That sounded like Tricia.

"Do you think Tricia killed herself?" Ruth asked after we'd started walking again.

Did I? I wasn't sure what I thought; there were too many unanswered questions, too many possibilities — all of which I couldn't bear to say out loud to Ruth. "I don't know."

We'd hit a clearing of sorts. More like an abandoned road. The end of the line. Beyond was Birch Hill Recreational Park and the cabin, Tricia's last known sighting. It was hidden somewhere in the thick snarled confines of the forest. We couldn't reach it without leaving the path.

I picked up a bunch of beer bottles. Too many. They wouldn't fit in my bag. "Even if we have to spray-paint her name on the whole school . . ." I said as I searched the area for a trash can. I gave up and piled them on top of a broken picnic table. "We won't let them forget Tricia the way they did Renny."

Three hours after we began the search, we headed home, cloakless and exhausted. Either the cloak was still in the water, tangled in sticks and weeds at the murky bottom, or it was someplace else entirely.

Like Dellian's apartment.

The more I thought about it, the more convinced I became.

"No cloak, huh?" Jonathan said when I called him after Greg dropped me off.

"You really think Dellian has it?"

"There's only one way to find out." He paused. "We shouldn't talk on here, you know what I mean? I'll be there in five."

I stared at the phone. Seriously? Would the police really tap our phones? There was this Tom Cruise movie I saw once where a couple's whole house had been bugged. They had to go outside to talk in private. I decided to do the same.

"Plan's simple," Jonathan said as he plopped down on the swing next to me. I scooted away. "We go look."

I started laughing. "Right. 'Hey, Dellian, mind if we search through your stuff?'"

"Don't be stupid. We go in when he's not there."

"No way." I stopped laughing. He was serious. "I'm not breaking into his house."

"We wouldn't be. We'd have the key," Jonathan said. "The way you did when you found that picture."

"It's not the same thing." I stood up. "Forget it; the cloak's not that important."

"I don't give a shit about the cloak!" Jonathan cried. "I need proof that Dellian was neck high in her crap so the cops get off my back! They told my parents to get a lawyer and make sure I don't leave town. They think *I* gave her the drugs that killed her."

"Oh, my God!" The swing shook violently as I dropped back on it. "Why do they think that?"

"Because some low-life called in an anonymous tip. Said I bought drugs for her."

"The pot?" Air slowly left me. I leaned back against the seat to keep from collapsing. "Somebody told them? Do they know I paid?"

Jonathan shrugged. "I don't think they have any real facts, you know? Just fishing. I bet it was Dellian. Pointing the finger at me because I told the cops about him and Tricia."

"I told them about him and Tricia too. Will the police tell me to get a lawyer also?" I said, more to myself than to Jonathan. This was stupid. We hadn't done anything wrong! I exhaled slowly. "Okay, we're scared, but we have to stay calm. Breaking in isn't the solution. With everything we told the police, they'll have to search his apartment, right? They'll find her cloak."

"Don't you watch cop shows? They can't go in without a warrant, and they can't get that without a good reason."

"They have one. His relationship with Tricia."

"You mean the one that only you and I—the two to last see her—told them about? They don't have proof he was screwing her."

"The photo . . ." It probably didn't exist anymore, and again, it was only me saying it ever did. "Maybe you're right. But don't you think he's got rid of everything already? He had six months to cover his ass, Jonathan. There may be nothing there. And if we get caught, we *really* look guilty!"

"What if he hasn't? This could be our only chance."

"God, Jonathan, I don't know —"

"Beautiful, you know he'll try to pin this on us if he can. He's already got the cops looking at me."

I heard the clanky chug that Greg's engine now made, thanks to me, approaching from down the street. "Great," I muttered. "Hurry, tell me the plan."

Jonathan smirked as Greg's purple Pacer pulled in. "How does he drive that beat-up old thing? The hood's a mess, and it's butt-ass ugly."

I winced. I hadn't seen his car since I'd wrecked it. I guess he had been right; it couldn't be fixed. "Just tell me." I felt the weight of Greg's stare as he walked toward us.

"You steal Dellian's keys. Coat closet, left pocket. I search, call in whatever I find anonymously, and, with any luck, he's arrested before school gets out." He leaned over as if to kiss me. "Don't think too long; time's ticking," he whispered, and then grinned over at Greg. "I'm done with her. Your turn."

"You know he's dating Sophie Reynolds," Greg said as Jonathan walked away.

"Good for him," I said. I got up from the swing and headed to my front door.

"You're not talking to Heather because of him, remember? If you're all hot to give him another chance, don't you think you owe Heather one?"

"Who I give second chances to is none of your business." I was so tired of fighting with him. "Why are you here? Shouldn't you be at Missy's or something?"

"Why do you always bring her into everything? I told you I don't —"

"Save it, Greg." I pulled the screen door open. "I saw you hugging her Thursday."

"Missy's mom might have cancer. She just found out."

I hadn't seen that one coming. The door slammed as I let go. "Is Missy okay?"

He shrugged. "It sucks when you first find out. You're totally helpless while waiting for the test results. That's what I told her, *Thursday*."

God, I'm an idiot. I turned toward him, staring at his jeans. "Maybe I'll call her."

"You should. So" — he paused — "I don't suppose Jonathan's mom is sick too?"

"Greg!" I turned back around and opened the door.

"Wait. I'm sorry. I didn't come here to fight." But he couldn't let it go. "After everything he did to you, why are you still talking to him?"

I whirled around. "Why are *we* still talking? How many times are we going to do this? Back and forth, back and forth. I'm sick of it, Greg —" Something about the way he was pushing his hands through his hair made me stop. After everything we'd been through, I still cared, and he did too, or he wouldn't be here.

"There's nothing going on with him, Greg." I tried to erase the anger from my voice. "We're both just in the same messed-up predicament."

"What predicament would that be?"

I wanted to tell him everything. I hated that my only confidant was a guy I couldn't trust. But every argument I'd ever had with Greg was proof that I shouldn't tell him anything. Greg was too straight and narrow to keep something this big a secret. His world was either black or white, with no grays in between. He'd make me go to the police with the truth—and I didn't know the truth, not really. I couldn't risk telling anyone anything until I was sure myself. "We were with Tricia before she disappeared. Until they figure out what happened, we're both under suspicion. We're looking out for each other. That's all."

Greg shoved his hands in the front pockets of his jeans and kicked at some mud with his tennis shoe. "I heard he was dealing drugs to Tricia."

"Not everything you hear is true, Greg."

He stopped kicking at the mud and looked at me. "Not everything he tells you is true, either. What if you're wrong about him?"

I kept my voice calm and even. "I'm not."

"You were wrong to trust him when you two were dating."

"That's different."

"Is it? You know that drug they found in Tricia? GHB? Mom said if given too much, it can immobilize you. It can make you black out too. Whoever gives it to you can do anything he wants; you can't fight back, and you won't remember."

A sick feeling crept through me. My throat went dry. If what I'd been slipped was GHB, did someone do something to me? Something I couldn't remember?

"Tricia's not the first girl to be slipped GHB at a party, Roz. Missy thinks she was, and Heather too. You know what they have in common? Jonathan. When it happened, they were both with Jonathan."

"Come on, Greg, anyone could've given it to them." Uncertainty nagged at me, though. Both times I blacked out, I'd been at parties with Jonathan too.

"Roz, without even talking to each other, they both accused him."

I shook my head. He was wrong; *they* were wrong. I might not remember much about that night Tricia died, but I did know Jonathan never touched anything I ate or drank. How could he have slipped me something without handling my cup? And would he have told me someone was slipping stuff in beer if he was the one doing it?

"Greg, I know he didn't do that, okay?"

"After everything he's done" — he clenched his jaw — "how can you be so blind?"

I set my jaw too. "I'm not being *blind*." He was the one being blind — blinded by jealousy and hatred for a guy he barely knew.

"You want to stand by him? Go ahead." He opened his car door. "It's your funeral."

Eight days after

The thing about alien life is there's no universally accepted proof that it exists. Belief is left to the individual. Some believe without needing proof. Others believe because they've seen proof. And some will never believe, regardless of proof.

Truth is like that too. It isn't necessarily universal. Sometimes what we see, what seems real, isn't real at all. When I didn't see the lamppost in front of us the day Greg tried teaching me to drive, the truth, for me, was that nothing existed in that space. But unfortunately, the truth for Greg and his car was that it did exist. The same thing happens on *UFO Sightings* when two witnesses give opposite accounts of the same event. Both believe their accounts are the truth, even when they are drastically different. So which is the real account? The *truth?*

It all comes down to faith and your examination of the evidence.

After Greg left, I struggled with this. What was truth, what was fiction, and could I spot the difference between the two? Once upon a time, I thought I could. Now I was questioning everything and everyone, especially myself.

What if I was wrong about Jonathan? What if he wasn't telling me everything? Then again, what if I was right? What if Dellian was guilty and would get away with it because everyone was too busy crucifying Jonathan?

If truth had to come down to evidence, then I needed to find some. Something tangible I could examine. Jonathan's idea seemed the best way to get that.

A few days later we had it all planned. I'd get Fritz to make a scene as he had before, and once Dellian was out of the room, I'd hang my jacket in the coat closet, steal the keys from Dellian's pocket, and give them to Jonathan, who would be waiting in the hall. Once he'd searched Dellian's apartment — taking pictures of anything incriminating, such as Tricia's cloak — he'd return the keys to me. I'd "remember" my jacket in Dellian's room and slip the keys back in his pocket. Simple. Smooth. Easy.

"Roz." Ruth stopped me as I approached the SPED hallway. "Ratner's waiting for you. Dellian got you suspended."

"What?" I should've been ready for this. Given Tricia's death and my attempts to find the truth, though, I'd forgotten how I'd followed up my Last Stand in AP by ditching the entire day of school.

"Sorry," Ruth said with a shrug. She handed me a book. "It's my yearbook from last year. Renny's in there."

I didn't have the heart to tell her I had the same yearbook at home, so I took it from her. "Thanks," I said as we rounded the corner.

Principal Ratner's silhouette blocked the hallway. "Roswell, come with me."

I rolled my eyes at Ruth and followed Ratner to his office. We passed Jonathan along the way. I shrugged at his questioning look and kept walking.

"Roswell, I am afraid I am going to have to suspend you for two days. I warned you about missing school; we also sent a warning notice home. With the death of your classmate, I was willing to forgo this, but Mr. Dellian feels suspension is necessary."

Of course he does. "Principal Ratner, I swear he's marking me absent because I won't sit in the back. Ask Mrs. Martin; she knows."

He picked up his phone. "Nurse Martin? Could you come to my office for a moment?" When she entered he said, "Roswell is about to be suspended for missing too many classes. She tells me you are aware of this situation?"

"Yes, my son actually mentioned something earlier this year. When I spoke to Mr. Dellian about it, he assured me he was simply separating Roz and my son for too much socializing. Roz came to me before break with the same story, though, so I observed."

He nodded. "Did you witness anything?"

Mrs. Martin glanced at me before she answered. "No, he marked her present."

"Because you were there!" I protested.

"I did skim her records," Mrs. Martin said. "The majority of absences do occur in that class. She's a good student too. I'm inclined to believe her and my son when they say she's there every day."

Ratner shuffled through the attendance records. "Thursday you were marked absent in all classes. I seem to remember you leaving before first hour."

"I wasn't feeling well."

"Your parents excused you then? I don't see a pass."

"No." What was I supposed to say? I saw Greg hugging Missy and took off? "I . . . just left." I'd lost my footing.

"Roswell, you cannot leave school when you wish. I'm suspending you as planned."

"How does that even make sense?" I looked at Nurse Martin for help. "If I *was* skipping class, how does keeping me out of school punish me?" She didn't say anything. I looked back at Principal Ratner. "That's every truant's dream! It's stupid!"

"It's policy," Principal Ratner said. "Go gather your books. I'll call your home."

I found Jonathan waiting in the hallway. "I only have a second; I have to meet Ratner in the front to wait for my mom." I told him. "I'm suspended."

"Shit, our plan was perfect!" He glared at me. "What do I do now?"

"Wait three days? Or get the keys yourself," I said, annoyed by his attitude.

"I can't get near that room, and three days is too long!" We heard someone coming. "I'll call you," Jonathan whispered, and left.

"I don't believe it." Heather walked up with some sort of cardboard tree. "You two are back together?"

I gave her a hostile look and started walking.

"How could you be with him again?"

"Why? Are you jealous?" I hurried up the stairs to my locker.

"Hardly." She took the steps two at a time to keep up. "I'm worried about you."

"Worried about me?" I ripped my locker open, tossed Ruth's yearbook on the floor inside, and grabbed my coat. "The way you were when you hooked up with Jonathan at Ethan's party?"

Heather ignored my dig. "Where are you going?"

"I've been suspended for skipping classes I never skipped."

"That sucks."

I threw my backpack over my shoulder. "Yeah, pretty much everything sucks these days."

"Roz, can we start over? Please? My dad's out of town tomorrow. We could hang out after school. Order pizza, whatever you want. Come on, please?"

"I don't . . ." Her dad's apartment was right above Dellian's. The perfect place to gain access. I nibbled my inner cheek. "I'll think about it."

"You know, after talking with that police lady, I almost believed you," Mom said as she peeled out of the school parking lot. "I thought maybe you were telling the truth this time. Maybe that perverted teacher really was out to get you."

"He is," I muttered.

"Rozzy, your principal said you admitted to skipping!"

I shook my head. It was no use. She was pissed and believed only what she wanted to believe anyway. While she ranted, I formulated a new plan. An easier one. From Heather's apartment I could watch for Dellian while Jonathan broke in and searched.

"One problem," Jonathan said when I told him my plan later that afternoon. "I don't know how to pick a lock."

"Can't you just pop it with a paper clip?"

"Sure, if we're breaking into his bathroom. A dead bolt's another story." He paused. "Hold up. Heather dates that Felix kid, the one in a wheelchair, right?"

"Fritz. Yeah, what about him?"

"Dellian wouldn't stop to lock his dead bolt if he had to leave in a hurry, say in an emergency, would he?"

"Probably not," I said, unsure of what he was getting at.

"This will work," Jonathan said. "Get Felix with you at Heather's tomorrow night."

"*Fritz.*" I corrected. "Why? How's he going to help?"

"Fire alarm. Can't use the elevator in a fire. You get Dellian to help Lover Boy out of the building. I'll search his apartment."

Nine days after

I liked my less criminal role in the new plan. No stealing of keys or sneaking around. I would simply get Fritz to Heather's and make sure Dellian helped him out of the building — something I'd do anyway if there were a real fire.

The first part was easy. I called Heather and said I'd come over, but Fritz had to be a buffer between us. She was more than willing to agree to that. As it neared the time to catch the bus the next day, though, doubt about carrying out the rest of the plan began to rattle me.

No matter what my role, I was helping Jonathan commit a crime. And what did we really hope to accomplish? Even if he did find the cloak, by the time the police searched the place it could be gone. It would still be our word against his — only this time our word would also get us arrested for burglary.

But at least I'd know.

My doorbell rang as I was about to walk out. "I'm on my way to pick up Fritz," Greg said. "You want a ride?"

"You and Heather are buddy-buddy again?" It figured she would ask Greg to pick him up.

"No, but I think inviting me was a gesture to make amends."

"Wait, she invited you?" He could not be there. He'd know I was up to something and ruin the plan. "You're staying?"

"If you don't want me there —"

"I don't." I saw the hurt in his face. I couldn't worry about his feelings right now. He could *not* be there. I pushed past him. "I'm gonna take the bus."

Greg and Fritz were sprawled out on Heather's couch eating chips when I arrived. Greg held his arm up and tapped his watch. "Took you long enough."

"I thought you weren't staying." It came out snotty. Fritz and Heather glanced at me in surprise.

"No, you said you didn't want me to stay," Greg shot back. "I never said I wouldn't."

He could be so annoying! *Okay, he's here, so what?* I told myself. *Just ignore him.* I strolled over to the window and pushed the curtain aside. "Can I open these? Let some light in?"

"I shut them so we could watch a movie," Heather said.

"Oh." I peered down at the crowded parking lot. I could barely make out the first row of cars. The rest were just a smear of colors. "What does Dellian drive?"

"Do we care?" Greg asked.

"A truck," Fritz replied.

I nodded, remembering the day he'd come looking for Tricia. "Dark green." Great. If there had been snow on the ground, dark green would be awesome. It would stand out against the white canvas. Most of the cars down there, however, were black, green, or blue. There wasn't enough contrast against the black asphalt for me to pick out his vehicle. Why did I say I'd be the lookout? I couldn't even *see* to look out.

"Why?" Fritz asked.

"I was curious to see if he was here. It's sort of creepy, with him so close by, especially if he had something to do with Tricia's death." I tried to focus on individual sections of the parking lot, darting my dots to the side so I could look.

The smell of dryer sheets sent my heart into a frenzy as Greg came and stood next to me. He pressed his nose up to the glass. "There's his truck." He turned his head toward me, face still against the glass, and gave me a serious look. "Why do you think Dellian was involved?"

"She was living here with him." I squinted in the direction Greg had motioned. I couldn't see the truck, but at least I could watch the area, make sure he didn't pull out between now and when Jonathan called. "They had a baby." I glanced at my watch. He'd be calling in a few minutes.

"Allegedly, according to you two." Greg gestured at me and Heather.

"Allegedly?" Heather said. "I've seen him with her a billion times! Or I used to anyway. They found me in the stairwell. If they didn't have something going, why would she be here after midnight on a Saturday? Plus, as Roz said, there's the baby."

Greg shook his head. "My mom said Tricia couldn't have had a baby. She never missed that much school. I think my mom would know if a student had a baby."

"What about when she went for rehab?" I said. "She could've been pregnant then."

"Yeah." Heather agreed. "And drug babies are small. She could've been pregnant without anyone noticing, especially with that smock thing she always wore."

My cell rang. "Hey." I turned away from the others.

"Is D. there?" Jonathan asked.

"Yeah." I wanted to warn him about Greg. "I'm at Heather's, hanging out with Fritz and Greg."

"You brought Loser along?" Jonathan sounded pissed.

"I didn't —"

"Whatever," Jonathan snapped. "Don't let him screw this up! Follow the plan. Okay?"

"Okay. Chill." I scanned the lot for Jonathan, thinking how easy his car was to spot. Too easy. If parked out there, he'd be noticed. "Wait, where are you?"

"Outside."

"In your car? It's kind of *loud,* isn't it?" I glanced at the others. Greg was glaring at me.

"*Loud?* Everyone's listening, huh? Don't worry. They won't see my Vette. I'm parked around the back" — he gave a sarcastic laugh — "in the *fire* lane."

"Zeus having car trouble?" Greg said when I hung up. "His golden chariot get too close to the sun?"

"I think that was Phaeton who did that," I said. "Not Zeus."

Greg wasn't amused. "He's not coming over here, is he?"

"I didn't invite him," Heather said, looking at me.

"Don't worry, he's not. His car's just acting up a bit."

"Your concern is touching." Greg plopped down on the couch again, shoved a handful of tortilla chips into his mouth, and stared at the blank television screen.

"Let's watch a movie," Heather said. "I'll make popcorn."

Fritz snatched up the remote. "What should we watch?"

"There's that new horror spoof," Heather called from the kitchen. The microwave door slammed. "Or that romantic comedy about the newscaster and a hockey player."

Greg snorted. "I'm not watching a hockey movie."

I rolled my eyes and looked back outside. What was taking Jonathan so long? He said he was here, around the back.

I moved to the sliding glass doors to see if I'd have a better view. I didn't, so I went back to the window and caught a whiff of something burning. "Heather, is the popcorn okay?"

I heard her yank the microwave open. "It's not the popcorn. But I smell that too." She walked back into the living room. "It smells like—"

"Smoke," Greg and I said in unison.

The wail of the fire alarm sliced through the silence. We stared at each other as the siren above Heather's front door began blinking blue.

"Oh, my God!" Heather cried. "Fire!"

In the few seconds we took to register the fire, the air in the room had become hazy. Terror ricocheted through me. What the hell? He had said fire *alarm,* not fire!

"Help me get in my chair!" Fritz screamed.

Greg and I rushed to the couch, where Fritz was desperately trying to drag himself to his wheelchair. I grabbed one side of him while Greg grabbed the other. We slammed him too hard into the chair.

"Are you okay?" I asked.

"Fine! Let's go!"

Greg gripped the handles and propelled Fritz out of the room. I squinted into the haze looking for Heather. She was flipping out, flitting around in shock, not getting anywhere. I grabbed her arm and beelined for the door.

When we got there, the boys were staring at it. A thick mass of smoke poured from underneath. My eyes started to sting. Heather whimpered next to me.

"If it's hot, we shouldn't open it," Fritz said.

I stepped around his chair and pushed my palms on the door. It felt warm, but maybe that was just me. "How hot is too hot?"

Greg yanked Fritz's chair out of his way and felt the door. "It's definitely hot. There might be flames in the hall. Go to the balcony."

"We're three stories up!" I said. "How will we get down?"

"We wait and hope the firefighters can help us." Greg turned the chair around and headed to the balcony.

I didn't follow. This was crazy. Jonathan wouldn't have started a fire. It was probably smoke bombs or something for effect. The hall had to be clear. "If we have to climb, Fritz is screwed," I yelled. "We should take the hall, stay low, and crawl down the stairs. Fritz can do that, right, Fritz? Dellian's here, he can help us." I winced.

That had been the plan.

Knocking on Dellian's door in a *real* panic? That had *not* been in the plan.

"Come on!" I flung the door open.

"Roz, no!" Greg cried.

Acrid smoke billowed into the room, choking me, knocking me backwards. Heather screamed. Somewhere down below, flames crackled.

This wasn't happening! It wasn't supposed to go like this. Smoke filled my lungs. I gasped for breath and dropped to the ground. Holding my sweatshirt collar over my mouth with one hand, I kicked the door shut with my foot and crawled back into the apartment.

I felt the panic rising as I realized I couldn't see through the smoke or my tearing eyes. *I don't need to see,* I told myself. With my mental map of the apartment, all I needed was the wall. I crawled sideways until my knee connected with it, and then scooted along knee to wall.

My hand hit someone's foot as I turned a corner. I reached up the pant leg. It was Heather. I curled my hand into hers and yanked her down next to me. "Crawl."

We clomped our way along in slow, jerky movements.

The smoke cleared a bit. The open sliding glass doors were ahead, curtains blowing back and forth. We stood and ran.

"I couldn't see," Heather sobbed into Fritz's lap. "I couldn't find you."

I slid the glass door shut behind me and looked for Greg. He was leaning over the edge, yelling to someone. I moved toward him.

Dellian balanced on the railing of an apartment one level down and to the left of Heather's. He was throwing a rope ladder with metal hooks to Greg. Every throw, however, missed Greg's outstretched arms.

"Crawl over the side of the rail!" Dellian screamed at him. "Come on!"

Greg shook his head. "I . . . I can't."

My heart ached at the fear in his voice. I'd done this to him. "I can do it," I said.

He turned, eyes wild, face white. "That was stupid! You could've killed us!"

"I know." This whole thing was stupid, and if I didn't act fast, my stupidity could still kill us all. "Move, okay?" I gently peeled him away from the ledge.

I tossed one leg and then the other over the metal railing, rested my butt on the top for a second as I twisted my body around, and then lowered myself to the outside ledge. My toes struggled to find a footing. Barely an inch of cement bordered the outside of the rail.

Below people were in chaos. Residents running, scattering. Scared.

I looked away. It was a long way down.

My heart hammered so hard, I could feel it pulsing through every inch of me, shaking me, threatening my grip. I looped one arm through the posts of the railing and clutched the edge with my elbow.

When I felt secure, I took a deep breath and turned toward Mr. Dellian. "Okay."

He nodded at me. "Good, now bend your knees. Crouch a little when you reach."

I did as I was told and leaned forward. He was farther away than I'd thought. My shoulder muscle tore. Pain ripped through my side and back.

I gritted my teeth and kept reaching. The tips of my fingers brushed the rough edge of the metal rings in Dellian's outstretched hands. With one last painful push forward, I folded my hand around the metal hook and grabbed the ladder.

"Good work. Now hang those hooks and throw the ladder down."

The hooks clipped easily on the edge. I tossed the ladder down to Dellian and climbed back onto Heather's balcony. Sirens wailed in the distance.

Dellian pulled himself over the ledge and moved quickly to Fritz as the fire trucks screamed into the apartments' entrance. Instead of pulling into the parking lot underneath us, however, they turned right, away from us, and disappeared.

"They're leaving!" Heather cried.

"They went around the back," Dellian said. "I'm sure they'll send someone to help us." We heard more sirens in the distance. Dellian smiled. "See? Now let's get Mr. Grandman down. Mr. Martin, I'll need your belt," Dellian said as he yanked his own belt off.

Greg fumbled with his buckle, fingers shaking, but managed to get it free and handed it to Mr. Dellian.

Mr. Dellian frowned at it. "You could stand to gain a few pounds, Mr. Martin." He attached the belts together and then nodded at us. "I'll need you all to attach him to me with this rather narrow strap and then help hold him while I climb over. I hope all those asinine tricks of yours have built some upper-body strength, Mr. Grandman. You'll need it to hold on."

The belts together were barely long enough to go around their bodies. We struggled to fasten the belts around them both, the leather edge cutting deeply into Fritz's skin. Once the belts were secure, we steadied Fritz as Dellian climbed onto the ladder. They slowly scaled their way down, Fritz's arms shaking violently with the effort to hold on. Two fire trucks pulled into the parking lot below. Within seconds, a firefighter had helped get Fritz the rest of the way down and carried him to the grassy area on the other side of the lot.

Dellian returned to the ladder. "You're okay up there. The fire was small. They've put it out. Just stay there!"

"No way," Heather said. "I'm not staying."

Greg and I watched her scurry down the ladder and run across the lot to Fritz. Things below began to look less chaotic. A few people wandered back into the building. A fire truck left. As a tow truck came into the lot and drove around the back, I realized my body was shaking. I hugged myself to stop trembling. "Did you want to go down?" I asked.

"I'll wait. You go if you want." He was trembling too.

"I'll wait with you." I moved closer until my arms, still hugging my chest, touched his. "Cold?"

"Just freaked out. Sorry I couldn't . . ." He dropped his eyes to our arms. I dropped mine too. "I hate heights," he said. "If you'd fallen . . ." A tiny tearstain appeared on his sweatshirt.

I made him cry. He was scared and vulnerable and defeated, and I'd done that to him. Me. *This was my fault.* I had to tell him. "I'm sorry —" I said, fighting against my own tears.

"No!" He nudged me with his arms. "You were brave! Like that time with Missy's cat, remember?"

"PJ Jamma Jamma?" I whispered over the lump in my throat.

"Yeah, when that bully — what was his name?"

"Pete Bowls," I said, still staring at our arms.

"Pete Bowls," Greg said. "He stole PJ and put her in a tree. You were only eight, but you scaled that tree as if it were a flight of stairs. A hero. Just like now."

I remembered that day. How Missy had praised me, thanked me. That had felt good. This didn't. This felt wrong. I wasn't a hero. I was the villain. A monster.

"Don't," I whispered. "I'm not a hero. This is my fault."

"No, it's not." He unfolded his arms. Pried mine apart. Clasped my hands in his. "I'm sorry I yelled. I almost opened the door too. Anyone could've."

"That's not what I mean." My lips trembled. I couldn't look at him. "The fire's my fault."

"Don't be silly. You were nowhere near the fire."

There was a loud honking below. Our heads turned automatically toward the noise. A group of people were blocking the back entrance of the apartment building, and someone trying to get through from the fire lane was laying on his horn. We watched as the bystanders moved aside and the tow truck pulled through — a red sports car attached to its tow.

The air between us thickened. Greg slowly pulled his hands away.

"Greg, let me explain, please?"

He backed away from me. His mouth opened and shut, a fish gasping for air.

"There wasn't supposed to be a fire, just a false alarm to get everyone out."

"Get away from me." He moved to the edge where the rope ladder was hung.

"Greg, I never would've agreed to help if I'd known this would happen. Never."

"What were you helping that asshole do? What was so important that you were willing to use your friends, *lose* your friends, to achieve?"

"I was trying to help Tricia."

He stared at me. "How exactly does this help Tricia? She's dead!"

Nothing I could say would convince him, because nothing I could say now would convince me. I no longer knew how I had thought this plan would help anyone. "I'm sorry," I whispered.

"You are." He gripped the ledge. "You know how humiliating that must've been for Fritz? He was strapped to his teacher's back, dangling three stories aboveground! How could you do that to him? To all of us?" He lifted a leg over the side.

"Stop! What're you doing?" I cried. "You hate heights."

"Yeah, I do." He lifted the other leg over and faced me from the other side of the ledge. "But right now, I hate you more."

His words punched the life out of me. I wanted to run after him, make him understand, make him take those words back, but I knew I couldn't. I hated me too.

I watched him inch his way down the ladder. When he reached the ground, he'd tell them. Then they'd all hate me. How long before the lynch mob came? The firemen? The police?

I fumbled for my cell phone. The asshole answered on the first ring. "Why'd you set a fire?"

"Ethan thought —"

"Ethan? How did Ethan become a part of this? You said a fire *alarm* — we had it all planned, Jonathan!"

"Yeah, well, I needed backup in case you screwed things up again — which you did, bringing *Loser* along. The plan had to change because of him. Ethan said a fire on the stairs would get Dellian out and us in through the glass doors. Can't deadbolt those puppies — and that way we were covered if Loser tried to carry Lover Boy out himself."

"They have names — Greg and Fritz! They're people, not objects you can just screw around with!" I snapped. "And where are you? Your car got towed —"

"I couldn't get back to my Vette — too many people freaking out around the back when we finished in Dellian's apartment, so we had to bail without it."

My head started to hurt. "God, Jonathan," I said, rubbing my temples, "you could've killed someone."

"With that fire? Please. Besides, it worked, didn't it? I just hid in the bushes and slipped right in while D. was rescuing —" He paused. "Cops are calling through; must've found my *stolen* car." He laughed. "Tell Loser to expect a call from them. I told them he stole it."

I stared at the screen as Jonathan disconnected. How could he mess with people's lives as if they were nothing?

Slowly I let my breath out.

How could I?

Not anymore. I flipped my phone open and called Detective King.

"You understand," Detective King said when I'd finished explaining about the fire, "you're admitting to a crime."

"I know." We were sitting in her office with my mother. "I understand."

"Okay, I'm going to go talk to the fire investigator and the officers questioning Jonathan and your friends. Is there anything else before I go?"

"Greg didn't steal Jonathan's car. It was towed from the fire lane. Jonathan knew Greg was there — and he knew the car proved he was at the fire — so he said Greg stole it. But Greg drove his own car to Heather's — ask Fritz. Greg picked him up."

"Okay," the detective said. "I'll see what I can do."

Mom glared at me as Detective King left the room. "Every time I turn around, you're in trouble. A fire, Rozzy? What the hell is wrong with you?"

"Mom, I didn't —"

"Save it!" She whipped out her phone and started texting. "Now I need to find someone to work for me. God knows how long we'll be here."

Detective King returned fifteen minutes later. "Roswell, you said you didn't arrive at the apartment building with Jonathan. You took the bus?" When I nodded, she said, "What time did you arrive?"

"I don't know. The bus dropped me off at the corner around four thirty, maybe? I walked to Heather's from there. Greg would know. He commented on how late I was."

Detective King frowned. "That's the problem. He said you arrived a lot later than he'd expected, and that he had offered you a ride, which you refused."

I ignored my mother's snort. "Because we were arguing."

"Well, unfortunately Jonathan is not corroborating your story. He claims he was with Ethan Baker at ShopCo when his car was stolen. Now, the report didn't actually come in until after the fire alarm went off, but —"

"Because he was there! Ethan too. They set the fire."

"No." Detective King shook her head. "Ethan Baker was working the entire time at ShopCo. His manager confirmed that with his time card. And several people remember seeing Jonathan there too."

"He could've slipped out without his manager knowing!" I said. "And those could be their friends, or people who remember seeing them before or after the fire, and are assuming they were there the whole time!"

"Maybe, but no one saw either boy at the apartment building, Roz, just the Corvette."

"Well that's something, right?" I said.

"It would be if he hadn't reported it stolen."

"*After* the fire was set," I said.

"That only means Jonathan noticed it was stolen at that time. With the witnesses placing both boys in ShopCo during that time frame, it looks as if it could have been stolen and the thief drove it to the apartment building."

"So what're you saying exactly?" Mom asked.

"I'm saying that while we know Greg Martin did not steal Jonathan's car, it looks as though it may indeed have been stolen. Which means"—Detective King leaned forward, folding her hands neatly on the desk—"there's not a shred of evidence that proves those two boys were involved in the fire. Right now, Roz is our only suspect."

"But I didn't start the fire!"

"But you confessed to being involved, and because you arrived late, alone, after refusing your friend's offer to drive you, it's plausible that you set the fire before entering the Torreses' apartment."

"No!" Telling the truth was supposed to set me free; instead I was scrambling to save myself. "Look, I got off the bus and walked to the apartment. It takes at least ten minutes to walk that distance. How could I have had time to set a fire?"

"Which bus did you take?"

"The six. I got on at Park and Renton."

"That route passes ShopCo, doesn't it?"

"Yeah?" Her meaning hit me. "I didn't steal his car! I don't even know how to drive—"

"We both know that's not true," Detective King said.

"No, now that *is* true," Mom piped up. "She's blind. She'll never be able to drive."

I cringed. *Of all the times to back me up, she picks now?*

Detective King was looking at me. "You never told your mother?"

I shook my head as Mom said, "Told me what?"

"I ticketed your daughter a few months ago for driving without a license," Detective King said. "She wrecked Greg Martin's car."

"What?" Mom leaped out of her chair. "You crashed someone's car? You can't drive, Roswell! What is going on in that head of yours?"

"Ms. Braylor — Priscilla — please, sit," Detective King said.

"Okay, so I tried to drive!" I said. "But you saw me! I rammed his car into that light pole! You think I'd try that again? With Jonathan's *Corvette*?"

"What I saw," Detective King said carefully, "was you driving — yes, you weren't doing a good job of it, I can vouch for that — but you *were* driving. For all I know, you could've been practicing since then and got better."

"But — ugh!" I raked my fingers through my hair in frustration and slumped back in my chair. "I didn't steal his car."

"Okay," Detective King said. "Then let's try to confirm your story. How about the bus. Did anyone get off with you? Did you talk to the driver or any passengers? Someone who can verify where you got off the bus and when?"

I'd been too preoccupied. I barely remembered the ride, let alone any passengers. I could've been sitting next to Big Foot and I wouldn't have noticed. "No." I slumped farther in my chair. "I don't remember anyone."

Mom was shaking her head. "You've finally done it. Always bent on doing your own thing instead of what's best for you. Are you happy with yourself now?" She looked at Detective King. "Are there any special considerations for disabled kids? An insanity plea or something?"

"Mom, I'm not disabled — and I'm not insane!"

"She hasn't been charged —" Detective King said.

"If her story doesn't check out, she will be. That's what you're saying, isn't it?"

"It's possible, yes. After all, she did confess. Normally that *would* be enough to arrest her, but" — she turned back to me — "I'm going to give you the benefit of the doubt. You did come to me, and so far, I have no reason to believe you aren't telling the truth. What I don't understand, Roz, is why you wanted into the apartment. What were you hoping to find?"

"Proof he's guilty, like Tricia's cloak or that photo I saw."

Detective King took a sip of coffee. "I'm still investigating. Don't you trust me to find the answers?"

I shrugged. "Dellian's trying to make Jonathan look guilty. He already has you believing Jonathan sold Tricia drugs."

"Jonathan isn't a suspect. He's a person of interest, but so is half this town."

"If he's not a suspect, why did you tell him to get a lawyer?"

"Is that what he told you?"

I stared at her ear, taking in the puzzled frown on her face. "I thought that's what he said." Doubt began to take over. I couldn't be sure of anything Jonathan had said, could I? He'd lied about being involved with the fire, lied about being a suspect. What else was he lying about?

"While you two were plotting illegal activities to find evidence against your teacher, I was following up on information you gave me." She sat back against her desk chair. "Would you like to know what I found, or would you prefer to break some more laws to get the information yourself?"

"I want to hear what you found," I muttered.

"First of all, the only relationship Rodney Dellian had with Tricia Farni was as her brother-in-law."

"Brother-in-law?" My mouth fell open.

"Yes, apparently he told the officer this when he and Abbey reported Tricia missing, although it never went into the report. I'm not happy about that at all."

I didn't care about police reports and missing information. "What about the baby?"

"Tricia's niece. Rodney and Abbey are separated. Tricia was the go-between to keep things civil."

What? No, there had to be something between them. "So he had an excuse to be around Tricia. That doesn't mean they weren't involved. What about the photo?"

"He claims he's never seen it, that if there is one, it was created digitally by you and Jonathan to get back at him. It seems you both have issues? You've been suspended for truancy, and Jonathan has been benched for grades?"

"He's lying! I mean, that's true about our issues, but I saw the photo in his desk!"

"Right now, it's your word against his. No one else has seen it."

I sighed, defeated. "I suppose he lied about being there that night too?"

"Actually, he said she did call, hysterical, needing a ride. But he couldn't find her when he got there; after looking a while, he went to get Abbey. They returned, still couldn't locate her, and that's when they reported her missing."

I sat up. "No! I *know* he found her that night!"

She tilted her head in surprise. "How do you know?"

"Because, you know, he said he knew about the loft thing." I wanted so badly to tell her the truth, to tell her Dellian had been there when Tricia attacked Jonathan and me. But I couldn't without admitting I'd lied, admitting we'd fought, and admitting I actually couldn't remember any of it.

"She could've told him that over the phone when she called for the ride," Detective King said. "It doesn't mean he saw her."

"I guess so," I said. But he *had* seen her. He'd been there for the fight.

I knew why *I* was lying. Why was Dellian?

Ten days after

My first day back from suspension, I tore through Chance High's usual mob of colors and smells with my war face on, but no one bothered me. Maybe the rumor mill hadn't been briefed on how I'd set fire to Dellian's apartment building? When I noticed a glittered wall-length PROM!!! sign, however, I figured everyone probably did know and didn't care. Finding a date before the deadline was more important than fires, burglaries, and a dead drug addict.

I ripped at my locker handle, expecting it to open. My fingers jammed into the locked metal, ripping two fingernails backwards. Dammit! I didn't have time for this. I needed to find Greg before class.

With my face pressed against the cold surface, I frantically turned the dial. The more I tried to hurry, though, the more I fumbled. Over and over, I dialed wrong.

I snatched my magnifier from my backpack, not caring who saw me. The bulky glass fit over the dial, enlarging the numbers, but I had to remove it to turn the knob. *Ugh!* I threw the glass into my bag and went back to searching out the numbers the hard way.

On about the fifteenth combination attempt, I got it. I threw the door open and tossed my stuff inside. There was Ruth's year-book on the bottom where I'd left it. I hadn't looked at Renny's picture. I would today, with Ruth.

On the way to first hour, I searched the halls for Greg, even though I knew if I found him now, I wouldn't have enough time to talk. I didn't want to be rushed. I still wasn't sure what to say.

Would he ignore me or lecture me? Lecture, I hoped — a scathing, bruising lecture. I deserved that. But if he ignored me — looked through me as if I didn't exist in his world any-more — I couldn't take that. It would mean he'd given up on me.

The *whoosh* of wheels on tile caught my attention. Fritz. God, how I'd humiliated him. Hanging from Mr. Dellian, helpless and scared. I didn't deserve forgiveness, but he certainly deserved an apology. I hurried around the corner to catch him.

I ran into Ratner instead. "Roswell, come with me."

Not again! What now? I reluctantly followed him into his office.

"There are serious allegations against you, most of which are not my jurisdiction. However . . ." He picked up his phone. "Miss Glendale? Please send in the officers."

Officers? What was going on?

The door opened. Detective King and a man in a gray business suit entered. The man stepped over to me. "Roswell Hart?"

The saliva glands in my mouth stopped working. "Yes?" I croaked.

"You've been served." He handed me a piece of paper. "This is a restraining order. You are not permitted to be within a three-mile radius of Mr. Rodney Dellian. If you and your parents have

245

any questions, the number is printed on the bottom. Have a nice day." He nodded at Principal Ratner and exited the room.

Restraining order? I stared at the paper blankly, the print too small to read. "What is this for?"

"Unfortunate it's had to come to this," Principal Ratner said. "I believe he's filing charges against you as well."

"For what? He's the one —" I looked at Detective King. "Tell him!"

Detective King stepped forward. Principal Ratner held up his hand. "Allow me." He turned back to me. "As I said before, most of the allegations against you are not my jurisdiction." He paused. "However, after Mr. Dellian apprised me of this situation, he and I both felt it would be wise to search your locker, to be sure there were no explosives or weapons —"

"What? Why would I have weapons?"

Principal Ratner ignored me and went on. "So this morning we conducted a search of your locker and found this." He pushed a clear plastic bag toward me.

"What is it?" A small green object was inside. It looked like — *Tricia's pipe?*

"It's used for smoking drugs. Of course, you already knew that, didn't you?"

"Yes." I frowned up at him. "But that's not mine!"

"It was in your locker." He handed the bag to Detective King. "Given this pipe and your other offenses — truancy, that field trip stunt you pulled, *arson* — I am expelling you." Ratner nodded at Detective King. "We're trying to reach her mother. When we do, I'll send her to the station."

"Station?" I looked from Ratner to Detective King. "But the pipe isn't mine! Someone put it there! Probably Dellian, while he helped you search my locker."

"Mr. Dellian wasn't there," Detective King said in a stern voice. "I was. With a warrant."

"Warrant?" I stared at her. "Why?"

"It's not just the pipe, Roswell. We received a tip that you bought crack for Tricia. The anonymous informant was very specific on the time and date — even said you left school to get cash at an ATM for the purchase."

Jonathan. That asshole! First the fire and now this? I started to shake my head. "No, I didn't —"

"We have a bank video corroborating the claim," Detective King said, shutting me up. "The video alone isn't enough to arrest you — though it does support the suspicion that you purchased drugs with the intent to distribute — but your confession to being an accessory to the fire and the possession of the pipe is enough." Detective King took a pair of handcuffs from her pocket.

Life slowly drained from my body.

"Roswell, I'm arresting you for the illegal possession of drug paraphernalia as well as arson and the suspicion of purchasing narcotics with the intent to distribute. You have the right to remain silent . . ."

Right to remain silent? I couldn't have spoken if I tried.

In third grade, Missy and I, and sometimes Greg, would play detective games with an old Polaroid camera and a fingerprinting kit. The villain was the sought-after role. There was something glamorous about having my mug shot taken and messy black powder smeared on my fingertips. Now that I was playing for real, it didn't feel glamorous at all.

Someone took my photograph. Then an officer shuffled me off to be fingerprinted. There was no messy black powder. The technician doused my fingertips with water and pressed each one onto a smooth glass surface; my fingerprints magically appeared on the computer screen — "Roswell Hart" was now listed in the fingerprint database, just like a real criminal.

"As soon as your mother gets here, we'll take you for interrogation," Detective King explained, unhooking my left hand from the handcuff. "Would you like some water while you wait?" She reattached the cuff to the chair.

"That pipe's not mine," I whispered.

"Let's wait until your mom gets here, okay?"

Hurricane Priscilla blew in twenty minutes later, still wearing a black smock from the hairdresser's, highlighting foil layered on one half of her head. "Now you're buying drugs?" she screamed.

"Ms. Braylor, please sit down," Detective King said. "I'm sorry to take you from your appointment —"

"Not as sorry as she'll be." She glared at me. "If I knew where your father was, I'd send you there right now."

Nogales, Mexico. Although chasing UFOs in the desert sounded good right now, I didn't share the information.

"We wanted you present while we interrogate your daughter," Detective King explained. "You should probably call an attorney."

"This is going to cost a fortune, isn't it?" Mom said.

"We have public defenders, ma'am."

"I don't need a lawyer!" I said. "I didn't do anything, I swear."

"I want to believe you," Detective King said, "but you haven't been entirely truthful." Mom snorted in agreement.

An officer tapped on the door. "Her prints match a few found in the Corvette — only on the passenger side, though."

Detective King smiled at me. "That's good — you didn't steal Jonathan's car."

"I told you I didn't."

The officer cleared his throat. "We also got a partial off that pipe." He handed her a sheet of paper. "Tricia Farni."

"That's not so good." Detective King said. "You'd better start talking, Roswell. Let's start with how a crack pipe with Tricia's prints ended up in your locker."

I felt out of breath. "I —" I shook my head. "Jonathan. It had to have been Jonathan. He put it there."

"Earlier you said Mr. Dellian put it there," Detective King said.

"I know, but that was before —"

"Before what?" Detective King asked. "It was less than an hour ago."

"Before . . ." If I said *Before I knew you had a tip about my buying drugs for Tricia,* I'd have to explain, and that meant admitting I was guilty of exactly that. Why would they even want to believe me about the pipe after I admitted I bought her drugs? I shrugged and slumped in my chair. "I don't know."

"Roswell," Detective King warned, "if you know something, now is the time to tell me."

"Okay. I think it was Jonathan because I think he called that tip in, about . . . me."

"What tip?" Mom asked.

"The tip that made us search her locker," Detective King said, sounding annoyed. She looked back at me. "But *why* are you so sure now that it was Jonathan, and not Dellian? What changed from an hour ago?"

"Because" — I tried to fill my lungs with air — "he was the only one besides Tricia who knew about that day. He was with me when I took money out at the ATM. But I swear, it was to buy Tricia pot, not crack." I ignored the "Oh, dear Lord" from Mom and continued. "Pot helped her keep off heroin. When Dellian took her pot away, she begged me to get more."

"Where did you buy the pot?" Detective King asked.

"I didn't. I gave the money to Jonathan to buy it."

"Why Jonathan? Did he have some? Or knew someone? What?"

I shrugged. "Tricia just said he'd know how to get it, so I asked him to help me."

"You didn't question why she said that? Didn't think maybe he was a dealer?"

"No." Why *hadn't* I questioned that? Why did I go to him without wondering how he'd know? Because he was Jonathan Webb, lightning-fast god of the ice? God, I was an idiot for ever liking him. The tips of my ears began to burn. "But he said he'd never bought it before and didn't know what it would cost. That's why I took out eighty dollars."

"Eighty dollars?" Mom said. "You used eighty dollars of *my* money? For drugs?"

"It's *my* money, from *my* Social Security check."

"Oh, that's even better, Rozzy. You have the government purchasing your drugs!"

"Ms. Braylor, please," Detective King said. "Roswell, did you see the pot? See who he bought it from?"

"No. That day, Tricia got really high, though. They sent her to the hospital. Dellian said it wasn't pot or heroin. I thought maybe something was in the pot, so I asked Jonathan. He said he gave the money to Ethan to buy the pot for her."

Detective King tapped her pen on her chin. "But you didn't see him give the money to Ethan or see Ethan give him the pot?"

"No, he just said he did." *And we all know how good Jonathan's word is,* I thought bitterly.

"Is it possible Jonathan told Ethan everything, and Ethan phoned in the tip?" Detective King asked.

I hadn't thought of that. The way those two were, it was entirely possible. Heck, Tricia could've told Dellian too that day he'd taken her to the hospital. Just because I hadn't told anyone didn't mean no one else had. "Yes," I said, feeling confused and defeated. "It's possible."

"Okay," Detective King said. "Let's assume for a moment that you are telling the truth about the pipe." Detective King ignored my emphatic "I am!" "How about your locker —"

Something flashed through my mind at that moment, distracting me from what she was saying. At that first party with Jonathan, when he put money in for the keg, he had a wad of cash — but hardly any when we'd gone to the ATM the day before. Was that *my* money in his wallet? Had I paid Jonathan for Tricia's pot?

If there even was any pot. Maybe he had lied to me. Maybe he kept the money and never gave her anything, forcing her to get another needle full of heroin from wherever she'd got the last one.

But there'd been no tracks, no needle marks.

What if Jonathan had given her something, just not pot? Something that would make her insanely high in the cafeteria? Something that would leave no tracks? Something like . . . crack?

I'd never seen her smoke it until after that day. Was he selling crack to her? When I saw her get in his car that time at lunch — he made me think I'd been mistaken, but what if I hadn't? Could he have been giving her crack? In the loft, Tricia had said she "just needed." Had she "just needed" the crack he could supply? Was she "paying" him that night in the loft? I shivered in disgust.

If he was supplying her with crack, there was a good chance he'd have a crack pipe with her prints on it — one he'd need to plant in my locker to keep the police from finding it on him.

"Roz?" Detective King said.

Then again, as Detective King said, it could've been Ethan who called in the tip. Maybe Jonathan did give him the money and he was the one who got her crack instead. He could've planted the pipe . . . or Jonathan could have been lying, saying he gave Ethan the money, saying Ethan started the fire. Was Ethan another scapegoat like me? Dellian too? Had the fire been about getting proof? Or something else entirely? The whole thing made my head hurt.

"Roz!" Mom yelled. "She asked you a question!"

"Sorry." I shifted my eyes to Detective King's face to fake eye contact. "What?"

"Who else knows your locker combination? Who else has access to it?"

"Nobody." I sighed. That wasn't true. "And everybody."

"Rozzy, don't play games!" Mom snapped.

"I'm not! Nobody knows my combo; everyone has access to it. I leave it unlocked." Jonathan knew that. He had to have planted the pipe. It was the only thing that truly made sense. And he knew that by calling in the tip, I'd take the fall for everything. Just as I had for the fire. Because he knew drugs had killed Tricia. His drugs.

"I think Jonathan is behind everything," I said, and laid out my suspicions.

"Sounds plausible," Detective King said when I'd finished. "Unfortunately, it's speculation. We need something concrete. I'll keep digging." She stood up. "I have to send you to the detention center now."

"Detention center?" What was she talking about? "But I just told you —"

"You're sending her to *jail?*" Mom turned to me, her head shaking back and forth. "You've really screwed things up this time."

For the first time in my life, I agreed with her.

A police officer took me to the detention center in handcuffs and handed me over to a female guard. After my clothes and shoes were replaced with an orange jumpsuit and slippers, the guard escorted me to a windowless room with ice-blue brick walls and a steel-framed cot nailed to the cement floor.

The thick metal door bounced shut.

The lock clanked into place.

I was alone.

I picked my way across the itchy wool blanket on the cot and sat with my back against the cold concrete. Knees hugged to my chest, I stared up at the gray, UFO-less ceiling.

It was quiet. Too quiet. So absent of sound, it suffocated me, like being underwater. At first I thought I'd lost my hearing. But there simply was nothing to hear. No hissing radiator; no thumping bass from a distant car; no squeaking shoes from a passing guard. Nothing. Just a thick, deafening silence.

"They could at least get some made-for-the-elevator canned Madonna music in here." My voice echoed off the walls and disappeared.

What the hell? How did I end up in a juvenile detention center? At what point did I take that wrong turn and land here?

"Wrong turn? Please," I told myself. "You mean *which* wrong turn. You've made so many." Trusting Jonathan. Not listening to Greg. Using my friends. Not being a friend. Being so wrapped up with my selfish self, I was blind to everything around me. "Guess when they said I was legally blind, they meant more than my eyesight."

What seemed like an eternity later, the door of my cell began groaning and then rumbled open. A guard nodded at me. "Visitor."

My spirits lifted when I saw Detective King. "Can I go home?"

She gave me a sad look. "Your mom and the public defender are working on it, but the process sometimes takes a while. They give you dinner yet?"

My shoulders slumped back against the cement wall as I nodded. "Yes."

"You know you can use the phone to call your mom. They allow a phone call each day." She handed me Ruth's yearbook. "You left this in my office. Thought you might want it."

I embraced it like a lost treasure. "Can I get my music and earphones from my stuff too? It's so quiet."

"Sorry, hon, not allowed. The earphones are considered a weapon."

"Right," I said with a laugh.

She made a choking motion with her hands.

"Oh," I said. "People really do that?"

"Roswell." She sat on the corner of my cot. "We searched Jonathan's house, car, and locker. No drugs."

"So he stashed them someplace." Her sigh made me feel hopeless. I sighed too. "Check my locker again. All the evidence you need is probably in there now."

"His prints weren't on your locker or the pipe, Roswell, and we tested the pipe in case your hunch about him and Tricia smoking crack together was true. The only DNA in that pipe was Tricia's."

"So?" I rested my head on the wall and looked up at the ceiling. "My prints and DNA weren't on that pipe either, were they? I'm still in here."

"Roswell, I'm sorry. But the pipe *was* found in your locker. Unless we can prove it was planted, it's hard to argue that charge — you were in possession and you admitted to purchasing drugs —"

"I didn't purchase them! I just took the money out. For all I know, Jonathan went and bought a pizza with that money."

"And I hope your lawyer argues that —"

Lawyer? My heart sank. "I'm going to jail for the pipe and the fire, aren't I?"

"You're still innocent until proven guilty." She shook her head. "Roz, I want to believe you're innocent, but nothing you tell me checks out. Mr. Dellian let us search his apartment. Nothing incriminating. No photos, no cloak."

"So, he's hiding them!"

"Or he never had them." Detective King sighed. "Roz —"

The exhaustion in her tone made me want to scream. "Look, obviously that pipe was Tricia's. Your fancy tests proved that, right?" I didn't wait for confirmation. "Well, Tricia kept her pipe in a pocket of her cape, which she was wearing that night in the loft. And when she was found, there was no cape. So, whether it was Jonathan or Ethan or Dellian or the boogyman — whoever put that pipe in my locker has her cape and is probably the person who killed her."

It's not that I thought I was handing her the smoking gun or anything, but I did expect some sense of urgency or excitement over this revelation. Instead, she just gave me a sad, sympathetic look. "We closed her case, Roz. With Tricia's past substance abuse, we think the lethal mixture was her doing — whether suicide or accident, we aren't sure — but we've ruled out foul play."

"What?" How could they abandon Tricia like that? "But the pipe . . . the cape . . ."

"It doesn't mean anything, hon. Tricia could've taken the cape off and left it someplace that night. And you two were friends. She could've left the pipe in your locker."

"But she didn't!" They couldn't do this! They couldn't just close her case. "What about the GHB? You said yourself it's used as a date-rape drug! Why would she give herself that?"

"I said *sometimes* used. People use it as a recreational drug too."

"But what about the other girls who think they were slipped GHB? They weren't taking it recreationally. Doesn't that prove a pattern or something? That maybe Tricia *didn't* take it on purpose? And even if she did take it on purpose, if Jonathan was supplying her with drugs, isn't that like killing her?"

"Yes, and we're —"

But I wasn't finished. "And how about Dellian? He lied about seeing her that night; I know he did! What if he drowned her and she was too messed up to fight back? Or what if Dellian or Jonathan or someone else forced her to take the drugs and then drowned her? There're so many things that could've happened!" My voice had reached a hysterical pitch and I knew I was about to lose it. I lowered my voice, but it still came out in a whine. "You don't know anything yet! You can't just give up on finding the truth!"

"Roz, ruling her death accidental doesn't mean we've given up. We're interviewing girls about the GHB, and if we can use her death to nail Jonathan or someone else for the drugs, we will. We can also reopen the case if we feel her death wasn't accidental. But right now, you need to worry about you because" — she paused — "the only person we have any real evidence against, for any crime, is you."

Eleven days after

Time stopped in my windowless tomb of a cell. With no clock or light from the outside, I had no idea if a minute or an hour had passed. If not for the guard's "lights out" command and then the plate of cold scrambled eggs and burnt toast hours later, I wouldn't have known night had turned to day. It was as if the world outside no longer existed.

Was this how Tricia's body felt all winter? Trapped in an icy coffin, unable to hear or see anything, with no chance of reaching out for help? I may as well have been at the bottom of the Birch River too. With everything stacked against me, did I have any hope of breaking free to the surface?

But I had to. I'd never figure out what really happened stuck in here.

Everything was so confusing, though, so contradictory. How could I ever sort it all out and find the truth? I wished more than anything that Greg were talking to me. He was the one person who I knew could look at everything objectively. The one person I trusted with absolute conviction to help me. He was also the one person I knew never would. He hated me.

More than heights.

My body ached at the memory. God, how I'd screwed everything up with him! With Heather. With Fritz. And Missy. The end of our lifelong friendship this past summer hadn't been her fault. It had been mine.

I had lashed out at her during a softball game. She'd just hit a home run, winning the game for us, everyone ecstatic at their golden girl. I'd always been jealous of her a little. She had a dad who was there every day, while I was lucky if I heard from mine once a year. And her mom was always taking Missy to the movies or to get their nails done, making her breakfast, packing her lunch, doing "mom" things, while mine seemed too busy with work or boyfriends or whatever to even bother. But that school year, my jealousy had really become intense. I'd been diagnosed with my eye disease only months before, and it made everything in my life worse. Mom seemed annoyed at me all the time; I had all these teachers and specialists telling me what I needed; I had people looking at me differently; heck, I had *me* looking at me differently — and yet, there was Missy. Her life still perfection — looks, sports, popularity, boys — everything just getting easier for her.

So, I guess watching everyone go crazy that day over her made me snap. Right after the home run, the coach's son asked if I thought Missy'd go out with him. I knew she would, she'd been crushing on him all summer, but the envy in me took over. I told him she was gay and dating Rona. I said it within earshot of Rona on purpose. She and Missy had been hanging out a lot, and I guess I was jealous of that too. Rona ran straight to Missy, and in a blink of an eye, I'd lost my best friend.

She got back at me. She told the coach I was legally blind. But I deserved that. Whether she did it because I didn't want anyone to know, or because she knew how he would react, I don't know. It doesn't matter. The coach started treating me like a glass vase, afraid I'd break. So I quit. Greg thinks I got kicked off. One more lie he'll hate me for when he learns the truth.

I flipped through Ruth's yearbook to distract myself. Memories frozen in time. Most of them probably weren't memories at all, simply moments staged by the yearbook staff to tell the story they wanted to tell.

She'd marked Renny's picture with a blue sticky note. His official name was Ronaldo Peter Jensen. His goofy grin made him stand out on the senior page — so infectious, I couldn't help but smile back at it. How could someone who looked so happy kill himself? If I had to guess who was capable of suicide, I'd choose Tricia hands down over this goofy, grinning boy in the picture. Yet, Renny did commit suicide. It was Tricia I doubted.

There was a page dedicated to deceased students. Renny wasn't one of them. But his death had been close to graduation. Maybe they'd added a supplement? I darted my dots around the pages while straining to read the small print of the index in the back, but I found only one other listing for him — RRSH, or Resource Room Study Hall — a class I quickly told Mr. Villanari I didn't need when he recommended it to me last year.

Ruth was right. No one cared. Dellian was yearbook advisor and he'd done nothing to honor Renny. Why would anyone else?

The RRSH photo was toward the back. There was JJ in the front row, with two boys kneeling on either side of him; Tricia, in her cloak, stood in the back row between Jeffrey and Dellian; Renny and Ruth, in the back next to Dellian, wore matching yellow smiley-face T-shirts. Renny wore an unbuttoned plaid shirt over his. He and Ruth smiled at each other instead of the photographer, lost in their own world, just the two of them.

I wiped at a hair in the corner several times before realizing it was part of the photo. The photograph above had one too. Heather had complained about the same thing with her and Greg's homecoming pictures. For the hell of it, I surveyed every photo in the yearbook. Two-thirds of the pictures had that stupid hair.

If Dellian used the yearbook camera to take that photo of him and Tricia, there'd be a hair on it too. Was there one in that photo?

I curled up, closed my eyes, and recalled the photo, examining my visual memory. Dellian's eyes had been closed. Tricia was kissing his neck. Both were wearing the same clothes from the dance . . . ugh. I opened my eyes. Trying to remember was pointless. I wasn't even sure if Dellian's shirt had flowers or palm trees. How would I know if there was a hair in the corner? I certainly hadn't been looking for one. Besides, the photo had been kind of blurry. Out of focus.

No. Not blurry or out of focus. Grainy.

My eyes flew open. *Grainy,* like a UFO photo taken by a cell phone. The yearbook camera hadn't taken that photo. A cell phone had. And nobody takes a cell phone picture with a tripod.

Dellian hadn't taken that photo. Someone else had. A third party.

"Jonathan."

Dellian's eyes hadn't been closed because he was into the

moment. He'd been asleep! Or passed out. With so many people thinking they'd been slipped something at parties, could Dellian have been slipped something that night to make him sick? Sick enough to sleep or pass out?

Asleep or passed out, either way, the photo had been staged. Just as Dellian told Detective King. Only it wasn't *me* who had staged it with Jonathan; it was Tricia. She was kissing Dellian; she would've known Jonathan was there. They must've done it to blackmail Dellian.

It all made sense. Dellian had been about to kick Jonathan off the team. Then suddenly he kicked Jonathan out of class, but not off the hockey team. That was the day I found the photo. Maybe Jonathan had just used it? It explained why Dellian was so angry with Jonathan — the photo, even if it was staged, was incriminating.

But if Dellian was telling the truth about his relationship with Tricia, why did he lie and say he never found Tricia that night? Even with the photo out there somewhere and the threat of blackmail, it made no sense to lie about seeing her.

Unless he hadn't lied.

"Guard! Guard!" I screamed into the intercom. "I need to make a phone call!"

Once the guard led me to the telephone, however, I stared at the receiver, unsure who to call. Telling the truth to Detective King had landed me in juvenile detention. I couldn't tell her Jonathan said the four of us had fought, without explaining I had no memory of it. And all she'd hear was that I'd lied. Again.

Innocent or not, I'd look guilty. And besides, I really didn't know the truth. All my suspicions were just that — suspicions based on a memory I'd been given by Jonathan. Maybe there was no fight. Jonathan could've made that up too so I'd help him get back at Dellian.

No, calling Detective King would be a mistake. I needed to talk to the only other person with answers — Dellian.

But how? I couldn't call him. He had a restraining order against me. Someone would have to persuade him to speak with me. Difficult, considering *no one* was speaking to me.

I glanced at the digital clock next to the phone: 6:30 p.m. School was out. Greg would be home. Would he take the call? I had only one phone call.

Maybe Heather?

Even if I could get Heather to listen to me, Dellian wouldn't listen to her. He wouldn't trust anyone he knew had a relationship with me — which left Fritz, Ruth, and the rest of Life Skills out too. No, it had to be someone he knew and respected, a student who never gave him problems; someone he'd never suspect would call him on my behalf. I lifted the receiver and dialed the one number I knew better than my own.

Missy's cell.

"Who is this?"

"It's Roz." I glanced at the guard. "Please don't hang up."

"Why are you calling me? Are you in jail? The caller ID says Juv Detention."

"Yeah, I am." I took a deep breath. Why was this so hard? Once upon a time I could tell her anything. "I need your help."

Missy snorted. "Why would I help you?"

"Because before I screwed everything up, we used to help each other. We used to be there for one another." There was silence on the other end. "I know I don't deserve your help. I haven't been there for you lately. Like with your mom. I should've been there when you found out."

Still no answer.

This was a mistake. I'd wasted my phone call. I sighed and tried asking a question this time. "How is your mom?"

"The lump was benign," Missy said finally. "No cancer."

"That's great —"

"You were the only person I wanted to tell, and I couldn't. I hated you for that," Missy said. "Only Greg understood, and I felt like a bitch telling him Mom was cancer free when Mrs. Martin's still in chemo."

"What? Greg's mom?" I felt as if I'd just been slapped. He had never told me. Never said anything. But why would he have? I hadn't been there for him either, or for anyone.

"You didn't know?"

I shook my head at the receiver. I knew she couldn't see me, but it was the only response I could give. My throat was closing.

"Don't feel bad. I know only because Mrs. Martin told my mom."

"When did they find out?" I managed to ask. I pictured Greg getting the news, needing a friend, me, to talk to, and where was I? Running around with Greg's least favorite person, Jonathan, trying to prove him innocent of something he most likely did.

"February," Missy said.

February? That didn't make sense. We were talking in February.

Then I remembered. The day I wrecked his car, he'd wanted to talk. I was too busy proving myself to notice he needed me. "Oh, Greg," I whispered.

Missy was quiet, probably thinking I deserved to feel like shit. She'd be right.

"Two minutes," the guard yelled.

"I have to go, Missy," I said, slapping tears away. "I'm out of time."

"What do you need?" Missy asked. "I'll do it."

"You will? Thank you!" Shocked, I almost forgot to tell her *what* I needed. "Persuade Dellian to come see me. I have to talk to him."

"He has a restraining order on you, Roz. You tried to burn his house down."

"I didn't —" I bit my lip. It didn't matter whether I had set the fire or not. I had helped do it. "I know. That's why you have to convince him. I'm tired of letting my friends down, Missy. Tricia was my friend, and she's dead, and I need to find out the truth. I can't do that without talking to Dellian." There was silence again. "Missy?"

"All right."

The guard yelled, "Time!" and the line went dead.

No one came.

I stared holes into the ceiling and waited.

My evening meal arrived, and then my morning meal. Still no one came.

The isolation drove me mad. I resorted to lunacy to save my

sanity. I screamed song after song, desperate for the sound of a human voice. I danced my dots along the ceiling, pretending I was home, safe under my UFO sky. I tricked my nose into thinking the sterile odor of industrial disinfectant was really those fragrances I missed — dryer sheets, watermelon bubblegum, lavender and vanilla body spray. I even twirled in a circle faster and faster until the air on my face felt like a spring breeze.

When these tricks finally failed, I sank down on my itchy cot and slipped into a motionless funk.

Twelve days after

Early the next evening, when my door groaned, I didn't react. I no longer let myself hope when I heard the rumbling, and the arrival of food had long lost its luster.

"Time to go, Hart," the guard said as the door rattled open.

My dots slid from the ceiling and focused on the guard. "What? Where?" My feet dropped to the floor.

"Home. Your mom posted bail."

"Home?" The concept seemed so foreign.

Mom had little to say. Her face pinched in a tight scowl, she merely grunted when I threw my arms around her. "I had to use the house to get you out," she said, throwing open the door of her hybrid.

"Sorry," I said.

She grunted again and said nothing until we pulled into the driveway. "Just because you're out of jail doesn't mean you're off the hook, young lady." She shoved the gearshift into "park" and glared across the seat at me. "You're under house arrest. You understand? No phone calls, no leaving the house. No more crap. Got it?"

"Got it." I opened the door. "Aren't you coming in?"

She shook her head, hands on the steering wheel. "I need a drink. I'm going out."

"Home sweet home," I muttered as I got out. When the familiar smell of stale coffee and carpet freshener met me at the door, though, I sighed. It *was* home sweet home. Leaping down the stairs to my room, I jumped on my bed and smiled up at my UFOs. "Missed you, guys!"

An image of Greg standing in the same spot, ogling my photos, popped into my mind and wrenched me back to reality. "I have so much to fix."

I dropped to my bedspread and stared over at my cell phone. Should I call him? Would he talk to me? Mom said no phone calls, but no punishment from her could top the juvie cell I had just vacated.

I cradled the phone in my hands, smoothed my fingers across the number two speed-dial button, but couldn't push it. What if he hung up when he heard my voice?

The doorbell cut into my thoughts. I bounded up the steps and peeked through the peephole. Missy.

I threw the door open and flung my arms around my ex–best friend. A familiar outline stood just beyond her, huddled next to the porch swing. My heart tumbled over itself. "Greg?" I let go of Missy.

All the conversations I'd rehearsed — telling him I was sorry, that I was wrong, how I felt about him — failed me. I could only blink at him and wish I'd taken a shower.

"Can we come in?" Missy said. "I need to pee."

"Yeah, yes, come on in." I held the door open.

"Priscilla said no visitors when we called to see when you were getting home, but I knew she'd leave eventually." Missy grimaced. "Did she even come inside?"

I shrugged, my face burning.

Missy ran into the bathroom, leaving Greg and me awkwardly alone. He leaned against the curio cabinet and fiddled with an imaginary object in his hands.

Could he smell me? How bad did I look? I tried to see my reflection in the curio's glass doors.

My movement caught his attention. He cocked his head slightly and looked up at me through his eyelashes. "So, how've you been?" He rolled his eyes and looked back at the air between his fingers. "I mean, besides being in jail and all that. Was it bad?"

I looked at my own fingers, picking at my nails. "It wasn't too bad. I had a lot of time to think." I tried to meet his gaze, but he wouldn't look at me. "I thought a lot about how I screwed up." His curls moved. Was that a nod or an involuntary jerk? "And you. I thought a lot about you," I said. "I'm sorry your mom's sick. You never said anything."

His head came up, mouth open to respond.

"Better!" Missy walked back into the room. "You tell her?"

"Not yet." Greg gave me a sympathetic frown. "Dellian won't see you, and without knowing what you planned to say, we didn't push it."

We? Greg was helping? That gave me hope. "I need to ask him about that night."

Greg threw his arms up in disgust. "Did jail mean anything to you? Give it up! Leave the man alone!"

"Wait, listen, okay?" I said. "Dellian was there that night. He told the police he came to get Tricia but couldn't find her. I . . . I remember him, sort of, but not much else. Nothing else, actually."

Missy slapped her hand to her mouth. "You got slipped GHB too?"

"Maybe." I glanced at Greg. "I'm not sure." Greg wouldn't look at me. Did he hate me for not telling him? "Jonathan said Tricia went kind of crazy after he and I had left the party. Tricia pulled me out of his car and we . . ." God, this was hard. Would they think I killed her? "We struggled. Jonathan was breaking it up when Dellian came. Tricia took off, and . . ." I shrugged. "Jonathan took me home."

"But you don't remember any of that?" Greg asked.

"No, and as I said, Dellian didn't say anything about this fight to the police. He said he never found Tricia that night. With everything Jonathan has lied about, he could've made that up too." I ignored Greg's sarcastic snort. "Which means maybe Jonathan knows more about Tricia's death than he's saying."

Greg nodded. "So you want to ask Dellian, to prove *Jonathan's* guilty? Hallelujah! She's finally seen the light!"

"Yes, that, and to ask about a photo of him and Tricia."

"Photo?" Missy asked.

"Of Tricia kissing him the night of the dance. I found it in his desk, but when I went back to take it, it was gone."

"You went through his desk?" Greg's tone shamed me. I waited for the lecture. He just sighed. "So you still think Dellian was more than her brother-in-law?"

"Well, yeah!" Missy said. "If they were kissing —"

"Actually, no. I think Jonathan faked the photo to blackmail Dellian. Dellian didn't admit to having the photo when the police asked, though." I held up my hand before Greg could interrupt me. "I know. Of course he denied it, right? He would've looked guilty for hiding it. I think there's more to it. I still think he's hiding something."

"Or, novel idea, humor me," Greg said. "Maybe Jonathan is the one hiding things, and Dellian is totally innocent?"

"They're closing Tricia's case, Greg! They think it was an accident or suicide. They're more interested in pinning the fire on me than finding the truth about that night. But I'm not giving up. I owe it to Tricia to try. Dellian knows about that photo, about that night. If he tells me what he knows, maybe we can find the truth."

"Will this help clear you?" Missy asked.

"For the fire? No. Only a confession from Jonathan or Ethan could. But I should be punished for my part in it anyway." *I'm sorry,* I thought, as I looked at Greg. He wouldn't acknowledge me. I turned back to Missy. "Finding Tricia's cloak might help with the drug charges, though. It might solve everything."

Greg's head snapped up. The accusatory look on his face hurt. He thought this was another plot to get into Dellian's place.

"Don't worry, Greg. I don't expect you to snoop around Dellian's apartment."

"What's so special about her cape?" Missy asked.

"Tricia kept her pipe in the pocket, and I know she wore the cloak that night. I'm positive whoever has it not only put the pipe in my locker to set me up, but was with her right before she died. I think it was Jonathan, but I can't be sure unless I find the cloak."

"Sounds as if the cloak is the *only* thing that can help," Greg said. "So why even bother talking to Dellian?"

"I don't know! Because he was there? Because he has answers?" I shrugged, frustrated. "It's the only place I know to start looking for the truth."

"Okay," Greg said with a nod. "I'll get Dellian to talk to you." His eyes met mine. My heart skipped across my chest. "And if we have to, I'll help you find that cloak too."

It was taking forever.

I sat on my bed, holding my cell phone, waiting for them to call with Mr. Dellian on the line. We figured a phone conversation would go over easier than a face-to-face meeting. As one hour rolled into two, though, I began to feel hopeless. Mom would be back soon, and then, even if they did manage to convince Dellian, I wouldn't be able to speak to him.

What's taking so long? I dialed Greg's cell phone. No answer.

I waited thirty seconds and dialed again. Still no answer.

Oh God, what if they decided to snoop around for the cloak and got caught? Or worse, what if Dellian really *was* responsible for Tricia's death? Would he do something to Greg and Missy? "Three more minutes, then I'm calling Detective King."

Thirty seconds went by. I called Greg's cell again.

"Hey," Greg whispered.

"Oh, thank God!" I said. "What's taking so long?"

"He won't talk. He says he's 'not buying what you're peddling.' Hold on. What?"

I heard Missy's voice, soft and muffled. I strained to hear. Dellian's angry voice suddenly barked through the receiver.

"Phone contact is prohibited, Miss Hart!"

"I know. I . . . I need your help."

"The help you need only an attorney can provide."

I rolled my eyes. I really couldn't stand him. "I'm doing this for Tricia."

"And setting fire to my apartment? Was that for Tricia as well?"

"I'm sorry about that. I didn't know —"

"Goodbye, Miss Hart."

"Wait, please, I'm trying to find the truth."

He gave a sarcastic laugh. "I wasn't born yesterday. I know audio can be cut and spliced into anything you want. Just like a photo, right, Miss Hart?"

"You mean like the photo of you and Tricia?" My heart began to thump faster.

"Are you admitting you created such a photo?"

"No. Are you admitting the photo exists?"

"You're recording this conversation, aren't you? That's the game we're playing here?"

"No, I swear! There's no game. I only want answers about that night. And the photo. Jonathan was behind that, wasn't he?"

"Once again you're using your friends to pull off some scam with Mr. Webb. Doesn't that make you ashamed, Miss Hart? Using your friends?"

"I'm not using them! They're helping me. I know Jonathan's been lying."

"Then why are you helping him?"

"Aren't you listening?" I yelled into the phone. "I'm not helping him anymore! I know you were there that night. What happened?"

Click.

"Ughhhhhhhhh!" I threw my phone across the bed. How do you find the truth when no one will give it to you?

My phone buzzed. I scrambled to grab it. "Meet me in front of your house," Greg said. "Be ready. Dellian said he'll meet with you. I don't want to give him time to change his mind."

I approached Dellian's green truck and peered through the passenger window. "Where's Missy?"

"We dropped her off at home," Mr. Dellian said without looking at me. "My vehicle is too small for all four of us, and I was not getting into Mr. Martin's car."

"Oh." I frowned at Greg. "So we're not talking here?"

Greg gave me a slight shrug of his shoulders.

"Mr. Webb lives in this vicinity, doesn't he?" Mr. Dellian said.

I nodded.

"Four streets over," Greg said.

"Then we're not speaking here. Get in. I'll choose a neutral place."

It was small inside, too small for three people not used to being crammed into a tight place together. The cramped cab made the mutual dislike between me and Dellian almost visible in the air, and I was grateful for the buffer that Greg provided, a protective blanket from the harsh elements on the other side. He sat almost on top of me to avoid straddling the gearshift. His long legs pressed against mine, our shirtsleeves touching.

I tried to focus on the baby picture that hung from a leather strap off the mirror instead of on the growing unease in the pit of my stomach. Even though I sort of believed Dellian was a victim in all of this, I didn't trust him. What if this was a trick? Being within a three-mile radius violated the restraining order. Maybe he was taking us to the police department to slap yet another infraction on my laundry list of offenses. If I were arrested and thrown back in jail, would we lose our house?

I shouldn't be here. A wave of panic rippled through me. Despite the cranked car heater, Greg's body, and my thick sweatshirt, I started to shiver. I gripped the loose cotton fabric of my sweatpants and tried to calm down.

Greg tore my left hand free and squeezed it. My eyes rolled over to his. He smiled and squeezed my hand again. I relaxed a little. It would be okay. Greg had my back. I trusted him.

Dellian pulled into the public library. It was well after nine o'clock in the evening. The place was dark and deserted, lit only by the orange streetlights. He shut the engine off and pointed at a picnic table in the park next door. "We'll talk there."

Greg and I leaped from the truck like inmates escaping from Alcatraz, our pace slowing only when we reached the table. Greg still had my hand clasped in his as we sat down. "Thank you," I whispered.

Dellian slapped a small tape recorder down on the picnic table, making us jump. "If this is a trap, I have this as insurance. The two of you, Roswell Hart and Gregory Martin, came to my residence and requested that I speak with you." He pushed "pause." "Let's keep Miss Cervano out of this, shall we?" He pushed "record" again. "I obliged, but demanded a public setting. We are now at the Birch Hill Library. Is that correct?"

Greg leaned into the tape recorder. "No, sir. That is not correct. *Greg Martin* came to your residence requesting this meeting with Roswell; she was not there. She maintained her three-mile radius at all times until you agreed to this meeting and drove to her residence in your green Toyota pickup truck, license number —"

"Enough!" Dellian hissed. "I stand corrected." Dellian slid the tape recorder in front of me. "Miss Hart, do you agree with this statement?"

I talked into the speaker. "Uh, yes sir, what Greg said."

"Okay." Dellian motioned at me. "You have a confession to make?"

"Not a confession, no." Frowning down at the tape recorder, I tried to assemble what I wanted to say. "I want to know about the night Tricia died, what happened."

"Well, don't we all? I don't know what happened to Miss Farni. If I did, I would have told the police already."

"Like you told them about the photo of you and Tricia?" I asked.

Dellian pushed the "stop" button. "What are you trying to pull here? You know those photos were digitally altered garbage. Of course I denied seeing them! Do you think I'm an idiot?"

Photos? There was more than one? I had to tread carefully.

"No, I don't think you're an idiot. I get why you didn't say anything at first. But Tricia's dead. Shouldn't you tell the police who took the photo? Was it Jonathan? Did he try to blackmail you?"

"Don't play Miss Innocent with me. You and your vile boyfriend made them!"

"I thought you wanted to record this conversation?" Greg asked.

"I want to record the truth, Mr. Martin. So far, I've heard only lies."

This was stupid. Why did I think I could get anything from him? "Look, I didn't help Jonathan with the photo, okay? But I think Tricia did. They set it up, and got you to leave the dance early to do it."

"No. T. would *never* do that to me. Besides, how could they possibly know I'd get sick?"

"Because they put something in your punch," I said. "And she would do it, you know she would, if Jonathan was holding something over her head, like drugs she desperately needed."

The fight seemed to leave Mr. Dellian. "Yes," he whispered. "She might, for that." He let his breath out, slowly. "The ipecac."

"What?" I asked.

"I found an old bottle of ipecac syrup in my truck. It had been in my home first aid kit for so many years, I'd forgotten I had it. I planned to ask T. why it was in the truck when she . . . came back."

"Ipecac induces vomiting, doesn't it?" Greg asked.

I thought about the umbrella Tricia had thrown in his punch at the dance. "That's what they used to make you sick."

Dellian nodded his head. "It induces vomiting, but that's all. I would've known if they were taking pictures — ." He paused and let out a long, sad sigh. "I did doze off after the vomiting finally ceased. I was so violently ill, so exhausted." His voice trailed off.

I softened my voice. "What did Jonathan want? To stay on the team?"

Dellian nodded. "At first, yes."

"Can we record this now?" Greg asked.

Dellian hesitated. "I'd rather not."

"Why?" Greg said. "If it was all staged, you have nothing to worry about."

Mr. Dellian rubbed his face with his hands. "There are too many people this could hurt. I won't have it recorded."

"Oh, come on!" Greg threw his arms up. "You can't just record what incriminates her! Either we record this whole conversation, or we're out of here."

"Greg, no!" I looked at Dellian. "It's okay. I just want the truth. What did Jonathan want?"

"At first he used it to keep his place on the team. I went along with it only because T. was missing. I knew without her around to dispute the photo, it would look exactly how he wanted it to, and there was too much at stake. Abbey was trying to get Tricia out of foster care. An accusation like that, true or false, would ruin that — and we still thought she'd run away. She'd done it before, and she was extremely upset that night. Abbey and I assumed she'd be back once she cooled down a bit. When they found her, I knew Jonathan was behind her death. I was planning to tell the police everything."

"So why didn't you?" I asked.

"He got to me first. He threatened me with things I couldn't afford to have exposed, and with you as his alibi for that evening, I really had no leg to stand on. I had to keep quiet."

"What do you mean 'alibi'?" Greg asked.

"Yeah, and what things did he threaten you with?" I asked.

"T. was a very troubled girl," Mr. Dellian said. "When she was ten, a piece of garbage named Wayne Fresno doped T. up and forced himself on her. Her mother walked in on the assault, stabbed him to death, and is now serving time for it."

"Jesus," Greg said.

I nodded. "She told me."

"Well, she blamed herself," Dellian said. "The girls were separated, placed in foster homes. I met Abbey when she was barely nineteen and fighting for custody of T. Because of her previous drug abuse and young age, they denied her custody. My position at the high school allowed me to get T. help and keep an eye on her, but because she was to have no family contact, we kept my relationship to her a secret. I sent T. to rehab this last time, after she was kicked out of her foster home. We knew if she went back to yet another home, she'd start again. Abbey and I were going through our own problems, but I agreed to let T. live with me, illegally."

"That's what he threatened you with? So what? How could that matter more than nailing Jonathan?" I said.

"It didn't! I told the police all that." Dellian blew an angry puff of air out of his nose. "T. had a way of persuading you to do things for her. She convinced me she could keep clean only by smoking pot." He flashed his eyes up at me for a second. "I had no idea where to find it. I made the mistake of asking Mr. Webb. I don't know where he was buying it from, and I didn't care. I just wanted to help T. He got pushy, cocky, using the drug transactions to elicit favors and special treatment. I had to end the supply to T. to end his harassment."

"That's when she asked me," I said.

"Yes, and thanks to you, Mr. Webb turned her on to crack."

"Are you serious?" Greg said. "How can you blame Roz for something you were doing too? At least Roz wasn't supplying drugs to her every day for what? Weeks? Months? How can you say you cared about Tricia when you were providing the crutch that crippled her?"

"Don't you dare lecture me!" Dellian exploded. "I did care for her! T. was like a daughter to me."

"Then why hide the truth after Tricia was found dead?" I asked. "I mean, I understand being afraid of going to jail, but if you were sure Jonathan was behind her death, why not take that risk?"

"Why not indeed." The look he gave me made me uncomfortable. "Tell me, Miss Hart, if you are truly interested in the truth, why do you continue to lie to the police?"

"I'm not lying about anything!"

Greg nudged me. "You did say you . . . you know," he whispered.

Mr. Dellian flipped on the recorder. "Explain what he's referring to."

"No." Greg snatched it off the picnic table. "We didn't record your indiscretions. We're not recording hers."

"Give me my tape recorder," Dellian demanded.

"Sure." Greg ejected the tape, popped it into his pocket, and handed Dellian the recorder.

While they had a standoff, I debated my next move. Here was my chance to find out if the four of us had really fought, or if Jonathan had made all that up to scare me into helping him. But what if he used my confession to incriminate me? And how could I be sure that whatever he told me was the truth?

Finding out what happened to Tricia was worth the risk.

"I didn't lie to the police," I whispered. "Not intentionally. But I did mislead them."

Dellian and Greg stopped scowling at each other and looked at me.

"I pretended to know about the entire night, but I don't remember anything after leaving the cabin with Jonathan. Except you. I think I remember you there." Dellian was very still, watching me. No, not watching, *examining* me. I stared down at the picnic table. "If you think I lied about something, please tell me what I'm not remembering."

Dellian was quiet for a second. "You told the police that Jonathan drove you home that night, so you obviously have some thoughts as to what did happen? Perhaps Mr. Webb gave an account of the evening?" When I nodded, he asked, "What was his account?"

Greg shook his head. "No, no, no. She's not going to tell you. You're going to tell her." He held up a finger. "One, were you there that night?" He held up a second finger. "Two, did you see Roz? And three" — he held up a third finger — "did you see Tricia? Tell her what you know or take us home."

Dellian shot Greg an annoyed look. "Mr. Martin, would you mind leaving us for a moment? I wish to ask Miss Hart something in private."

"No way," Greg said. "Whatever you need to say, say it in front of me. I'm her human tape recorder."

"Well, human tape recorder or not, I'm trying to protect her privacy. Miss Hart? Do you wish to have him here?"

My privacy? Was he talking about the loft incident? "I want him here, and he knows what happened that night with Jonathan."

"If what you say is true, I doubt very much that he knows what happened with Mr. Webb." He cocked his head. "You asked me what I think you're lying about. Quite frankly, Miss Hart, I don't think, I *know*. You lied about Jonathan taking you home."

I frowned. I'd expected him to say something about the fight with Tricia, not my transportation home. "He didn't take me home?"

"No." Mr. Dellian lowered his voice. "I did. After Mr. Webb tried to force himself on you."

My heart fell to my feet. He tried to . . . ? How could I not remember that?

"He tried to rape her?" Greg said. "And you didn't report it?"

"No," I said. "Tricia attacked me, not Jonathan. He tried to get Tricia off me. That's what you saw—"

"That's what you remember?" Dellian asked me. "Or that's what you were told?"

"Told." I squeezed the word out. My mouth was dry. I needed something to drink. Despite being outside, I needed air. "He said he fought with you."

"Yes." Mr. Dellian nodded. "He did fight with me. That is true."

My hands began to tremble against the metal picnic table. My fingernails scraped the surface with each shake, typing out an SOS.

Greg curled his fingers around mine and held them still. "Why don't you tell us what happened?" Greg said to Dellian.

"I was no longer ill, simply weak and tired when T. called me from the party." He shook his head. "I didn't want to drive. However, T. was frantic, and I couldn't reach Abbey. I took a wrong turn and was coming back around, when I spotted Mr. Webb's vehicle. When my headlights flashed across the side, I saw movement."

I held my breath, afraid to hear what came next.

"He and T. were struggling; T. was trying to drag him from the car. You were sprawled across the front seat. T. said he attacked you. Do you remember that?"

I shook my head. Cotton coated the inside of my mouth. I tried to swallow.

"I threw him off T. and was helping you into my truck when T. attacked him again. I grabbed her, told her to get in the truck too. Mr. Webb took off on foot. T. said she had to 'make things right with you' and went after him. I waited for her. When she didn't come back, I took you home and returned with Abbey. We couldn't find her."

"You just took Roz home? You didn't call the police or tell her mom or take her to the hospital? You just left her there alone?" Greg said.

"Her mother wasn't home. Besides, I had no reason to think

she was not conscious of her surroundings!" He looked at me. "You seemed inebriated, slightly disoriented, but you were speaking. You said you were okay, and you were able to give me your address and tell me where to find your keys. Quite honestly, I expected you to report the incident yourself."

He said it as if I were to blame, as if I should've known.

I should have.

How could my memory betray me like that?

"And when she didn't? Did you bother to ask her about it? Ask her how she was? Anything?" Greg asked.

"I thought she had told the police!" He looked at me. "Remember I asked you if you were able to tell the detective everything?"

"I thought you were talking about the loft," I whispered.

"The loft?" Mr. Dellian asked. When I nodded my head, he continued, "Well, I *thought* you understood me, and when you asked if *I'd* disclosed everything too, I assumed . . ." He sighed. "Your memory loss explains your attitude, I suppose. But at the time, I thought it was an admission that you and Mr. Webb were in on the blackmail together."

Greg shook his head. "She doesn't remember that night. How do we know you're telling her the truth? She's already been told an entirely different version. How do we know which is correct?"

"Did you bring me into my house?" I asked.

"Yes, I helped you in, looked around for your mother. When I determined she wasn't at home, I returned to your sitting room. You were resting on the couch, so I —"

"Covered me with a blanket?"

"Yes, I believe it was orange. It was on the back of the couch."

That ratty old throw blanket. "He's telling the truth." My stomach hurt. "Can we go? I don't feel so good."

Mr. Dellian stood. "I'm truly sorry, Miss Hart. I didn't realize you weren't aware of this. I'll go with you to the police, tell them all of this, and hand over T.'s cloak."

"Tricia's cloak?" I stared at him. "*You* called in the tip and put the pipe in my locker?"

"The tip, no. Until you confessed to helping her buy, I didn't know anything about that day. But I had my suspicions you were involved, especially after the fire—so, yes, when I found the pipe in her cloak, I put it in your locker and suggested to Principal Ratner that your locker be searched."

"But why my locker? You knew Jonathan was knee-deep in this—you'd been getting pot from him. He was blackmailing you! Why plant it in my locker, instead of his?"

"Because I thought you were both to blame, and the way he's always able to talk himself out of trouble, I didn't want to waste the opportunity. You were the easier target."

"Easy target?" Greg said. "Is that why you've harassed her all year? Because she's an easy target?"

Dellian gave me a solemn look. "I'm sorry. I'm not proud of a lot of things I've done regarding you, Miss Hart, and I owe you a thousand more apologies. When I met you, you reminded me of Renny. In denial about your handicap, stubborn, refusing help—and so capable. Renny was sharp like you. I mean truly sharp—his intelligence astounded me. But his body didn't always cooperate with that intelligence and it made him stubborn. I thought it was okay to let him refuse help. I thought he could still make it out there, that he'd fight the odds and win. When he committed suicide, I" — he rubbed his face with his hands — "I really was trying to help you, Miss Hart. I didn't want you to fall like Renny. But my God! You are so stubborn and pigheaded! The more you fought, the more I lost sight of the fact that I was trying to help you — I let my temper get the best of me, and my tactics went a bit overboard."

"Tactics? Overboard? Let's forget suspension and expulsion. How is planting evidence a teaching tactic?" Greg said. "You make me sick."

I knew I should be angry too, angrier than Greg. But my body was too numb to react to anything anymore. I could only stare, disbelieving.

Dellian nodded. "I make myself sick. I apologize profusely, I do. I thought you were working with Mr. Webb."

"She doesn't want your apology —"

"If you cared so much for Tricia" — I interrupted — "why didn't you bury the cloak with her?"

"I loved her, very much," he said. "I didn't have it then. It appeared in my apartment during the fire, along with copies of that photo."

"Jonathan," I whispered.

"Yes, and Ethan perhaps; the two are never far from one another. Luckily, neither has any real intellect. I found the items long before the officers entered the room. If you wish to go right now,

I'll tell the police this. Maybe between the two of us, we can finally put Jonathan away."

Away? I thought as we walked across the dark lot to Dellian's truck. I didn't want to see Jonathan put *away*. I wanted to see him *fry*.

"How can you lie there and say nothing?" Greg said as he paced back and forth in my room. It was almost one in the morning. He wasn't supposed to be over, but Mom wasn't home from her "drink" yet, and I didn't feel like being alone. There was a murderer-attempted rapist-arsonist-drug dealer-asshole extraordinaire in my neighborhood. "I'm so mad, I could punch something!"

We'd returned from our unsuccessful trip to the police station. Detective King told us that because Mr. Dellian hadn't actually seen Jonathan attempting to rape me — he had only witnessed Tricia attacking Jonathan — our new information was merely "speculation and circumstantial"; she couldn't issue an arrest warrant for Jonathan.

It wasn't fair. Jonathan was walking around free while Tricia was dead and I was stunned and numb, feeling betrayed by my own body. How could my body let Jonathan near me after what he tried to do? And the fact that I couldn't remember wasn't a blessing anymore. Detective King said attempted rape was hard enough to prove with a clearly witnessed account — the fact that I had no memory, and Dellian hadn't seen the attack, meant the district attorney probably wouldn't even bother.

I tried to picture that night, over and over, tried to focus my brain, but got nowhere. Just as my macular degeneration blocked objects, my mind was blocking the assault.

"Roz?" Greg sat on the edge of the bed. "Talk to me. What are you thinking?"

"He's gonna get away with it," I said. "Doesn't it matter that he's guilty? That all the evidence points to him? Why isn't that enough to arrest him?"

"They'll get him," Greg said. "You heard Dellian. Jonathan lacks intellect. Stupid people slip up eventually. When he does, they'll have their proof."

"Maybe we could help him slip up?" I rolled over on my elbow. "Remember how we helped Jonathan when he was stuck in the snow? When I got his jack out of the trunk?"

Greg nodded.

"His spare was on a brown cloth, the same color and texture as Tricia's cloak. Do you think it was?"

He shrugged. "Even if they find fibers in the trunk, it's still circumstantial. Like trapping Sasquatch. Plenty of footprints and fur have been found, but it's always explained away. You have to catch Sasquatch to prove he exists."

I sighed. I knew he was right. "The only way to catch Jonathan is to get him to confess. But how? What would make him talk?"

Greg shook his head. "No idea."

Fear. Fear would get him talking. I sat up. "What if a witness claimed to have seen Jonathan with Tricia that night after everyone left the party? If he thought he was about to be arrested, maybe he'd try to set Dellian up again."

"What could he possibly frame him with? He's already left the cloak, the photos — what else would he use?"

I thought for a minute. "What if I tell him I remember that night — tell him I won't press charges if he tells the police what happened to Tricia and fesses up to the fire? At least we'd get him on something, right?" But even as I said it, I knew I couldn't do it. I wanted him to pay for everything he'd done — or tried to do.

"But you *don't* remember. All you know is what Dellian claims to have seen."

"Are you saying you don't think it happened?"

"I'm saying you don't remember what happened and he knows that. You'd have to give him some details to prove you suddenly remember. What if you say the wrong thing and Jonathan catches on?" Greg shook his head. "No. No way will you be alone with that creep again. We'll come up with something else."

"Well, there is nothing else!" I flopped back on the bed.

Greg stretched out next to me. "Then we let the police handle it."

"Please," I said with a snort. "Tricia's corpse could walk in and tell the police every sordid detail, and they'd still say it's *circumstantial* and *speculation —*"

That's it! I sat up again. "Who would have the most incriminating things to say? Who would Jonathan fear most?" I didn't wait for a response. "Tricia!" I leaped to my feet. "I know how to get Jonathan to talk!"

My excitement was drowned out by the hum of the garage door opening. "Crap! You have to go."

"But what's the plan?" Greg asked as he pushed his feet into his shoes.

"I'll explain tomorrow. Just get Dellian and Heather over to your house tomorrow afternoon, okay? Fritz and Missy too. I think this is more of a group project."

I spent all day planning Jonathan's demise. It really was like planning a school project—except the outcome had more weight than anything I'd ever done for school. The plan depended most on Heather, Dellian, and me. Dellian I wasn't so worried about, but Heather? I hadn't spoken to her since the fire. I wouldn't blame her if she refused to help. But I needed her. I wasn't sure if I could trust anyone else with her part.

As soon as school got out—three o'clock on the dot—Greg called. "I'll be there soon. I'm bringing Fritz and Heather with me. Missy will meet us there. Mr. Dellian said he'll help if he can, but"—Greg mimicked Dellian—"'I cannot risk tarnishing my reputation any further with illegal antics.' He said I could be his human tape recorder, though."

"I thought you were *my* human tape recorder." I laughed.

"I was protecting you when I said that," he said.

A ton of emotions rushed through me. "I know. Thank you." I bit my lip to keep my voice steady. "Greg? I couldn't have done it yesterday without you. I mean it. You were great. I'm so sorry about the fire and Jonathan and—"

"Stop, I forgave you hours ago. I'm leaving school now. As soon as I round everyone up, I'll be by to get you."

"I'll meet you at your house," I said, then explained. "Detective King's bringing me. We can't afford to screw this up."

When Detective King and I arrived, Missy was just walking over, and Heather was dragging Fritz's wheelchair out of Greg's back seat. "Here." I grabbed the handles from Heather with a nervous smile. "Glad you came. I —"

She threw her arms around me. "I missed you! I can't believe everything! First the fire, then jail, now rape." She slapped her hand over her mouth.

"It's okay. I figured he'd tell you." My bottom lip trembled. "I'm sorry about the fire. Really. I never should've used you like that. There's no excuse."

Heather shrugged. "You didn't know they'd really set a fire. You thought you were helping."

I shook my head. "It doesn't matter what I thought I was doing. It was wrong." I turned to Fritz. "Fritz, I feel sick about what happened that day. I am so, so sorry."

"Hey, we're cool, okay?" Fritz smiled. "Totally cool."

"So what's the plan?" Greg asked once we were all inside.

I grinned at him. "We're going to catch Sasquatch to prove he exists."

"Huh?" Heather and Missy said in unison.

Greg waved his hand to quiet them. "Explain."

"Remember that article my dad sent about Big Foot in the Alps? It turned out to be a hoax some guys pulled with an ape costume. But until the lab ran the tests, the guy who found the alleged corpse thought he'd seen the real thing. He told people all sorts of stories about seeing Big Foot, while his friends were laughing it up because they knew it was a hoax."

"Fascinating," Missy said.

"Yeah, seriously," Heather said. "I thought you had a plan?"

"Just let her talk, you two," Fritz said.

Greg's eyes were glued on me, a smile creeping across his face. "I like the way you think."

I couldn't help smiling. "I like that you get the way I think."

Heather rolled her eyes. "I'd like to *think* you both upside the head! What are you two yammering about?"

Detective King looked at her watch. "Could we speed this up a bit?"

"Okay, okay," I said. "Right now, Jonathan's free because Tricia's about the only person who could pin a crime on him. And she's dead."

"But if she weren't, she'd know everything. All the details. The perfect witness," Greg finished.

"Exactly," I said.

"But she *is* dead," Heather said.

"Maybe not," I said. "Maybe the coroner made a mistake and misidentified the body, or she faked her death."

"Or she's come back from the grave for revenge," Greg said. "I've seen her. Haven't you, Roz?"

Fritz chuckled. "I've seen her."

"Her ghost?" Missy asked. "You've seen it?"

"Not for real, doofus!" Heather said. "We're going to pretend."

"Maybe I talked to her," I said, "and she told me all about that night —"

The playful grin on Greg's face clouded over and dissipated. "No way are you putting yourself in jeopardy! Twirling around a few yards away from him or leaving messages is one thing, but you are not going to be alone with him. He'll hurt you."

"How else would we get a confession from him? It's the only way," I said.

"Can't we just pretend she's alive and see what he does?" Greg looked at Detective King for help.

"It's worth a try," Detective King said. "If we get him rattled enough, he may incriminate himself on a wiretap or even confess. It has to be planned carefully, though. What exactly did you have in mind, Roswell?"

"Nothing too dramatic. I figure for him to believe she's alive, he has to hear it indirectly, you know? From people who aren't tangled in any of this."

"You want to spread a rumor," Missy said. "I could totally do that in my sleep."

"Starting it is cake," Fritz said. "It's the rumor that's tricky. People have to believe it — and there was a funeral, man. A casket, with a body."

"That hardly anyone went to," I said. "If everyone who was there knows we're doing this, there're no problems."

Detective King shook her head. "We'll have to tell a few people, obviously, like Abbey and Rodney Dellian, but I recommend keeping as many out of the loop as possible."

Ruth, JJ, and Jeffrey would be ecstatic to hear she was alive — and I didn't want to hurt them like that. But Jonathan knew them. What if he asked them? Tortured them for the truth? As much as it hurt to let them believe she was alive, I realized it was safer for them not to know what we were doing. "Okay, we don't tell anyone the truth unless Detective King clears it, agreed?"

Everyone nodded in agreement.

"All right. We say the coroner somehow misidentified the body. That Tricia really ran away to Seattle. She called her sister and is coming back in a few days. Detective King, can you put surveillance on Jonathan?"

"Already have."

"Good. Once Tricia is supposedly in town, you know Jonathan will be curious. When he comes looking, the police will alert Abbey, and we'll make sure Jonathan sees Tricia. If I can't contact him" — I looked at Greg — "then hopefully seeing her will be enough to get him rattled and talking."

Missy frowned. "How's he going to see Tricia, though?"

"Heather lives in the same building." I smiled at Heather. "How are you at playing dead girls?"

Heather grinned back. "Do I get to wear her cape?"

Seventeen days after

Missy and Fritz started telling Tricia's bizarre story at school on Monday. Like the flame from a lit cigarette dropped into dry grass, the rumor quickly spread and took on a life of its own. Since I was expelled, I didn't get to hear it told over and over, but the day after it was set in motion, Mom came home from work talking about it. She'd heard the rumor from one of the other cosmetic reps, who'd heard it on some morning talk radio show.

Most people focused on the incompetence of the police and coroner's office — which meant Detective King had to inform the coroner of the plan — but a few radio and TV hosts began calling Abbey, requesting interviews with Tricia. Detective King said we'd need to speed up the timeline before the situation got too out of hand. So Wednesday, Fritz and Missy set the second rumor in motion: Tricia would be arriving home on Friday.

That morning I sat alone at home watching a *Ghost Team* marathon, wishing I could be at school with the others to see how the news was received. At 10:35, just as the ghost hunter was telling the ghost to bang on the wall, my doorbell rang. I thought maybe it was Greg, skipping class to hang with me — crazy, yes, but what else did I have to fantasize about?

I flew to the door and ripped it open without peeking through the peephole.

Jonathan stood there.

It wasn't that I didn't expect Jonathan to contact me. I did. We all did. We knew that if he talked to anyone other than Ethan, it would be me. That's why they put a tap on my landline and cell. And they said if he attempted a face-to-face encounter, they'd warn me, since Jonathan was under surveillance at all times.

No one had called to warn me, so why would I have expected him?

"Jonathan?" I stuck my body in the way and tried to casually close the door to eliminate any available space.

"Hey, Beautiful," he said with a grin as if we were still friends. "What's going on?"

My pulse rocketed. I tried to stay calm. "Oh, just watching some TV —"

"I mean with Tricia." He pushed at the door with his palm. "You hear the rumors?"

I buckled my arm firmly against the door. "I can't have anyone over. Mom's . . . sleeping."

He nodded and lowered his voice. "I thought it was a practical joke, but everyone's talking."

"Yeah, crazy, huh?" I aimed my eyes on his to give the appearance of eye contact, even though I was looking at the door frame next to his head. For once I was glad for my disability. I couldn't pull this off if I had to look into his eyes for real.

"Seems weird. You think it's for real? That she's really alive?"

"Of course it's for real!" Could he hear my heart pounding?

See it jumping from my chest? "I mean, why wouldn't it be? Everyone's talking about it. Who would be sick enough to make that up?"

"Yeah, pretty cool if she is alive. Just seems crazy." He was quiet for a second. "You went to her funeral — didn't you notice it wasn't her? I mean, damn!"

"Yeah, I guess no one looked closely — she was, you know, in the water a while and all." I had to make sure he believed this. I took a deep breath through my nose, letting it out slowly to calm myself. "I heard she's coming home Friday."

He nodded. "I heard that too." He smiled. "You wanna go with me, check it out?"

Go with him? Was he insane? After everything he'd done to me? "I don't think so, Jonathan. Last time I did something with you, I landed in jail."

"Sorry, Beautiful." His hand reached up to touch my face, but I flinched away. He cocked his head. "You scared of me?"

"No," I said, hoping my snort sounded sincere. "I'm pissed at you! I was jailed *and* expelled, thanks to you."

"I was afraid they'd get me in the slammer too, you know? Was it rough?"

"Jail? No, it was a trip; a real kick in the pants."

He gave me an amused smile. "You really crack me up sometimes. Why'd we break up again?"

I glared at him.

"Oh, yeah." He smirked. "Come with me Friday, please? She'll talk to me if you're there."

"Why do you need to talk to her? She's alive, right? That means we're off the hook — well, you are. I still have a drug charge and the fire . . ." *God! I'm not supposed to talk him out of going,* I thought as panic over the whole plan began to rise. *But if he tries to speak to her, Heather's cover will be blown and he'll realize it was a trick.* How was I supposed to get him to drive by or hide in the bushes and watch for Tricia without talking to her?

He studied me for a second, as if deciding to tell me something. "Look, I gotta talk to her because — you know that photo you found in D.'s desk?"

I swallowed. "Yes?"

"Tricia and I set that all up. I know as soon as Dellian gets the chance, he'll get her to confess to the police. I gotta get her to keep her mouth shut. If you go, I'll tell the cops I made that anonymous tip, that I was with you when you took that money out" — he paused — "and I'll tell them Ethan started the fire."

He had just confessed! And . . . I had nothing on me to get it. Damn it! This plan was working, though. "You'd do that?" I said. "Tell the police the truth? All I have to do is go with you to see Tricia?" With me there, I could keep him from talking to Heather, and maybe I could get him to confess on the way over too.

He held up two fingers. "Scout's honor."

Scout's honor? Did he even know what a Scout was? "Okay," I said, "I'll go with you Friday." I cracked a smile as I shut the door. For once with Jonathan, I was running the show.

"No, no, no!" Greg said. "Absolutely not! She's not going with him."

It was Friday afternoon. Everyone, including Mr. Dellian and Abbey, had met at Greg's house to go over the plan and get ready. I told Detective King what I had learned from Jonathan about our change in plans but had purposely not told Greg. I knew he would try to talk me out of it. And I *was* doing this. I had to.

"Greg, it's fifteen minutes between my house and Dellian's apartment, okay?" I said. "Besides, he'll be too focused on seeing Tricia to do anything on the way there." My stomach was in knots. I hoped I was right.

"No. You're not going in his car alone!" Greg said.

"We'll have an officer tailing them," Detective King said.

Dellian frowned. "Jonathan is an imbecile, but he is observant. How do you think he got to Miss Hart's house without your officers knowing on Wednesday? If he spots this tail, he will get suspicious. A jilted lover following them might work, however." Dellian looked directly at Greg. "Your presence will not only give you peace of mind, it will occupy Mr. Webb the entire ride. He can't resist playing the conquering king."

"I don't want him 'conquering' anything!" Greg said. "That's the whole point!"

"Greg, calm down," Detective King warned. "Roswell will be fine. I'll be listening to the conversation with a wire the entire time, police cars seconds away if needed, and at the apartment, officers will be positioned inside and out."

Greg's concern rattled me. What if he was right? Jonathan couldn't be trusted; he'd proven that time and again. What if he *did* try something? I needed reassurance. I left Greg pleading his case and sought out Heather and Missy. They were bleaching Heather's hair in the bathroom.

Yikes. "Too blond, don't you think?" I asked when I saw her hair. "And your complexion is several shades darker." I slumped down on the edge of the tub. This wasn't going to work. "He won't be happy with a quick glimpse. We can't pull off a close-up. This plan was stupid."

"Come on, it's a great plan, Roz." Heather scrubbed her hair dry with a towel. "Have faith, I'm a professional."

"With professional makeup." Missy waved a large cosmetic trunk at me.

"Roz?" Detective King peeked in. "You ready for the bug?"

The fear in my stomach twisted tighter. I followed her back into the living room.

I expected an elaborate wiring system taped under my clothing. Instead, Detective King handed me a tiny button-shaped microphone. "This should be as close to your mouth as possible. Your lapel is best." She frowned at my gray, logoless sweatshirt. "That's too plain. You need a collar or buttons, something to attach it to that won't be obvious."

"I've got something." Greg came back a few seconds later with a black Nine Inch Nails T-shirt. "The microphone should blend in with this, but just in case . . ." He handed me a collared dress shirt. "Wear this overtop to cover it."

Greg's dryer-sheet smell emanated from the shirts and filled the tiny bathroom where I was changing. Just breathing it in calmed me, made me confident. I pulled the T-shirt over my head, slipped my arms into the dress shirt, and rolled the sleeves. *I can do this,* I told my reflection. *I can totally do this.*

Detective King mounted the receiver near my collarbone. "Try not to fiddle with this too much, okay? These wireless receivers have a decent range, but reception can be spotty if they're not placed correctly."

"That's reassuring," I mumbled.

"You'll be fine." She began putting an identical receiver on Mr. Dellian. "If things look dicey in the car, get away from him and call me. You have your cell phone?"

"That's the backup plan? Get away and call you?" I shoved my phone in the front pocket of my jeans. "What if he's going one hundred miles an hour? What then?"

"If he's going that fast, we'll have cause to stop and arrest him for speeding. Relax, okay?" She nodded at Greg. "Keep your eye on her."

"Oh, I will," Greg said.

"Now when you get there with Jonathan, you go straight to the apartment, even if you haven't recorded any info from him yet, okay? Abbey will open the door; Heather will be visible from the doorway in the other room. As soon as Jonathan's seen her, Rodney will confront him. You come inside then. You hear me? Rodney will do the rest."

A sudden gasp from Abbey interrupted the detective.

Heather had emerged from the bathroom wearing Tricia's cloak, her eyes deep black circles, her face a pasty white. For a split second it really did seem as if I was looking at Tricia's ghost.

"How'd you do that?" I said. "You look so . . . real."

"I know, right?" Heather said. "Missy's a goddess with the makeup."

"Well done, Miss Cervano," Mr. Dellian said. He put his arm around Abbey's shaking shoulders. She'd started to sob.

No one spoke. I'm sure we were all thinking the same thing, though. How sobering it was to have Heather standing there as Tricia's look-alike, when the real Tricia would never get a chance to stand there.

Determination and anger overtook me. This plan had to work. Jonathan had to fry for everything he'd done. He was nothing but a user. He had used Tricia and then just thrown her away. Heck, he'd used us all in one way or another, all to serve himself. I wasn't going to stop until I had recorded a confession from him for something. I didn't care what. As long as his ass was sitting in jail, I'd be happy.

"It's nearly six," Greg said. "I should get Roz home before he gets there. Fritz? You coming with me?"

"Yeah." Fritz moved his chair toward the door. Heather bent down to give him a hug. "Be careful," Fritz whispered.

The slight tremble in Fritz's voice tore at my confidence again. I expected it from Greg — anything out of his control made him nervous — but Fritz? He was Mr. Daredevil. Maybe this *was* a bad idea. If something went really wrong, would we be okay? Could the police keep Heather and me safe? I pulled the collar of Greg's borrowed shirt up to my nose, hoping to reclaim some of that calm I'd had earlier.

As if reading my mind, Mr. Dellian put an unexpected arm around me. "Don't worry, Miss Hart. You're a survivor. Use those instincts of yours." He held out a small canister. "Pepper spray, just in case," he said. "We both know the law can't always protect us."

Pepper spray? What the hell was I doing heading into a situation that might require pepper spray? "Thanks," I said, willing my voice to be steady despite the sense of horror that was taking place inside me. I clenched the spray in my fist and gave the room a shaky smile. "Break a leg!" I told Heather, then followed Fritz and Greg out the door.

On the way to my house, Greg and Fritz made small talk about the weather while I rolled the pepper spray around inside my palm, going over the plan in my head.

"I recorded a playlist for you," Greg said as he walked me inside.

"I'm going to be talking to Jonathan, not listening to music, Greg."

"I know. Actually it's just one song." He pushed "play" and handed me an earphone. "'Roswell's Spell' by Chevelle." He blushed. "It reminds me of you."

I put it up to my ear. The music was harsh and shrill and . . . perfect. Anything softer would've made me lose it. "Thanks." I handed the player back to him.

"No, keep it," he said, "until this is over." He tried to hug me.

I pushed him away. If I let myself feel his arms, I'd crumble. If I crumbled, I'd never go through with this plan. "I can't," I whispered. My voice cracked. Tears came to my eyes.

"That's okay," he said, walking backwards toward his car. "We can save that for later too." He opened his car door and looked at me. "Be safe, Roz. For me?"

Waiting inside for Jonathan proved too claustrophobic. The plan plowed through my mind like a freight train, over and over, on a never-ending track. The more I thought about it, the more the walls seemed to close in on me, until there didn't seem to be enough air for my constricted lungs to breathe.

I went outside and tried swinging on the porch to derail my thoughts. The motion made me queasy. I stopped and tried listening to the song Greg had given me. The loud, abrasive music, perfect only moments before, contributed to the chaos in my head. I ripped the earphones out and tried to just breathe.

Greg made several approaches in his hovercraft of a car while I waited. Although I couldn't see him, I could picture him, that intense look on his face as he passed. The image was enough to shoot blast after blast of unwanted adrenaline through my veins until my body was so overdosed, I thought I'd explode.

"I just want to get this over with already!" I fingered the corner of my shirt, folding and refolding the cotton material while I waited.

The bass vibration warned me before the flash of red sped down the street. I slipped Greg's MP3 player into my shirt pocket and, with an all-too-familiar rush of panic, stood up. I groped my back pocket until I felt the pepper spray, and then walked toward Jonathan's car.

"I saw Loser driving around the neighborhood," Jonathan said. "What's his deal?"

Showtime. I rolled my eyes and tried to sound annoyed. "He's mad." I climbed into his car. "I told him we were going to see Tricia, and he kind of got pissed."

Jonathan grinned. "A little jealous, huh?" He threw the gear into reverse and squealed out of the driveway. A few seconds later, he glanced in the rearview mirror. "Loser's tailing us."

Before I had a chance to respond, Jonathan slammed his foot on the gas pedal and floored it. Instead of turning right toward Heather's, he yanked left. We flew through two stop signs and an intersection, and then barreled down a side road.

"Ha!" Jonathan checked the mirror again. "Loser!" he screamed out the window. As if Greg could hear him. He was now miles away in a cloud of dust.

I peeled my fingers off the armrest. "You didn't have to do that. He was just —"

"Stalking you? You don't need a loser like that following you. It's creepy."

You're creepy. I wanted out of the car. Away from Jonathan. I was wrong. I couldn't do this.

I looked out the window for the familiar purple blob. Greg was long gone, frantically searching the route to Dellian's, while we sped along in the opposite direction. "You can turn around now. I'm pretty sure you lost him."

"Oh, I *know* I lost him." He grinned at me. "Forgot to tell you. Change of plans."

"What?" Change of plans? He couldn't change plans. *I* was making the plans, not Jonathan!

"You know Dellian won't let me talk to Tricia if I go there. So I e-mailed her, told her to meet me at our spot."

"Your spot?" Oh God. What was I supposed to do now? Where was he taking me? "What if she doesn't check her e-mail? Shouldn't we go by the apartment first? I could go in, tell her where to meet us."

"Already got that covered, Beautiful."

Covered? I was really starting to freak now. If Greg had been there, he'd have a quote for me about best-laid plans. Why hadn't I come up with Plan B? Why hadn't the cops? Oh wait, that's right. There *was* a Plan B. What had Detective King said? Get away and call?

I glanced out at the houses and trees zooming by the window. Great advice. Jump at this speed? How fast was he going? Sixty? Eighty? Could I survive that?

He slowed a bit as he changed lanes. My chance to get out.

I clutched the door handle.

Took a breath.

But I couldn't open the door.

What if my head hit the concrete? Or the car behind us ran me over? I rubbed the cold metal between my fingers, debating. Stay in danger, or jump into danger?

He took the on-ramp to the highway and sped up again. Crap. We were heading out of town. Going fast again, too fast to escape.

Now what? We'd lost Greg. No one knew where we were going. Even if Abbey thought to read Tricia's e-mail, nobody would know where Jonathan and Tricia's "spot" was.

I reached for the pepper spray and remembered. My microphone. Were we still within range? I had to hope we were. It was all I had. I looked out the window again. Where could we be going? What was out here? Woods? Campgrounds?

Birch Hill.

"Are we going to Birch Hill?" I said into my collar.

"You'll see."

His smug look made my skin crawl, my mind race, my heart pound. Was he on to me? Had he figured out this was a hoax, and I was the key player?

"Could we stop at Birch Hill? I have to pee."

"Sure." He shrugged.

His response made me feel better. If he was on to me, he would've said no. I sat back, trying to relax. Even if they couldn't hear me, maybe Greg or the police or Dellian would think to go to Birch Hill. It was the last place Tricia had been seen; it was a logical place to look for me.

The big yellow sign announcing Birch Hill Recreational Park came into view up ahead. Once Jonathan pulled onto the park's dirt road, I'd run. There were trees, trails, and thick tangles of bushes to lose myself in until the police or Greg showed up.

I took a calming breath and released the panic inside me.

We blew by the sign.

"Wait! Where are you going? It's back there!" I whirled around, watching the sign disappear behind us.

"Forgot," Jonathan said. "Sorry."

I slowly turned around, swallowing the fear in my throat. Was he sorry? Had he really forgotten? Or was he messing with me? Toying with me because he knew I was toying with him? "I can go in the bushes, I guess."

"Cool." He nodded. "It's not much farther." He slowed as he said this and turned onto a paved road almost hidden by over-grown grass and stark bushes.

"Where are we?" I said into the microphone. "Another camp-ground?"

Should I jump? He was driving slower now to keep his precious car from getting scratched by the low-hanging branches. I'd scrape myself up a bit if I jumped out, but I'd be in those bushes and running before he could stop the car and chase me.

My pulse pounded. It was now or never. Again I grasped the door handle. Again I hesitated. It wasn't my safety that stopped me this time, though. It was Jonathan's.

If I ran, I'd probably be safe, but so would he. This was all for Tricia, for justice. Who would stick it to this pompous prick then? We'd still have no proof of anything. And he'd be wiser, more cautious; he'd never fall for another trick. This would all be for nothing. He'd be laughing, thinking he was too clever for us. Meanwhile, I'd be serving some sort of time for the fire, and Tricia? She'd still be dead with no hope of vindication for her death.

I loosened my grip on the handle and slid my hand under the tails of Greg's shirt to my back pocket. My fingers pushed against the denim of my jeans and slowly rolled the canister up until it fell into my palm. My fist closed around the cold metal.

The pepper spray would buy me some time if I did need to run. But I was here to find the truth. Truth seekers like my father, searching for proof of extraterrestrial life, paranormal beings, Big Foot, the Loch Ness monster — none of them would get this close only to run in fear. I wouldn't either.

Jonathan turned left at a fork in the road and parked.

I perked up at the sight of the clearing ahead. There was the picnic table, the lineup of beer bottles Ruth and I had left. "We're by the river, right?" I leaned into the receiver. "We looked for Tricia's cloak here after her funeral. The Birch Hill Lodge is upriver a ways, right? The ice bridge downriver?" I looked around. "I don't see Tricia." Or anyone. How long would it take the police to get here? *If* they were coming. Maybe they hadn't heard me.

Jonathan wasn't listening. He had his phone in his hand, reading a text. "A frickin' trap. I knew it!"

That didn't sound good. I popped the door open, ready to sprint. "What's a trap?"

He shook his head. "Just says 'a trap, on my way.'" He handed me the phone.

"Who's on the way?" I took it from him and pretended to read the text. If he was showing it to me, my cover wasn't blown.

"Ethan. I sent him to grab Tricia."

Oh no. Ethan knew it was a trap. Time to go. Even if I did get a confession before Ethan got here, there was a good chance this microphone was a bust, since there was no sign of the police anywhere. What good was a confession if only I heard it?

I stepped out of the car, intent on maintaining total calmness. "I really have to pee. I'm gonna go in the bushes over there."

"Okay, you want a beer?" he asked, popping the trunk.

His question took me aback. "A beer?"

"Yeah, I brought some to celebrate with Tricia. For being alive and all. No sense in wasting it. Something to do until Ethan shows anyway."

"Uh, sure. Be right back." I rushed into the woods, focused on escaping. Barely a yard in, my toe caught in a root and I hit the ground with a thud. The canister of pepper spray flew through the air and out of sight.

"You okay?" Jonathan ran up behind me. "You're about to lose your music."

I looked down. Greg's music player dangled from my shirt pocket. The one Dellian had banned from class. The one Greg once recorded lectures with. I could get a confession after all! I casually pushed "record" and set it back in my pocket. "I think I'll wait to go." I walked back toward the clearing. "Don't want Ethan surprising me midpee. He'll be here soon, right? What do you think he meant by 'a trap'?"

"Whatever it is, Dellian's behind it." He pointed to my cheek. "You're bleeding. I've got napkins in the glove box." He returned to the open trunk.

I ducked into the car and found some fast-food napkins poking out from underneath what looked like a bag of pot. "Bag of pot, glove box," I muttered into the recorder.

"Find some?" Jonathan came around the side of the car and handed me a beer.

I wiped at the blood and then took the beer. "A trap does sound like Dellian." I pretended to take a sip. "You know he planted her pipe in my locker?"

"No shit?" He took a big swig of beer. "He's trying to get me too, for that photo. That's got to be what this is about."

"How exactly did you get it?"

"I planned it. I needed ammo to get him off my back, and she'd do anything for a fix. He wasn't supposed to start puking, though; that wasn't planned. But we still got the shot." He grinned. "A picture worth a thousand bribes."

I frowned to myself. Wasn't supposed to puke? What did he think ipecac syrup did? "What was he supposed to do if not puke?"

"I gave Tricia some stuff to slip him, to loosen him up, make him out of it, you know? We were gonna get him out to his truck, then take the picture. The puking messed that up a bit, had to think on our feet."

"What did you give her to" — I tried to keep the disgust out of my voice — "loosen him up?" It was hard to be casual and friendly. So hard.

"A party drug," he said with a shrug.

"A party drug? What Tricia had in her when she died?" I said. "What I was slipped? That sort of thing?"

"Yeah, that sort of thing." He studied me over the top of his bottle. Fear crept through me, but I wasn't backing down. I couldn't let him scare me. "We're in this together, right?" he asked. "You and me?"

"Are you joking?" My hand trembled. I gripped the neck of the bottle. "Why would I be? You just admitted to slipping me a date-rape drug!"

"What? No, I didn't! I said that's what I gave to Tricia for Dellian. I swear. I never gave you any!"

"And I'm supposed to believe you?" I wanted to scream *You tried to rape me,* but I knew if I did, he'd shut down. I had to get more first, get it all, before I accused him of that. "You told the police I bought Tricia drugs and you let me take the fall for the fire!"

"I said I was sorry. I couldn't admit I'd been there with D. on my back, telling the cops I was selling drugs to Tricia. If they knew I put the photos in there, my ass would be toast."

"Your ass should've been toast! You *were* selling her drugs, weren't you?"

"Not like some dealer on the corner, the way D. was telling it. I helped her score sometimes, to help her out. Same as you did."

"No. *I* tried to help her get pot so she could stay off the heroin. *You* went and bought her crack — with *my* money!"

He gave me a sheepish look. "Actually, that's why I'm cool with telling the cops I was with you at the ATM. I didn't buy any drugs with your money. I just pocketed it."

"What?" I stared at him. "Then how'd she get the crack that day?"

"Ethan said he couldn't score the pot until the next day. When I told him the situation, he offered up some crack for free, said he'd let it slide, this being her first time."

"Of course he let it slide! He knew she'd get addicted and be back, you idiot! Geez, Jonathan — she was trying to pull herself up. To finally take control of her life, on *her* terms. You took that from her. You pushed her right back into the gutter! How could you do that to her?"

"Come on, you saw her. She was desperate! If I didn't get her something, she would've just gone somewhere else. She's an addict! That's not my fault."

"You could've said no. You could've turned her away." Bile rose up in my throat. "But you liked her desperate, didn't you? It made getting what you wanted easy, right? Like that night in the loft? That was just another drug deal, wasn't it?"

"Yeah," he said, and actually sounded remorseful. "But it's not the way you make it sound. Tricia never had enough money and was always begging me to spot her so she could buy. The girl was maxing me out. I couldn't afford to pay for her habit anymore without getting paid back. So I made a deal with her. If she helped me take down Dellian by setting up that photo, I'd wipe the debt clean and score her crack a few more times. But then she wanted to back out — she came upstairs begging me to erase the photos. I told her she owed me way too much money to back out, and I'd already scored more crack for her from Ethan that night. That's when she came up with an alternative payment plan." He shrugged. "It was her idea. It was mutual."

"Mutual? That's what you call sex for drugs?" Anger took over. "And how about when it isn't mutual? When you use drugs for sex? What do you call that?" I was shaking all over. "I call that rape, Jonathan! Rape!"

"What?" He stared at me. "I told you it was mutual! I didn't rape her!"

"How'd it all go, exactly? When I interrupted the alternate payment, what? You got mad? Thought you'd get the rest from me?" My body was in convulsions, trembling uncontrollably now. "But Tricia saw you. She wasn't screaming crazy shit! She was telling you to stop! She attacked you because you were trying to rape me!"

"What the—?" Jonathan's mouth was on the ground. Eyes wide. "Beautiful, I never—" He reached for me.

I swung the full bottle of beer at him, smashing it between his eyes. It hit his forehead with a dull thud but didn't break. Beer foamed up, spilling everywhere. He stumbled backwards, a shocked look on his face.

Something rustled in the bushes behind us.

The police!

I didn't wait to see if Jonathan regained his balance. I flew into the bushes toward the noise. Leafless branches scratched and tore at me as I leaped through the underbrush, desperate to fall into Greg's arms.

I slammed into Ethan's arms instead. He was carrying a limp cloaked body.

"Going somewhere?" Ethan shoved me backwards with Heather's body. "Party's just starting. We're all here now."

"What'd you do to her?" I said to Ethan.

Jonathan came up behind me, grabbed my hands, and pulled me to his chest. "Why the hell'd you hit me?"

Ethan stepped around us and tossed Heather on the ground like a rag doll.

"What did you do to her?" I said again, trying to pull free from Jonathan.

"You need to chill," Ethan said as he took a bottle of beer from the six-pack Jonathan had brought, twisted the top off, and threw it into the bushes. He stuck two fingers into his pants' pocket and pulled out a pill. He grinned at me as he dropped the pill into the bottle. "This'll help us all get friendly." He shoved the bottle at me.

"Don't give her that shit!" Jonathan let go of me and slapped the bottle away.

I rushed over and knelt beside Heather. She was breathing. That was good. Good? What was she doing here? How did Ethan get ahold of her without anyone stopping him? She was supposed to be with Dellian and Abbey, surrounded by police, protected. Safe.

"Is that really Tricia?" Jonathan said.

"No, it's a trap. Go look at her. Really look at her."

How much did Ethan know? Had he tortured Heather until she told him everything? I watched Jonathan approach, my mouth going dry. I had to get out of here, but how with Heather drugged? I couldn't drag her. I couldn't leave her either.

Jonathan crouched down in front of Heather. I got up on my knees, turning my back to Ethan, and pretended to give Jonathan room. "What did he give her?" I asked while I slipped my hand into my front pocket and folded my fingers around my phone.

Jonathan gave me a solemn look. "A roofie, same shit he just put in that beer." He lowered his voice. "Same shit he pops in chicks' drinks at parties to loosen them up — get too much, this happens." He nodded at Heather's limp body. "That's why they call it a date-rape drug. I don't use that shit, Beautiful. You gotta believe me."

I ignored the pleading look he was giving me. "Will she be okay?"

"It'll wear off." He looked at Heather and then frowned at Ethan. "What? I don't see anything."

"Take the hood off, dude, really look!"

Jonathan slipped the hood off. "What the — that's not Tricia!"

In one smooth movement, I pulled the cell phone out and sat down against Heather, sliding the phone underneath the folds of the cloak.

Ethan chuckled. "Yeah, you were right about it being a scam. But much bigger than you thought." He guzzled the beer. "Tricia's dead as a doorknob. Has been for months. Rona told me

Fake Tricia here is working with her freak friends to trick you. She didn't say anything about your little Wouldn't-Do-Me-Wrong over there. But I'm thinking they planned it all to get the goods on you, so she won't go to jail." He looked at me. "Am I right?"

If I got through this alive, I would kill Rona. With my bare hands.

Jonathan frowned at me. "Were you in on this?" He looked hurt. "Because you think . . . ? I didn't touch you. I swear. Tricia just freaked. I told her I wasn't doing anything, but she kept calling me Wayne, just kept hitting me, scratching me."

Wayne? The drug dealer Tricia's mother had killed? The one who had raped Tricia? Suddenly I wasn't sure anymore. Dellian said he'd arrived while Tricia was attacking Jonathan. He hadn't actually seen Jonathan do anything to me. Could Tricia have mistaken what she'd seen? Lord knows I'd done that a bazillion times with my eyesight; maybe she'd done something similar, linked her past with the present and come up with the wrong conclusion. My emotions began a tug of war inside me. Jonathan seemed genuinely hurt. Could he be telling the truth this time?

"If nothing happened, why'd you lie? Why'd you say you took me home when Dellian did?"

"I never said I took you home. You did. I just went along with it because I didn't have an alibi after I left her." His eyes narrowed. "You still don't remember, do you? If you did, you'd know I didn't touch you. Dellian tell you that shit? You *are* working with him, aren't you? And the cops? Is that it?"

Ethan laughed, the whole thing apparently amusing to him. "No dude, no cops. No Dellian either; just that wannabe football

318

player and his crippled friend." Ethan slapped his leg. "Oh, it was sweet! They were trying to be all James Bond, hiding that purple car in the back of the apartment complex by the dumpsters. As if you can't but see that eyesore! Dude, it was classic. I walked up, knocked on the window, surprised the crap out of them. Said I knew all about their little game and wanted to borrow Fake Tricia for a bit."

What? My mouth dropped open. "They just let you take her?"

"Hell, no! I grabbed her when she came out of the building. Those idiots are prob'ly still waiting for her to come out. Freaking hilarious, dude!"

Freaking hilarious. What the heck was going on? How could the plan have gone so wrong? I slipped the phone forward, pushed Greg's speed-dial button, and then shoved the phone back under the arm folds of Tricia's cloak to smother the ringing. "So, why'd you bring her here if you knew she wasn't Tricia?" I said.

Greg answered on the first ring. "Roz!"

My hand shot out to muffle the sound.

So did Heather's arm. She was awake?

"Yeah, why did you bring her here?" Jonathan said. "I've got nothing to say to her."

"I thought you'd want to screw with her a bit." Ethan smiled. "She's supposed to be Tricia reanimated, right? Thought we'd show her how the real Tricia had fun."

I wasn't sure exactly what he meant, but I had an idea — and I didn't like it. "You're sick," I said.

"Oh, relax. I'm just talking a little fun." He held up the beer bottle again. "Here, have a sip, loosen up."

"Loosen up? Is that what you told Tricia when you gave her a roofied beer after she was already high on crack? Was it right here by the river?" I looked at Jonathan. "At your 'spot'? Did you watch her die too, for fun?"

"Whoa, hold on!" Jonathan held his hands up. "*No one* watched her do anything. We weren't with her."

Ethan gave me a dirty look. "You're more of a bitch than I thought. I think she's lying to you, dude. I think she's here trying to get us to admit something. Aren't you, bitch?"

"I . . . no." My brain failed me. With all the things Jonathan had done or I'd thought he'd done, he'd never spoken to me the way Ethan just had. It was hateful and vile and . . . scary.

"No?" He moved toward me. I crouched back against Heather. "I'm supposed to believe you're just here, hanging? Prove it. Drink this beer." He shoved it at me.

"I said don't give her that shit!" Jonathan snatched the bottle and threw it to the ground. "Just leave her alone, okay?"

Ethan scowled at him. "She's playing you, dude." He wandered over to the picnic table and sat down. "You're a frickin' wimp."

"I am not!" Jonathan said.

"No?" Ethan chugged the rest of his beer and tossed the bottle into the woods. It hit a tree and shattered. "Didn't you say she hit you earlier?"

Jonathan glared at Ethan, not saying anything.

"And since your girl brought it up, how about Tricia?" He snatched another bottle from the cardboard holder. "She smacked you around hard and you didn't do *nothing*. You're a wimp."

"I don't hit girls, dickhead!"

Heather's hand touched my leg. I kept my face forward and looked through my peripheral vision at her. Her eyes were slits, but she winked at me. She was definitely pretending to be unconscious. Did that mean the police were out there somewhere? The thought gave me confidence. "What's he talking about, Jonathan?" I asked.

"That night, when she thought I was hurting you. After Dellian took you home, Tricia came after me. Went crazy—"

"Like a wild animal," Ethan interjected. "She was on his back, goin' nuts!"

So Ethan had been there too. "What happened? Did she fall in when you were fighting?"

"No!" Jonathan jumped up. "I told you. I wasn't there! I left her right there at that picnic table. She said if she didn't see me erase the photos, she'd tell everyone I was selling drugs. I went to get my phone from my Vette; when I came back, her cape was here, but she wasn't. Tell her, Ethan! Tell her I wasn't there."

"How the hell would I know that?" Ethan said. "Maybe you were."

A snarl escaped Jonathan's lips. "Asshole!" He got in Ethan's face. "You know I wasn't! You were hanging out with her when I left."

"Psst." Heather motioned toward Jonathan and Ethan. "Watch them," she mouthed, cautiously sitting up.

"You'd better shut your mouth." Ethan jammed his finger into Jonathan's chest. "I don't know nothing that happened after that, and you know it! I left right after you. You're the one who came back."

"What are you talking about?" Jonathan said. "You saw me leave!"

"You just said you came back! How do I know you didn't do something to her?"

"'Cause I told you she wasn't here! How do I know you didn't do something to her while I was gone?"

Ethan grabbed Jonathan around the neck and yanked him forward. "Shut the eff up!" His voice was low and guttural. "I didn't touch her! I left right after you!"

Heather and I didn't need to hear anymore. We bolted into the woods.

"Hey!" Ethan yelled after us.

His voice made me run faster. I snapped twigs and tore at branches as I flew through the brush, Heather next to me.

Tricia's cloak caught on a low-lying bush. Heather jerked backwards with a cry.

I ripped her free, then grabbed her sleeve and tugged her forward.

We'd run only a few feet when another branch caught her, tearing her from my grasp. "Pull it up around you!"

"I'm trying!" Heather cried. She scooped the folds into her arms.

The sounds of pursuit intensified behind us, like a herd of cattle tearing through the woods. There was a yell and more thrashing.

We ran faster.

"No, this way!" Heather cried behind me.

I glanced back to see her sprinting left. I swerved toward her, narrowly missing an outstretched branch, but collided with the bare thorns of a raspberry bush. The sharp points tore at me as I untangled myself and caught back up with her.

We came out on a path. Heather slowed.

"Don't stop," I cried. Relieved to have a clear path, I pumped my legs faster. "Come on! The lodge is —" Arms grabbed me from the bushes. I threw my head back. It connected with a hard smack.

"Ow!" The arms dropped.

I propelled myself forward to run again just as the wind blew the scent of watermelon bubblegum toward me. I slammed to a stop and whirled around. "Greg?"

He stood behind me, blood pouring from his nose.

"Oh God." I rushed back over. "I didn't know it was you." I tilted his head up to stop the bleeding. "Where have you been? Where are the police?"

"They just went in to grab Jonathan and Ethan." He pinched the bridge of his nose. "I'm sorry it took a while to find you. Are you okay? Did they hurt you?"

"I'm fine." As soon as I said it, though, my throat tightened and tears filled my eyes. "I'm gonna kill Rona," I said. "She told Ethan. She ruined the plan."

"Detective King told her to. We thought he'd lead us to you."

"Yeah." Heather panted from the bushes behind us. "Rona totally saved your butt." She was bent over, hands on her knees, trying to catch her breath.

"So if you were going to follow Ethan to Jonathan, how did Heather end up with him?"

"That was my idea. I let him take me." Heather threw a sideways glance at Greg. "Not everyone approved."

Greg brought his hand down from his nose. "Because it was a stupid plan. We didn't need two in danger, and we knew he'd go to Jonathan eventually."

"Yeah, well, it worked, didn't it?" Heather said. "It was easy once I fake-drank the water he spiked. He didn't pay any attention to me once I pretended to pass out. Could you tell?"

"No." My voice wavered. "I thought he'd really drugged you." The lump returned to my throat.

"Sorry. I had to keep pretending." Heather put an arm around me. "All that stuff you got them to admit? I got it on tape." She pulled Dellian's tape recorder from the cloak pocket. "Dellian gave me this, in case my wire failed too."

"I *knew* that thing wasn't working." I pulled Greg's recorder out. "I had a backup too."

This struck us as hilarious. We erupted into laughter. Then, my hysterical gasps turned to choking sobs. Greg wrapped me tight in his arms. I buried my face in his chest and crumbled.

"It was my fault," he mumbled in my hair. "I lost you guys. I'm so sorry."

I wanted to say it wasn't his fault. Jonathan lost him on purpose. That he had no way of knowing Jonathan wouldn't go to Dellian's. But I couldn't stop sobbing long enough to form the words. I just buried myself deeper in his fleece.

"Are you okay, Roz?" Detective King asked me.

Wiping my tears, I looked up from Greg. Detective King and two other officers had walked out of the woods with Jonathan and Ethan in handcuffs. Ethan's bottom lip was bleeding. He glared at

Heather and me. Jonathan stared down at the ground, not making eye contact with anyone.

"No. Ethan gave me a drugged beer." I glanced over at Jonathan. "Or tried to, anyway. Jonathan stopped him."

"He drugged my water on the way out here," Heather said. "Come to think of it, the night I was slipped something, Ethan gave me a beer."

"Jonathan said Ethan does that a lot," I said.

"He's lying! They all are!" Ethan stared daggers at Jonathan. "Frickin' loser."

"Make sure you bag the water and beer for evidence," Detective King told one of the officers.

"I lied about the fire and my car being stolen. But I'm not lying about Ethan," Jonathan said quietly. "I was buying drugs off him for Tricia, so I know — he's always got roofies on him. Check his pockets."

"Dude! Shut up!" Ethan said as an officer began to frisk him.

"Ethan's the one who got Tricia hooked on the crack too," I said. "It's all on here" — I handed Detective King Greg's recorder — "including how my eighty dollars never bought pot or any other drugs. Jonathan kept it."

"What —" Ethan started to say, and then clamped his mouth shut and just glared at Jonathan.

Jonathan ignored him and looked at Detective King. "Yeah, he was dealing, but I'm just as guilty for giving it to her." He shrugged. "Maybe her OD'ing *was* my fault. That night when she attacked me, Ethan gave her a beer while I went to get the phone I'd used to take the photos. I was going to erase them, the way she wanted. She was already high on the crack I had given her at the party." He glanced up at me. "I swear I never touched you. And Tricia was gone when I got back with the phone. Only her cape was there. I grabbed it, to give it to her later."

"You never saw her in the water?" I asked.

Jonathan shook his head.

I turned to Ethan. "Did you? Did you see her get in the water?"

"No, and I didn't roofie her beer either! We hung out a bit, but I got frickin' cold waiting, so I took off."

"You expect us to believe hers was the one beer you didn't spike?" Greg asked.

"I don't give a shit *what* you believe," Ethan said.

"I think she gave it to herself," I said. "She was supposed to use it on Dellian, but she used ipecac syrup instead and kept the GHB for herself."

"Why?" Heather and Greg both said.

"'Cause she's a drug addict." Ethan smirked.

"Take him and Jonathan downtown," Detective King told the officers, then turned to Heather and me. "Let's get those wires off you two." She took the tiny microphones and kept both of our recorders too, just in case, and then headed down the trail. The three of us followed slowly behind.

"Do you think Tricia committed suicide?" Heather asked.

"I don't think she would've taken her cloak off if she meant to kill herself." I shrugged. "But I don't know what to believe." We'd reached the cars. I looked up at the sky — the sun was illuminating the horizon with soft strokes of orange, pink, and gold, while the moon hung nearby.

"I wish I knew for sure," I whispered.

Greg folded his arms around me. I leaned back against his chest, his heart thudding in rhythm with mine.

"You may never know," he said as he rested his chin gently on top of my hair. "Some truths stay hidden, no matter how much you want to unearth them."

"T. S. Eliot?" I mumbled.

"No." He hugged me tight. "That was all me this time."

Forty days after

It was junior prom, and after a crazy couple of weeks full of hearings and legalities, which had resulted in my reinstatement at Chance with a short stint of probation, Greg and I decided we would rather spend prom night watching a movie with our friends.

That afternoon, however, Abbey showed up at my door.

"I want you to keep it."

I stared at the soft brown bundle in her out-turned hands. "Your mom made it for her. You should keep it."

"She admired you. You didn't take crap. Her words, not mine." Abbey forced it into my hands. "I know she'd give it to you if she had the choice. Especially after everything you did to find the truth about what happened that night."

"But I didn't find the truth." I tried to shove it back.

Abbey just smiled and backed away. "You tried, though, like any good friend would. Have fun at prom tonight, for Tricia. She never missed a chance to dance."

"Oh, I'm not —" I hugged the cloak to my chest. "I will."

And I would. For Tricia.

● ● ●

The prom theme was Life Is Beautiful. Everyone was dressed accordingly. Billowing ball gowns and parasols, fancy updos and tuxedos. Satin, taffeta, lace, and silk. All Chance High's beauty was there in soft spring colors, layered with elegance, sophistication, and grace.

"This isn't Halloween," Liz Cobler gasped when we walked in. "This is prom!"

"We're in the right place then." I smoothed Tricia's cloak before giving Liz a big smile. "Come on, guys, let's go dance."

The rest of my caped entourage followed me — Greg, Heather, Fritz, JJ, Jeffrey, and Ruth. We descended onto the dance floor like vampires attacking an unsuspecting city. We pulled out cans of Insta-Whip and began spraying T-R-I-C-I-A across the polished floor.

Dancers shuffled to the side. Girls clung to their dates. Everyone stared.

The music stopped.

No one breathed.

"Don't worry," Greg told two teachers approaching us. "We plan to clean it up."

Dellian stepped from the shadows. "I'll make sure they do."

Heather smiled at the stunned band onstage. "Hey, you guys know 'Copacabana'?"

The lead singer and guitarist shook their heads, eyes fixated on the caped gang that had crashed the party.

"Wait." The guy at the keyboard cocked his head. "Manilow's 'Copacabana'? Yeah, I know it."

"Play it for us?" Heather cooed.

The keyboardist grinned. "A little sappy for a party-crashing song, don't you think?"

"Just play it!" Rona's deep voice threatened from the crowd.

He shrugged. "Okay."

Heather climbed onstage. "This is for Tricia Farni; may she be happy wherever she is!"

The keyboardist began to play. Heather sang, "Her name was Lola . . ."

Ruth and I stepped carefully into the center of the whipped-cream floor and began to twirl, twirl, twirl, like little girls on Easter morning. The more I turned, the freer I felt. I didn't think about how silly I looked or how much I stood out. I just twirled.

Greg and Jeffrey joined us, while JJ and Fritz spun wheelies in their chairs. Missy climbed onto the stage and began belting out the lyrics alongside Heather. Like zombies awakening from a trance, the rest of the prom came to life. Some who knew the words joined Heather and Missy onstage, while others danced.

I twirled close to Greg and said, "There's something I've been dying to do all night." I reached my hand up to his face.

Instinctively, his hand wiped at his chin. "Ink?"

"No." I gently pulled his face down to mine and kissed him.

As our lips parted, he grinned. "Just all night?" He drew me closer. His lips found mine again and he kissed me back. "I've been dying to do this for years."

Acknowledgments

That old saying "it takes a village" also applies when writing a book. There are so many people who have helped me along the way. I'd like to give a shout out and a thank you to all of them.

First and foremost, I owe so much to my awesome editor Karen Grove who, from the beginning, understood my vision for *Blind Spot* and knew what I needed to do to achieve that vision. I owe just as much to my agent-extraordinaire Jill Corcoran. If she hadn't taken a chance on me, *Blind Spot* may still be a file on my computer, instead of a novel in a teen's hands.

When it *was* simply a file on my computer though, *Blind Spot* and I went through many bumps, bruises, dead-ends, and drafts, and through it all I had the unfaltering support of my critique group: Sharon Blankenship, Jennifer Carson, Todd Gerring, Dawn King, Katena Presutti, Jacqui Robbins, Diane Telgen, and Jacey Yunker; my writing friends: Linda Gerber, Patty Hoffman, Kristin Lenz, Elizabeth Mosier, Su Shekar, and Renee Matthew Singh; and my Eastern Michigan University grad school writing group: Kate Ahmann, Teresa Asiain, Bill Barr, Pam McCombs, Dina Sowers, and Alicia Vonderhaar. To each and every one of you, thank you. You guys rock.

I also want to thank the SCBWI Michigan chapter for the great support system you have given me through the years, as well as the editors, agents, and authors who have critiqued my work at both regional and national SCBWI conferences—I learned something from each and every one of you and my novel was better for it. I want to especially thank Michael Stearns, the first industry professional to make me believe in myself. I will forever be grateful to him for taking the time, not once, but twice, to read my novel and give me invaluable advice that pushed me out of "potential" into "publishable". Thank you, Michael. I know you say it was nothing, but to me, it was everything.

Thank you to Larry Voight who teaches psychology courses at Washtenaw Community College for answering all my questions about date rape drugs and their psychological effects; Ann Arbor police officer Dawn King (and fellow writer) for her expertise and fact-checking as I wrote *Blind Spot*; and my beta readers: Cheryl Bullister, Leslie Figueroa, Patty Hoffman, Nikki Lang, and Jenny Tith for making me keep it real.

Writing and having a family don't always mesh as well as one would hope, so thank you to my children Breanna, James, and Megan for eating more than their fair share of pizza and for understanding when I needed to shut my office door and write; thank you especially to my husband, Jeff, who, through the years, has supported me, rearranging his busy schedule so that I could attend conferences, critique meetings, and grad school, and for taking the kids out, often overnight, when I needed quiet time. You are the biggest reason this dream became a reality.

Thank you also to Jenny Tith and Julia Stier for always stepping in and babysitting when my oldest daughter or my husband couldn't be home. Thank you to my family and friends who have stood by and cheered me on through this entire process.

And finally, in writing *Blind Spot* I based much of Roswell's experiences on my own as a teen struggling with macular degeneration, and a big part of that struggle occurred at school. I have the greatest respect for all the teachers I have had through the years—even those who didn't understand and therefore unintentionally made my life harder. But I'd like to acknowledge my high school English teachers BJ Craig and Susan Stitham, and the school nurse, Laura Rima. Their understanding and support taught me that there is always a way around an obstacle.